SONGS
OF THE
CAUVERY

Kalyanaraman Durgadas is an alumnus of both IIT Madras and IIM Calcutta, and has been an entrepreneur. He has written and produced plays. He currently lives in Bangalore.

Songs of the Cauvery is his first novel.

SONGS OF THE CAUVERY

Kalyanaraman Durgadas

RUPA

Published by
Rupa Publications India Pvt. Ltd 2016
7/16, Ansari Road, Daryaganj
New Delhi 110002

Sales centres:
Allahabad Bengaluru Chennai
Hyderabad Jaipur Kathmandu
Kolkata Mumbai

ISBN: 978-81-291-4205-4

First impression 2016

10 9 8 7 6 5 4 3 2 1

The moral right of the author has been asserted.

Typeset by SÜRYA, New Delhi

To Leela,
my wife,
and other strong,
courageous women like her

The holy river Cauvery, daughter of the gods, a gift to mankind, is born in an unassuming little tank at Tala Cauvery in the Western Ghats of south India. Were she to turn westwards, she would glimpse the handsome Arabian Sea. But that is not her lover and betrothed. He is eastwards, over 400 miles away. It is towards him that she must obsessively journey forth.

At the source, she has the energy and the playfulness of youth. As she flows ahead, rushing recklessly through the hilly terrain, she is joined by her companions—Harangi, Hemavati, Kabini and others, all daughters of the Western Ghats. She grows in confidence. She gushes forward, gathering not just the rich alluvia but also the culture, history and the stories of the lands around her, in turn influencing them.

At the plateau of Mysore, she realizes that she has a long way to go; as far as the eye can see, the plains stretch with no sight of her lover. She slows down, with the tentativeness of the adolescent, but absorbing to a greater extent the music, art and culture around her.

By the time she reaches Sivasamudram, she is a maiden at the peak of her strength and vitality and her blood begins to sing. All doubts vanish. She speeds through, anxious to keep her tryst, leaping over falls, cutting a narrow gorge through mountains, gathering more life-giving soil. She gambols and leaps, coming over rocks amidst a fine spray of mist at Hoganekkal.

By the time she enters the ancient Tamil land of the Cholas, she is a mature woman, mindful of who she is.

As she sees the undulating greenery of the rice fields around her, she is reminded of her duties.

1877–1896

TIRUVAIYARU

ONE

January 1877

If she were older than thirteen, or had someone with whom she could have shared her problems, Mangalam wouldn't have decided to kill herself. She was at an age when the smallest problem grew larger and larger to blot out her mental horizons entirely, till she was guided, not by the clear voice of reason, but by the ghostly whisperings of pale ideologies that distorted time by yanking her to and fro between the imagined guilts of the past and the fearful uncertainties of the future.

Sambu Sastry, her husband of three years, was away, transitioning the day into the evening by performing the sandhya vandanam at the temple tank after attending the midday puja at the temple.

Sambu's mother lay down in the covered thinnai that ran all along the wall in the front part of the house. She 'had just kept her eyes closed for a few minutes', though the snores that issued from her belied that.

It was an afternoon hour when, if the village of Tiruvaiyaru wasn't actually sleeping, it was definitely brimming with torpor. Mangalam stood in the inner courtyard in the middle of the house. The sky was darkening; a brown leaf on the packed earth swirled around and stopped; the musty smell of rain on fresh earth rose even before one or two spots of raindrops began to spread. For a moment, it awoke an automatic response within her. 'God, the clothes on the line at the back…' She smiled at the thought—a lopsided grin that didn't reach her eyes.

She turned with a sigh and entered her room, her toe-rings, a size too big for her, making a tiny scraping sound on the floor.

A steel trunk, painted green, the corners picked out in black, rust showing on the edges on which it rested, lay open. Two new woven-grass sleeping mats, rolled tightly, decorated a corner of the room. Nearby, a table with carved legs, one of which was propped up with a piece of folded cardboard; on it, a heap of dried palm leaves, threaded through and tied together with string. Upon it, a brass kooja, short and bulbous with a brass tumbler inverted on top. Another corner of the room overflowed with palm-leaf manuscripts. On one wall, a painting of baby Krishna, bejewelled but naked, lying down on a large fig leaf, hands grasping at his legs to position the right toe at his mouth. A slightly browned string of jasmine flowers decorated the picture, below which a small mirror hung crookedly on the wall, part of it rendered transparent where the quicksilver had peeled, black paint blistering on the carved frame. Two hooks were fixed on a rafter on the ceiling, two lengths of chain hung with links half the size of her palms, each chain folded back upon itself so that the loops hung higher than her head in mute reminder of the absent swing.

For a moment, she looked at the hooks, set one of the chains in motion with a flick of her wrist, watched it creak back and forth. With a shake of the head she bent at the trunk. She took out a small wooden box, carved with intricate floral designs, inlaid with ivory. She opened it and a faint smell of sandalwood filled her nostrils. She put her hand in and stroked the velvet lining a couple of times, marvelling at its feel. A teardrop fell into the box. She dried her eyes with the end of her sari, took out the piece of jewellery from inside the box. It was a simple circular gold pendant, attached to a gold chain. But the diamond in the centre—it dazzled! It was more than a quarter of an inch wide.

'This is the latest setting from England, Sir. They call it an open setting. This catches and reflects light much better. Of course you have to handle it more carefully...' Mangalam remembered the goldsmith's words to her father.

Despite the setting, it was not easy for her to prise the stone out, pushing the prongs aside with a pin that she had found in a box where she had kept buttons, needle, thread and other odds and ends. She then took out a lace handkerchief from her trunk, spread it out on the table and placed the diamond on top. She reached out to the kooja, lifted the tumbler, unscrewed the top and poured out the milk in it, using both her hands, filling the tumbler up halfway. She then lifted up the ends of the handkerchief to cover the jewel entirely and looked for something to pound it with.

She had one more thing to do. She had to do it quickly before her husband returned.

Two more things.

She looked at herself in the mirror. Satisfied, she stood on tiptoe to remove the string of flowers from the picture. She placed the flowers in her hair, looked around for a piece of paper to write on and picked up a thick paper with official-looking English writing on it. She turned the paper over, licked the pencil lead once and began writing in a beautiful copperplate Tamil.

There was an unusual rush at the temple and the priest took a long time to complete the puja. Not that Sambu blamed him, for there had been at least a dozen requests, accompanied with coconuts, bananas and flowers, for a puja and the priest was conscientious in taking down these requests, including the astrological birth information.

'Subramanian, Visakham,' the shawl-with-gold-filigree in front said.

'Visakham, Tula rasi,' the priest said, turning his face to one side either because he was in a hurry to move on or he was deafer in one ear.

'I think it is Vrichchikam.'

'Gotram?'

'Bharadwaja Gotram.'

As the priest moved away, the shawl said, 'Please add my wife, Saroja, Makha Nakshatram, Simha Rasi—'

'—along with family, wife and children,' said the priest as he moved to the next devotee.

At last the screen in front of the idol was drawn back. The priest showed the lamp to the deity, moving it in a circular motion, lingering at the face. The idol of the goddess never failed to move Sambu. He closed his eyes to blink away his tears.

'She who inhabits the heart of the pure and delights in eternal bliss, she who controls both actions and knowledge, and grants all desires...'

Sambu Sastry murmured the lines from Muthuswamy Dikshitar's composition.

When he went to the temple tank to complete his noon sandhya vandanam, the skies were darkening. As Sambu was finishing, standing in knee-deep water, a large drop of rain fell on his scalp where his shaved forehead met his knotted hair. He looked up. Rain clouds were directly overhead, but elsewhere the sky was clear. He stepped out of the water, on to the steps, sprinkled some water on the granite floor and applied some of it between his eyebrows. The raindrops were falling much faster now. Sambu rushed to the colonnaded pavilion nearby.

It should clear up soon now. Is this some kind of metaphor for my life?—the poet in him wondered. He recalled the Sanskrit poem that his father had taught him:

The night is past;
The day is soon to dawn.
When the sun rises,
The lotus will smile:
Thus thought the bee trapped in the lotus,
But alas, an elephant dashed it to the ground.

Sambu shook his head. *Certainly not a metaphor for my life.*

Sambu waited a while, looking at some of the sculptures in stone. One carving held his attention. The man had his hand around the waist of his lover who looked up at the man's face with eagerness and anticipation.

Sambu decided to walk home, braving the rain. Luckily, even as he stepped out, it stopped raining. Deciding to do something for the first time in his life, he stopped at a florist.

'Jasmine string,' he said, 'Four hand widths.'

'And be careful with your hands, and don't pull to stretch one hand width to two,' he added. The shopkeeper measured out the flowers generously, adding a couple of inches to each width, taking care to keep the string slack. He cut the plantain fibre with which the flowers were tied on the sharp edge of a stone and wrapped them in a leaf and placed the parcel on the counter. Sambu took the package and dropped a quarter-anna coin. The shopkeeper started to protest.

'This itself is too much. I will take something else from you later,' said Sambu and walked away without a glance at the shopkeeper.

'The rain has intensified the heat,' he said to himself as he reached his house.

His was the third house in the Agraharam Street. The street ran east to west and the house faced south. He joined his hands once at the Easwara temple at the western end of the street and muttered prayers under his breath.

'Amma,' he called out before entering the house, even though the front door was open. He had always done this and therefore did not quite recall the various methods his mother had employed to condition him, though he did remember that on one occasion she had scolded him, 'Why are you entering the house like a street dog wandering into an open house? Can you not give me a shout?'

His mother got up and adjusted her sari. 'I was just closing my eyes, thinking about the goddess—chanting the Lalitha Sahasranamam. Why do you have to shout so?'

'Where's Mangalam, Amma?'

'Must be inside, sleeping.' Disapproval was writ large in the way her lips curved downwards. 'I don't know how I am going to teach her to take care of you and the house. Her mother must have thought her duty was at an end as soon as she delivered her. Everything has now descended on my head. What to do? Wait. What's that in your hand behind your back?'

'Nothing, Amma. I just got some flowers for the god-pictures at home.'

'Aha. When have you ever done that? I know. It's your young bride, isn't it? Your wife has come home only three months ago and already you get her flowers? Your mother has been around, large as life, like a pounding stone, sacrificing everything, doing everything for you, even wiping your bottom till you were six.'

The defensive weapon that was her expressive sari-border was now poised at her nose and mouth and the sniffles ensued.

'Any day, any time in your life, has anyone—you or your father, got anything for me? What is the point if everyone praises you and your father for having dissolved all the Vedas and God knows what other books and drunk them? What have I got out of throwing out garbage in this house for so many years with a man like that?'

Sambu realized that the tirade had just been transferred to his absent father.

'Let my father come back from Kasi. Then you can roll his head. Is the food ready?'

She didn't seem to have heard him. 'This girl has come yesterday and you keep going around her, wagging your tail.' The sniffs now became louder.

'In this house, anything I do is wrong,' said Sambu, turning his head up, rolling his eyes and projecting his voice to the heavens, his hands flapping up only at the wrists in a pale simulacrum of the full effort that is required to convey the dramatic appeal. Like an actor muffing his short lines and wanting to be offstage quickly, he walked furiously towards his room.

It might have been the stillness in the air or the sight of the half-open door to his room that alerted him. Something was wrong. Sambu stepped into the room.

Mangalam lay sprawled on the ground. A thick band of blood had stained her cheeks and her mouth. Her hands were clutching at her abdomen. More blood had pooled on the ground and congealed. An upended brass tumbler in an unstable equilibrium rested against her body.

His hand tightened on the packet of flowers.

Sambu kept his composure all through the initial rites. He took no notice of the immense procession of relatives and friends who came to the cremation. He did not realize that his father-in-law hardly spoke to him, nor did he notice his brother-in-law Vichu glaring at him throughout. He broke down when he had to light a small fire at the body's mouth. He recalled that the last time he saw his young bride's mouth, it was on fire too.

He tried sleeping that night. He tossed and turned.

He decided he was not going to be able to sleep. He sat at the table hoping to get solace from the Gita. That was when he noticed it. The thick paper scroll announcing a title that he had been awarded was lying open on the table, a copying pencil balanced on it.

The writing was even, slanting back a little, the loops and whorls of the script small and emasculated, the purple showing clearly in some places and smudged in others, the black lead marks appearing in between, only the impression showing on the thick paper in some places. He read with shaking hands.

The letter started with a symbol of Om, a whorl continuing on to the right with a horizontal line, with another short line below it. She had written the traditional 'safe' in the top left-hand corner. She must have thought better of it; it had been scratched out.

To my loving husband,

The word 'husband' had also been scratched out and rewritten. Wives didn't call husbands by their names. They didn't even refer to them by name. Sambu remembered with a pang of grief, the 'Enna' with which she addressed him.

Countless crore namaskarams.

  I have to tell you why I came to this decision. That is why the letter.

  Even if one does not live in prosperity, one should think that people around should live in prosperity. I have been taught this again and again by my father. You have also told me, often, even in this short time, that your prayers are always for 'everyone to be happy and comfortable'.

Sambu nodded in assent.

  When I was in my parent's place, three days back, I overheard a conversation. Definitely wrong of me. But I could not resist. I was hidden behind a pillar. You know Subramania Jyothidar—he is the one who fixes all the auspicious times for everything good or bad that happens in my parents' house.

Sambu noticed that 'parents' had been an afterthought. It straddled the 'my' and 'house' above the line.

  The summary of the conversation is this. Apparently my birth horoscope is one with a grave defect. The planet Mars is in the seventh with Saturn. This kind of a combination means certain death for the husband and is also bad for the father-in-law. There were other things that I didn't understand. In short, I came to know that they had changed my birth details in the horoscope that was given to you for matching with yours. What a sin they have committed! Because of this, even my twin brother Vichu's horoscope has been changed.

Sambu turned up the wick on the lantern to make it brighter and continued reading.

Anyway, among us, for every sin, isn't there an expiatory act that is possible? This is why as an act of atonement, I have decided to end my life. I have heard that if you commit suicide you go to the seventh hell. This cannot be true. In any case, I will definitely not roam as a ghost. The last words on my lips will be the five-syllabled mantra that you have initiated me into.

Sambu blinked a couple of times to squeeze out drops of tears that were forming.

I am writing all this in detail to you after much thought. I have scarcely thought of anything else for the last three days. The reason for this is simply that people will be blaming you: they will say you have tortured me. Some will even blame Amma. Already, my brother Vichu, one who shared a womb with me, who is dearer to me than life itself, is upset for some reason. I ask of you that you be your generous self and do not mind him. Forgive him if he insults you.

In any case as I said, with the Lord's name on my lips in my last moments, I will have no rebirth. Even if I am reborn, I wish that I will be your wife in my next birth too.

Sambu's tears smudged the already smeared lines. He put his head on the table and gave in to tears. He forced himself to read further.

One last thing. I am told that prisoners who are about to be executed get a last wish. Don't read any further till you promise.

The next couple of lines were left blank.

This is what I want you to do. You know I have a beautiful parrot-like younger sister. Her name, you may remember, is Bhavani. She just grew up last year. Yes, I want you to marry her. Enna, won't you do this for me? You can't say no. Anyway, by now, you have already promised. Who else will take a girl from the house of someone who has committed suicide?

I am feeling light and I am very clear about what I want to do.

Your loving wife,
S. Mangalam

Two

February 1878

In the proclamation of 1877, Queen Victoria had assured native Indians that '...all may feel that under Our rule the great principles of liberty, equity and justice are secured to them; and to promote their happiness, to add to their prosperity, and advance their welfare, are the ever present aims and objects of Our Empire.' More specifically, 'And it is Our further will that, as far as may be, Our subjects, of whatever race or creed, be freely and impartially admitted to office in Our service, the duties of which they may be qualified by their education, ability and integrity duly to discharge.'

This might well have been called the Royal Prevarication as subsequent British policy and administration did very little in this direction. Disbelief set in quickly and even as early as 1878, *The Hindu,* an English-language weekly, was founded in Madras to support the candidature of Sir T. Muthuswamy Iyer for a judgeship at the Madras High Court, which the Anglo-Indian press opposed virulently. The first print run of eighty copies or so were a modest beginning, but a beginning all the same, for the role the Indian press was to play in the affairs of the country. The impact, however, had certainly not reached the politically somnolent village of Tiruvaiyaru, whose concerns were more spiritual than political.

The building was set deep inside the encircling compound wall, hidden from the road. The wall was painted in the traditional style with alternating stripes of white and crimson. The sun overhead reflected off the white stripes, making Sambu shade his eyes in an attempt to protect them from the harsh glare. Sambu went through the narrow entrance, which had an ornate pillar on either side with an arch above them, a board proclaiming the name of the monastery in Tamil.

Trees were planted all around the neatly swept compound. As soon as he entered the compound, he felt calmer. A sudden breeze blew and the heart-shaped leaves of the peepul tree stirred in a gesture of welcome.

'I would like to see the Swamigal,' he said to the young devotee at the door.

'And you are...'

'I am Sambu Sastry from Tiruvaiyaru. I want to meet him for a few minutes.'

'I will tell the elder Swamigal. He should be finishing his puja any time now. Can you wait here please?'

He indicated a mat of woven korai grass with stripes of green, red and black running across its width. Sambu sat cross-legged on the mat. His thoughts went to the previous time he had seen the monk. Sambu had been almost in tears when he begged him to admit and initiate him into the monastic order. The elder sanyasi was firm in saying 'No'. 'You have to experience the life of a householder,' he had said, and advised him to marry.

'Swamigal will see you now,' the young man came in and announced.

Swamigal, in ochre robes, was sitting, legs crossed, on a deerskin. His eyes were half-closed. Sambu was wondering how he should announce his presence when the Swamigal's eyes opened and he asked Sambu to sit down in front of him.

'Swami, what am I to do now? The only thing I have wished for is happiness for everyone around me. But that is not to be.'

'Yes,' said Swamigal. 'I heard about your wife's death. The important thing is that you do not blame yourself.'

'I understand, but I have had enough. I have been pestering you to give me sanyasa diksha. I want to be a monk now more than ever.'

'I think you are not ready. I will come and initiate you myself when you are ready.'

'Swami, I beg you.' Sambu had tears in his eyes now.

Swamigal closed his eyes and was quiet for a long time. Sambu was beginning to wonder if he was lost in meditation, when he opened his eyes.

'Do you know the central message of the Gita?'

'Krishna explains three possible paths to attain salvation. The path of knowledge, the path of devotion and the path of action.'

'Are you saying there are three central messages in the Gita?' Swamigal had a faint smile on his face.

'Well, these are various paths and all of them lead to the same result—salvation, though the paths are different.'

'No, there is a more fundamental message in the Gita. Ramakrishna, a saint who lives in Calcutta, sometimes asks his followers to repeat "Gita" several times. What you get, is tagi—or tyagi. You know what that means.'

'Yes, Swamigal, one who sacrifices.'

'Yes, meaning one who gives up something. On the path of devotion, as the Gita says, you must give up all ways of living and surrender to God.'

'The final chapter, verse 66,' murmured Sambu.

'On the path of knowledge,' said Swamigal, 'you must be able to reason out and give up through analysis, the distinction amongst the doer, the deed and the object of the deed.'

'One who thinks of it as the destroyer or one who thinks of it as the destroyed—neither knows; it neither destroys or is destroyed,' quoted Sambu.

'The idea of "giving up" while following the path of action is even more subtle. You must give up the fruits of your action, yet continue doing the right thing—the will of God.'

'You have a right only to act and not to the fruits thereof,' quoted Sambu.

'You seem to know the Gita rather well, Sambu. It is not enough if you know the words. You must bring them into your life. Becoming a sanyasi is not an end, but a beginning. There are experiences that you will never have if you become a sanyasi. You have to become a householder to learn some things.'

'Swami, Sankara took sanyasa when he was a young boy. And he was, to me, the greatest monk that ever lived.'

'You know the story of Sankara's debate with Mandanamishra, don't you? Mandanamishra's wife told Sankara he had to defeat her as well in debate. She then proceeded to ask him about relations between a man and a woman. Sankara had to experience being a householder before continuing the debate. But even that is not strictly relevant. You are a different person from Sankara. What is true for Sankara is not necessarily correct for you. If you value me as a guru, you must let me make the decision.'

'Yes, Swami,' said Sambu in a low voice as he prostrated himself and prepared to leave.

'And so, you will marry her sister according to Mangalam's wishes?'

Sambu wondered how Swamigal knew.

He merely said 'Yes' and was about to leave.

'Wait,' Swamigal said, 'I have one more thing to tell you. In tyaga, the important thing is selflessness. The object behind the sacrifice is less important. So, don't think any less of Mangalam's actions because they were, according to you, needless.'

Sambu felt lighter as he left.

Sambu stood in front of the large house with a tiled roof.

The sky was a delicate blue. With no cloud cover and not enough body cover for Sambu, the sun penetrated straight into his body and the thick topknot he wore trapped the sweat upon his scalp. He pleated the ends of his upper cloth and stood uncertainly, fanning himself.

An old man snoozed in the thinnai. A brown dog that looked like a hundred other dogs on the streets of Tiruvaiyaru was picking delicately at the leftovers on a banana leaf in front of the house.

'Anyone at home?' Sambu shouted. The old man hardly stirred.

'ANYONE HOME?' Years of training in reciting the Vedas had given him strong vocal chords.

It was then that he noticed the thirteen-year-old Vichu standing in the doorway, hands on his hips, chest thrown forward, lips drawn together.

'Vichu, is your father home?'

Vichu did not reply. He continued scowling at Sambu.

'Can't you recognize me? I am your brother-in-law.'

'Who is it...why are you keeping a guest waiting at the doorstep?' A voice sounded from inside.

Despite the voice of authority, Vichu remained where he was and Sambu had to jostle his way past him.

'Come in, come in.' Shankaraiyer's voice held formality rather than a welcome.

'I need to speak to you alone,' said Sambu.

Even before Shankaraiyer looked at Vichu, he was gone.

They sat on the swing at the mittam. Neither of them made an effort to set the swing in motion.

'Kamalam...' Shankaraiyer called out, years of practice enabling him to drag out even the short syllable at the end of his wife's name.

'Coming...' replied Kamalam, her reply lasting for exactly the same duration as her husband's call. She entered after waiting a little behind a pillar, pulling her sari tighter around her chest, hitching up the border of the sari at the same time.

'Come, come,' she said. 'You have been in the afternoon sun. I will get some buttermilk.' She walked back without waiting for an answer.

'How is it you have come this far?' Shankaraiyer asked. Not that Sambu had travelled all that much of a distance; it was not too far from Tiruvaiyaru to Thillaisthanam. It was just a way of asking, not too politely, the reason for his visit.

'Maybe he has come to return Mangalam's jewellery.'

'Will you shut your mouth and go inside?' Shankaraiyer's tone was flat and did not reflect the heat of the words, but had the effect of sending Vichu back deep into the house.

'Maybe I have not come at a good time. Anyway,' said Sambu, 'I will tell you why I came.' As he spoke, he reached into the veshti at his waist and brought out a thick sheet of paper that had been folded and re-folded.

'I think this letter that your daughter wrote will explain things.' He handed over the sheet to the older man.

Kamalam joined them with a brass pot full of buttermilk. Shankaraiyer read the letter out loud.

As he reached the end of the letter, both of them were weeping openly; Shankaraiyer held Sambu's hands and said, 'Please forgive me son-in-law,' a couple of times, claiming a relationship that had been absent in his words so far. 'The worst thing that can happen to a father,' he continued, 'is falling in the esteem of his own son. So...'

He looked around furtively.

'So, you don't want Vichu to know?'

'Thank you very much for your understanding. If you were older, I would have fallen at your feet. Anyway, even in a sad situation, God sows seeds of His grace. Will you honour us by becoming our son-in-law again, marrying our second daughter Bhavani?'

'Truly speaking,' said Sambu, 'I don't want to marry at all. If I can get sanyasa diksha from the seer of Kumbakonam, I will take the monastic orders immediately. Since childhood, this has been an ambition. However, I feel a strong sense of commitment towards Mangalam. It seems as though God has willed it thus. Even if God has not willed it, my guru has certainly willed it. Even so, normally, I would have said that I have to ask my father. You know, my father did not return from Kasi. We did not even get his ashes. Since I am the head of my house, may I ask you to fix a suitable date for the engagement and marriage?'

Sambu married Bhavani in the Bahudanya year of the Indian calendar—paradoxically the year of 'abundant grains'—on the twenty-fourth of February 1878, in the midst of one of the worst famines known.

The great famine had devastated over a quarter of the population. No one seemed to notice the irony, least of all Robert Bulwer-Lytton, first earl of Lytton, Governor General and Viceroy of India, when he had been happy to export that year a record 6.4 million hundredweight of wheat from India. Nor did anyone see anything amiss in holding the indecently opulent Proclamation Durbar designating Her Majesty as the Empress of India, making her a first-time Empress and allowing her the affectation of signing as VR&I— Victoria Regina et Imperatrix.

The delta, as ever, was insulated from the shortage of food, thanks to the bounty of the Cauvery, but families had to face the influx of relatives and friends from other parts. The celebrations for the marriage were muted. There were no musical and sadir performances and no procession of the son-in-law on a decorated horse-carriage. Despite that, the kudir in Shankaraiyer's house, which could store one hundred and fifty measures of paddy, was almost empty by the end of the wedding. The number of people in Tiruvaiyaru had more than doubled as people from famine-hit areas flocked to the houses of their relatives there, and all considered themselves invited for the wedding. A notable absentee was Vichu who ensured that he missed most of the three-day function, a younger cousin performing the role of the bride's brother. But he could not tear himself away from blessing the couple for a long married life by sprinkling yellowed rice on the newly-weds when Sambu tied three knots in the sacred thali around Bhavani's neck. Vichu was nonetheless careful to make sure that the rice grains he threw landed exclusively on Bhavani.

Bhavani's father paid a steep price for the wedding in spite of not having to get too much jewellery made. Sambu had offered to return all of Mangalam's jewellery. He had also offered gallantly to 'take Bhavani with just the sari she was wearing'.

'No, son-in-law,' Shankaraiyer had said, 'Anyway it is for my only daughter. For the sake of tradition I will need to make a few ornaments.'

The 'few ornaments' turned out to be an oddiyanam, a waist belt in gold that weighed in at twenty-five sovereigns, and the traditional M-shaped gold thali with the goddess Meenakshi in one arch of the M and the linga representing Lord Sundareshwara in the other, and polyhedral beads, all of which were strung together with thick, twisted strands of cotton threads yellowed with turmeric, and gold bangles that covered half the length of Bhavani's forearm. He also bought half a dozen silk saris. His relatives did not share the generosity of Sambu; they wanted their full complement of new clothes. While these did set

Shankaraiyer back a bit, what broke the bank, like the Cauvery in the month of Adi, was the emptying of his granary. He also had to sell a considerable portion of his landholding, which wasn't considerable to begin with, at a time when land prices were depressed.

Thus, when Krishna Iyer from a well-known dubashi family from Madras proposed that he would adopt Vichu and ensure that he completed his education, he jumped at the offer. Krishna Iyer had said, 'I don't think we have any chance of a son,' all the while looking at his wife, who was busy looking at her toes, shaking her head almost imperceptibly, attempting passively to deny the imputation of her husband's glance. Shankaraiyer was overjoyed and to his only comment—'An English education, I suppose'— Krishna Iyer answered in the affirmative.

'Anyway, I have another son who can light my pyre,' he told his wife, who alternated between ranting incoherently with the edge of her sari buried in her mouth and wondering aloud whether lucky times had begun for Vichu.

Vichu left Thillaisthanam on an auspicious day and hour and boarded a train from Tanjore, his eyes metaphorically filled with stardust at the prospect of an English education and the consequent job opportunities with Her Majesty and actually full of coal-dust from putting his head out of the window.

He loved the rhythm of the train on its tracks, the changed rhythm when it went over a bridge, the occasional steam whistle that was let off without warning, and the green fields and solitary trees that rushed past.

Amidst all this excitement, his thoughts soon turned to revenge. Against the one person who was responsible for all the misery he and his family had had to undergo—Sambu.

Three

In 1885, when A.O. Hume, a leader of the theosophical movement, was laying, perhaps unwittingly, the foundation for independence by starting the Congress party and preparing for the Poona meet that was plagued by, well, plague, and had to be shifted to Bombay, Sambu and his wife of six years were taking a dip in the Mahamaham tank at Kumbakonam. They rushed to the Cauvery after the dip to wash off the thick sludge caused by 500,000 people immersing themselves in twenty acres of water that had been deliberately reduced to a level of about two-and-a-half feet by the government for reasons of safety. Jupiter had entered Simha and the moon was in Makham, something that happened once in twelve years. The couple had an agenda; they wanted a child, specifically, a son.

Four years ago, there had been a bit of excitement when Bhavani missed her second consecutive period and told her husband, 'I haven't had a bath for three months.' He hadn't immediately understood; nor did he relate the fact that for the past two months he hadn't had those four days when he cooked a meal just about fit for human consumption. Bhavani had to look down pointedly in simulated shyness and trace patterns with her toes on the ground. The joy Sambu felt when he finally understood was somewhat short-lived as his mother predicted with prophetic certainty, 'The first-born won't stay.' Bhavani wasn't sure if it was the voice of experience or an outward expression of sheer malice; she suspected the latter and feared its evil impact; within a week of her announcement, Bhavani had a miscarriage.

Sambu's mother was not one to be ignored. She would often say, 'Every joint pains when I sit down, it pains when I get up, it pains when I bend my back.' The pains seemed to be particularly bad when attempting any housework.

'I don't know why I am a burden to the earth like this. If only I can see a small child on all fours in this house, I will die happily,' were her oft-repeated words, particularly in the presence of Bhavani, all the while looking at her, perhaps feeling that at least her looks could be pregnant—with meaning. 'What is the point in going around sacred ficus trees, in going to all the temples? Only if there is something in the vessel will you get something on the ladle,' she would add with a sigh. Sambu was oblivious to all this as Bhavani remained unfazed, putting on a meek blank look when his mother said such things. She refused to complain to her husband. When the time came, she would handle matters herself.

For Sambu, the relationship was something that would improve with time, although when his cobbler expressed a similar sentiment regarding the leather slippers he had made for Sambu, he didn't agree. Sambu's personal hell was the possibility of falling into the hell called 'puth'—which was what would happen if, at his death, he had no son to light his pyre and perform the last rites.

At Rameswaram, he had prayed along with Bhavani at the Siva temple. They had sprinkled on themselves the water from the twenty-two wells along the huge tank. At the end of the pilgrimage, for one last time, Sambu pinched his nostrils and sat down on the tank bed with his head completely under water. He got up and saw Bhavani in the sari that she had tied in the traditional madisar style, that even when dry revealed a leg, a hip, a waist and the under-curve of a breast. Now it clung to her body revealing even more.

'You look like Mahalakshmi risen from the ocean of milk,' said Sambu.

'Don't look at me like that,' said Bhavani with a teasing lilt to her voice, as she turned and walked back, but not before holding the pose for a beat. As Sambu watched, unable to tear his eyes from her, there was a hint of a sway in her hips.

They made love that night; full of passion, but with restraint so as not to wake the others in the house where they were staying. The Swati asterism was ruling that day. There was a coolness in the air and the smell of wet earth spoke of distant rain.

'I somehow feel that today is going to be important in our coming together,' said Sambu and quoted: 'When, during Swati, a drop of rainwater falls into an oyster in the ocean, a pearl is formed.'

He made Bhavani repeat the mantra 'Ahirasi sutam' as he recited it softly.

You are the serpent god, you are the life, you are the support
for everything.
May god Dhatr release you, may god Vidhatr maintain you.
May Brahma, Brahaspati, Vishnu, Soma, Surya, the Ashvins,
Bhaga, Mitra and Varuna
Provide me with a brave child.

Bhavani was somewhat breathless when she repeated it; but managed the words without error.

When they returned to Tiruvaiyaru, Sambu fell ill and ran a fever for two weeks.

It was so much more difficult for Sambu to wait in expectation of a non-event than an actual event. As the day of the full moon neared, Sambu's average heart rate seemed to increase, till on the day of the full moon, Bhavani's monthly flows, which occurred with clockwork accuracy, commenced once more and Sambu found himself cooking vaththakkuzhambu and roasted appalams again, for those four days.

Bhavani, on the other hand, never seemed to lose hope and on her insistence they visited the Rajagopalaswamy temple at Mannargudi. The journey was pleasant, green paddy fields stretching to the horizon on both sides, a gentle breeze playing across, the 'jhal jhal' of the bullocks and the sway of the cart providing a soothing lullaby. At least, Bhavani seemed comfortable, Sambu being seated somewhat uncomfortably albeit with mathematical precision, in the middle of the covered bullock cart.

They performed the archana and abhishekam. The old priest of the temple took one look at Bhavani and made them sit in front of the main idol. He gave them the small bronze idol of the baby Krishna to hold. Krishna, sucking his big toe, lay prone on the many-headed serpent Adisesha. The priest then sang a lullaby to Krishna from the Thiruppavai in his high quivering voice.

Bhavani was moved. She thought of a young lion cub on her lap, face radiant like the moon, praised in a million adoring voices.

'Certainly you will have baby Krishna crawling around in your koodam,' the priest said.

Bhavani's face blossomed. After they had done their namaskaram to the old man, Bhavani stared pointedly at Sambu, till he untied the knot at his waist and was in the process of counting out some copper coins. The priest said, 'wait' and turned back to bring the archana plate. Bhavani leaned over and picked out the silver rupee from the untied knot and held it tightly in her fist, only to release it on to the plate when the priest returned.

The priest's face seemed to be one big grin.

'Live long,' he blessed Bhavani, 'Live long as a married woman with your flowers and kumkumam.' The priest told Sambu about the Sri Vidya chakra that was established there. Sambu decided then and there to initiate Bhavani into Sri Vidya worship; he himself had been initiated by a scholar in the disciple lineage of Bhaskararaya. From then on, every single day, Bhavani was in the puja room for an hour, seated in front of the silver Sri Chakra, showering it with red kumkumam.

However, even as the months progressed, Bhavani's monthly flows continued, regular and copious as ever.

The first time she missed a period, she wanted to be sure and did not tell anyone for two more months. She also wanted to avoid evil eyes despite the fact that the one person who had given her grief on that account, her mother-in-law, had died the year before, but not before extracting a promise from Bhavani that she would look after her son, who 'did not know anything'. Whether or not Sambu was as innocent as his mother claimed, he certainly did not suspect anything till it became obvious from the swell of her belly that started showing even through her madisar. While Sambu was happy, he was also deeply worried. Bhavani was due in December of 1888. He read the ephemeris—he did not use the vak panchangam, which assumed that the planets all started forth on their peregrinations at the same time from the first point of Aries at the beginning of the Kali era and derived their positions at any point in time using their mean motions. He used the drik panchangam, which made corrections for planetary positions based on observations. By February, there would be a Rahu–Saturn conjunction in mutual aspect with Mars. This would not augur well for the child's married life.

December 1888

Sambu had finished teaching his students, who came to him to learn the Vedanta and mimamsa, for the day and was busy with the monthly tharpanam during the new moon day. He was praying for the peace of his forefathers on his mother's side, when the news about the baby arrived. He was a little disappointed that it was a girl since it did nothing to cancel his reservation in puth.

'I think it is my mother who has come down in the form of the child,' Sambu told Bhavani, who was too tired to say anything though she rather fervently hoped not. It was a foregone conclusion that the child would be named Janaki, after his mother. She wanted to name the child Srividya, but Sambu prevailed.

They waited for one and a half years for Janaki to be weaned, and commenced their pilgrimage again.

'After all,' Bhavani said, 'God has begun to open His eyes. Now I am sure we will have a boy.'

This time they travelled to the temples of all the seven grahas— the Sun temple at Suryanar koil, the Moon temple at Thingaloor, Mars at Vaideeswaran koil, Mercury at Thiruvenkadu, Jupiter at Alankudi, Venus at Kanjanoor and Saturn at Thirunallaru. They even visited the shadowy ones, Rahu at Thirunageswaram and Ketu at Keelaperumpallam, which were, as Sambu pointed out, more mathematical points in the sky rather than physical bodies. Even though the temples were all located within a circle of a radius of twenty miles, they needed to make allowances for the travelling time and the closing of the temples, most of which closed after the midday puja. It took them nearly fifteen days to complete the circuit, travelling by oxcart and foot.

April 1890

By the time they came back to Tiruvaiyaru, Sambu found that he had to put in extra folds in the pancha kachcham he was wearing. Bhavani, too, had lost some weight. Bhavani retrieved Janaki from the neighbours who had undertaken to look after her in their absence.

Every house had an elaborate kolam with red borders drawn

around it. Someone had even drawn one in front of Sambu's house. The occasion was the festival at the Panchanadeeswarar temple. All of Tiruvaiyaru wore a festive look. Houses were decorated with mango leaves and flowers. They heard the periya melam. Even at that distance, Sambu recognized the fist of Viswanatha Pillai at the nadaswaram in the 'Saadinchane' that flowed through the air with ecstatic vigour. He was certain that it must have been Ponnuswami Pillai who set up such complex percussive resonances in the air with the thavil.

It was the special day of the full moon in the twelve-day celebration. All the neighbouring temples were participating in the festival that celebrated the marriage of Nandi Deva, personal assistant to the principal deity of Tiruvaiyaru and a god in his own right. The deities were paying an annual visit to all the six holy temples that were connected to the temple at Tiruvaiyaru. Deities from each of the temples would join in the procession, adding to the ever-swelling crowds. Sambu and Bhavani forgot their tiredness and walked with the procession, slaking their thirst at the many water stations that were put up on the way. Bhavani's gaze was fixed on the swaying idol of Siva on the palanquin. They had a dip in the Cauvery to finish the day.

Bhavani slept uneasily that night.

The procession-idol of Panchanadeeswarar was dancing, swaying this way and that. A snake that lay wreathed around the deity's neck loosened and fell down. It started moving towards her, bathed in light, the middle of its sinuous body looped high. In her dream, Bhavani was awed but not afraid.

When she got up and woke Sambu, 'It is indeed an auspicious dream,' he said. 'It is significant that the snake was shaped like the hump of a bull. It signifies Nandi, who was born from the side of Siva.'

From that day, till Panju was born almost nine months later,

Bhavani added the repetition of the 108 names of Siva to her daily puja.

November 1896

As was the routine every day, Sambu woke up an hour and a half before dawn, before the beginning of the Brahma muhurtam—a forty-five-minute period that he believed was most suitable for meditation. He took his trusted, albeit somewhat dented brass jug, filled it with water, went to the field behind the agraharam and completed his ablutions. He was careful to wind his poonal around his ears and afterwards, made sure that the excreta were buried properly. He had his bath at his usual place, stepping down gingerly into the water, as the last few steps were always slippery. He then performed the sandhya vandanam, the daily ritual to be done thrice a day, once at dawn when night turned into day, once at noon when day morphed into evening and once at the twilight hour when evening turned into night.

As always, he repeated the Narasimha mantra, into which his father had initiated him.

My obeisance unto the ferocious and powerful Mahavishnu, the fiery one, who faces all directions, the fearful one, Narasimha, who is death to death itself.

This was in honour of Narasimha, the god of transitions who killed Hiranyakasipu when it was neither day nor night at the threshold of the house where it was neither inside nor outside in the form of a man-lion that was neither man nor beast by hoisting him on to his thighs where it was neither in the air nor on the ground.

He changed into the veshti that he had brought, reapplied the sacred ash on his body and washed his wet veshti, approaching with some reverence the 'Dikshitar kal', a stone that had been named after his grandfather because he always washed his clothes on that stone.

He had a smile on his face as he walked back, thinking of the method he was going to use to teach his students.

Sambu's face seemed brighter with the 'U' of sandalwood paste that now shone on his forehead like the crescent moon. As he entered the thinnai, the group, consisting of around ten children of various ages from six to sixteen, stood up, hands folded in front of their chests. He sat down fastidiously on the wooden seat that one of the students dragged in place. He waited for the students to settle down and began in a sonorous voice that would have served another twenty students easily.

'Today I am going to start with literature,' he said.

He looked around and started reciting from the *Ramodantam* without referring to the palm leaves in front of him. He started with an invocation to Valmiki, the author of the Ramayana, and stopped only at the third verse, where the rakshasas are allowed to ask their boons. He now looked at the oldest boy.

'Setu, can you repeat the verses?'

The boy stood up, hands folded across the chest; his face a blank palm leaf with nothing writ on it.

'All right then. I will chant again.' Without missing a beat, he continued, repeating the verses. Even after he finished, the boy's face remained blank. He commanded him to sit down.

'Anyone?' Can anyone repeat the verses?'

The rustling of the leaves of a nearby tree could be heard. A crow cawed loudly.

Sambu sighed deeply, looked towards the door leading inside and raised his voice.

'Panju!'

He waited for a minute and shouted, louder this time.

'Panjuu—'

'Yes, Appa,' Panju's voice sounded from the doorway.

Panju looked short for his five years but carried himself with a quiet dignity.

'Stand here,' he ordered his son and continued, turning towards his disciples. 'I am going to recite the verses again. Pay attention this time,' he said and started. '*Sripathim pranipathyam—*'

'—Appa, how many times are you going to repeat this? I am bored,' interjected Panju.

Sambu stopped reciting. 'If you know the verse, why don't you recite it?' he said.

'I learnt it the first time around Appa. I heard you from the mittam.'

Panju's voice was melodious, with a barely discernible lisp; he accentuated the hard consonants to compensate for it.

My son memorized the verse after listening to it only once. He is an ekachandagrahi!

His smile said it all.

1897–1908

Tiruvaiyaru, Madras

Four

In 1897, Bal Gangadhar Tilak wrote an article in the *Kesari* justifying the killing of Afzal Khan by Shivaji more than two hundred years before. He had written, 'God has not conferred upon the foreigners the grant, inscribed on a copperplate, of the Kingdom of Hindustan. The Maharaja (Shivaji) strove to drive them away from the land of his birth. He did not thereby commit the sin of coveting what belonged to others. Do not be circumscribed in your vision, like a frog in a well; get out of the Penal Code, and enter the extremely high atmosphere of the Srimad Bhagavad Gita, and consider the actions of great men.'

The metaphorical allusion was not lost on the subtle Indian mind. On the twenty-second of June, the Collector of Poona, Mr Rand, who was responsible for the plague measures, and a young military officer, Lieutenant Ayerst, were shot dead.

The jury found Tilak guilty of sedition, sentencing him to eighteen months rigorous imprisonment, Judge Strachey having explained the intended meaning of 'disaffection' in the act to them as an 'absence of affection' rather than 'hatred'.

Panju was just five and too young to be influenced by the nationalistic storm in Poona, but in the delta, which had always had a strong connection with the Marathas, there were whispers of protest among the youth.

Panju's brilliance began to manifest itself early. By five he was being routinely hauled before older people, reluctant guests who had come to have a meal from the fabled hand of Bhavani, whose morkkuzhambu was to die for, whose paruppusili often sent guests into transports of ecstatic delight. They felt obliged to listen to this near-toddler after having incurred a debt of salt. Their initial bored expressions soon turned to amazement as Panju, with a lisping but otherwise flawless diction, started reciting the *Ashtavakra Gita*. By the time he finished reciting the first stanza wherein Janaka asks Ashtavakra about the means for self-knowledge, the expressions would turn to envy. When Sambu asked him to explain the meaning and Panju obliged, his tender lips mouthing the Tamil as proficiently as they did the Sanskrit, the envy was replaced by the certain knowledge that their children or grandchildren would never ever be able to achieve this. The comparison between the original Ashtavakra and Panju was *meant* to be made—both scholars at a tender age, the only difference being that Panju's body was not deformed like Ashtavakra's.

He had one fault, one that his sister Janaki was acutely aware of, particularly since Sambu often said, 'Why can't you be bold like your sister?' Panju was one frightened boy. He was scared if no one was around him; he was scared if there was a crowd, when someone spoke in a whisper or in a loud tone. He wet his bed at night regularly till he was five and sporadically till he was seven.

Bhavani's life centred on her son's.

Bhavani almost always served most of the vegetable pieces in the sambar to Panju. The unbroken portion of curd from the pot and the cream would be ladled out to him, others often getting a slushy mixture of curd and whey. Janaki had to make do with pavadais meant for someone far older and bigger, the hem tucked up and stitched, to be gradually let out as she grew older. Panju was the only boy in the agraharam to wear half pants without stitched-in suspenders. His clothes fit him well and Bhavani insisted on new ones being bought every year. If Panju fell sick, Bhavani would stay awake, keep checking him for fever and in general fulfil his every fancy.

If there was one trait that Janaki shared with her mother, it was love for Panju.

Janaki had been initiating Panju into the secrets of Pallanguzhi since morning and Panju proved a fast learner. The fish-shaped wooden board lay between them. Most of the fourteen carved-out concavities had cowries in them, a few tamarind seeds standing in for missing cowries. It was Janaki's turn to play. She picked a cavity and started distributing the cowries, one in each hole, going clockwise around the board. When she stopped before an empty hole, capturing a rich haul of cowries from the next one, Panju was shocked. 'How is that possible, Akka?' he remonstrated. 'You told me that if I pick up from that cavity, I would lose.' Janaki then showed him her upturned palm that was largely empty. Only her little finger was bent and it held a cowrie.

'But that's cheating, Akka!' shouted Panju.

'Yes. I just wanted to show you how you can cheat in the game. I learnt this from Chitti who had come home last year. Even cheating should be done intelligently.'

'But that's still cheating, Akka.'

'Who is cheating?' asked Sambu as he entered. He took in the Pallanguzhi board in one glance. 'What is this?' he said, 'So many shells seem to be missing. At this rate you will be playing only with tamarind seeds. Every time, when you put away the board, you must count the markers. I had a hundred and fifty of them when my father gave it to me and I didn't lose a single one. Now fifteen or twenty of those seem to be missing.'

'We will put the board away, Appa. Anyway, I am tired of this cheating game,' said Panju.

Janaki started gathering the shells and the seeds and putting them into the biscuit tin in which they were stored. Panju stared morosely at his father.

Sambu seemed to be in a good mood. 'Don't be upset, Panju. Have you played Paramapadam before?'

'No, Appa,' said Panju.

'I might have the Paramapadam board with me,' said Sambu. 'Let me check.'

Sambu was back a few minutes later. He spread the stiff cloth he had brought on the ground. A matrix of individually numbered squares was drawn on it with snakes and ladders all over. Each of the beginning squares of the snakes and the ending squares of the ladders were named. The snakes were all named after the mythical ones, Karkotaka, Takshaka, Mucalinda, Sesha and others. The letters were faded, the pictures were beautiful, drawn in pen and ink. The ladders were named after noble qualities like wisdom, valour and truth.

Sambu also brought out a pair of rectangular dice. 'These are made of ivory,' he said, beaming.

The game started.

Panju and Janaki loved the game, giving in to whoops of joy when they went up ladders, shouting in disappointment when they went down snakes.

Sambu, too, got into the spirit of things and when Panju landed on Takshaka, going down all the way to the starting square and started to protest, he told them the story of Takshaka.

'Janamejaya performed a yajna to destroy snakes everywhere in retaliation against Takshaka, a snake who had killed his father Parikshit. Snakes from all directions started falling into the sacrificial fire, quite against their will. Takshaka tried to hide by coiling his body around the cot of Indra, the king of gods. The sage performing the yajna saw this with his supernatural vision and offered a large ladle of oblation to the fire god, saying,' here Sambu paused and brought his hands down with dramatic finality. '"Sendraaya swaha"— let Indra be consumed along with Takshaka.'

The children shouted with laughter at this.

'So, Takshaka and Indra fell into the fire?' asked Panju.

Sambu looked away as though he had done something illegal. His voice changed to his everyday teaching voice.

'No, another sage, called Astika, stopped the wholesale slaughter of snakes. That is a story for another day. Actually, I meant to tell you about the ladders. I got carried away. You will notice that it is impossible to finish the game—attain salvation—without climbing up the ladder called "Sacrifice".'

Sambu looked at Panju whose eyes were focused on something far away.

December 1899

Panju excelled at most games of dexterity and mental agility. However, when Janaki wanted to play kittippul, which involved hitting a sharpened piece of stick with another larger one, he demurred because he was afraid that the smaller wooden piece might pierce his eyes or fall on his head. He was also too scared to play the 'green horse', which involved vaulting over one another.

When other boys were not looking, he enjoyed playing paandi, a game usually played by girls, with his sister.

But tomorrow was going to be different.

Panju woke early even though he didn't have classes; his father was away to Mysore where he was to be awarded the title of Sahitya Sagara in recognition of his contribution to Sanskrit literature and teaching. Panju was in a hurry to finish his breakfast that consisted of the previous day's rice soaked in water with added buttermilk and salt.

He got in everyone's way. He very nearly broke his sister's pride and joy, a writing slate, by bumping into her while she was trying to work out arithmetical sums on it. 'Sorry, Akka,' he shouted in reply to Janaki's 'What's wrong with you today?' as he ran out and promptly collided with an old lady who had come to borrow some sugar from Bhavani, causing her to go back muttering into her house about another bath that her ritual purity demanded.

He ran into the storeroom where he had carefully secreted his prized top that his father had bought him during the last Brahmotsavam festival. The top was red and blue. He had rubbed the metal nail on a granite slab till it was blunt and spun beautifully without jittering. Janaki had made a hole in a bottle cap and threaded the spinning rope through it, knotting one end of the rope to keep it in place. Over the last week, Panju had spent practically every waking moment in learning to spin the top and pick it up by looping the rope once around it while it was still spinning. He would then flick it up by tightening the rope and catch it neatly. Though he tried several times to spin the top and whip it back directly on his palms, he didn't come close to succeeding. The top was now to go on its maiden voyage. Kuppu who lived in Kudiyanavan Street had agreed to a match. Today was the day!

He polished the top once more with his veshti, tucked it at his middle, and was off.

It was the first of December. The year, 1899. Kipling had published his *White Man's Burden* and Lord Curzon had assumed it presumptuously, believing that 'the highest ideal of truth was to a large extent, a western conception', instituting an education policy that was geared towards producing clerks.

There was nothing to indicate that there was anything special about the day. Nothing to indicate that the century was in its dying moments and a new one would begin in a month. The sky though was an unusual blue. Layers of white clouds tinged with grey had gathered on the western horizon, looking like bundles of cotton stacked higgledy-piggledy one on top of the other. The air was still. A couple of piss-poor huts, flanked by a few stunted coconut trees, dotted the landscape in Panju's view.

Kuppu was already waiting. 'Nice top,' he said and sniggered. The game began.

Kuppu undid his hair and retied it once before flicking his rope. He caught the top neatly, whipping it up into his hands without it touching the ground. Panju was much slower, despite winding the rope around the top only halfway through to save time. Consequently, he had to keep his top inside the circle drawn on the hard, packed earth. This time, Kuppu's top hit his squarely, knocking it off the circle, and spun on the ground for Kuppu to pick up with his rope. Panju had lost the match almost before it had begun. Time for the forfeits. The forfeit allowed the winner to inflict damage on the loser's top by stabbing it with his top five times. Now Kuppu produced his surprise, a top that he exclusively used for giving and receiving forfeits. It was a huge top, bigger than Panju's fist, made of hardened wood with a thick, inch-long nail, honed impossibly sharp, gleaming wickedly.

Panju started to protest but Kuppu's top had already struck once. When Kuppu lifted his top, Panju's top stuck to his.

'Noooo...' shouted Panju as the second blow sank the nail deeper.

'Don't, don't...' Panju's breathing became heavier and was coming out in big gasps.

The next blow broke Panju's top cleanly in two.

For a moment, Panju stood still. The veins on his neck stood out. Arms flailing, he launched himself at his much taller opponent. Kuppu was unbalanced and fell down. He recovered quickly. He got up and caught hold of Panju's left arm and twisted it. He then kicked the legs out from beneath Panju. He kept Panju's arms twisted behind his back as he rained blows on his head.

Blood streamed out of Panju's nose. He tried to ask Kuppu

to stop but no words came out of his mouth. He was finding it difficult to breathe. He was certain he could not last much longer. That's when it happened. He heard Kuppu's high-pitched howl before the pressure on his back eased. His hands were entirely free now.

He got up with difficulty. Janaki stood, her hair open, looking like vengeful Kali, with her fists full of Kuppu's hair.

Janaki yanked.

Fear and horror showed on Kuppu's face. His eyes were frozen on the fistful of hair in Janaki's hand.

'You have pulled out my hair,' he started wailing and ran away when Janaki took an aggressive step in his direction.

'What's that smell?' Janaki asked, wrinkling her nose. 'Have you wet yourself?'

The pained look on Panju's tear-laden face was an answer.

'I won't let you suffer in any way.' Janaki hugged him fiercely.

'I won't let it happen either,' said Panju. There was determination in his voice.

The western sky now looked like white cotton candy that had been given a good licking over.

FIVE

Panju looked around and spotted the signboard on the neem tree. It said 'Bhimasena Akhara' in faded Devanagari lettering. There was a drawing, presumably of Bhima, his waist impossibly thin, muscles grotesquely accentuated, holding aloft a huge Indian club in the shape of a frustum of a cone by the short handle at the smaller end.

Panju entered and a serene beauty enveloped him. The akhara belonged to a different world. The area was bounded by mango and neem trees. A square sandpit of about twenty feet by twenty was laid out in the middle, covered with a tin roof resting on stakes driven into the four corners of the pit. The sand was of a reddish hue; the texture different from the surrounding soil. A fresh aroma rose from the sand.

Panju approached the pit.

Two young men grappled in the pit, their oily bodies glistening in the afternoon sun. The wrestlers wore identical clothing, a piece of cloth that covered their loins, wrapped around their waists, forming three triangles, one in the middle with its apex pointing down and the base on top, the apexes of the other two triangles attached to the base. On the far side of the pit, a middle-aged man sat on a stone bench in the shade of a mango tree. A streak of a red paste of kumkumam and sandal flamed across his forehead. A wall of brick encircled the tree. Underneath was an idol of a muscular Hanuman in profile, one hand holding aloft the Sanjeevini Mountain and the other holding a mace poised on his shoulder, the left leg bent a little and off the ground. The right leg was balanced on the toes; on the whole an impossible posture unless he was flying. The idol itself was smeared with a red powder, too red to have been made with saffron. Fresh flowers lay strewn on the ground, evidencing a recent puja.

'Have you had a bath?' The man on the stone bench hadn't moved; the voice boomed across.

'Yes,' Panju shouted back, puzzled.

'Come here.'

Panju skirted around the pit and approached the man who was dressed like the wrestlers except for a shawl around his shoulders. The shawl had fallen open on one side to reveal a muscular chest, a thick wrist and a prominent vein that started at the wrist and went up nearly to his collarbone.

'What do you want?' asked the man, stroking a moustache that turned up to end in fine points.

'Why did you ask me if I have had a bath?' asked Panju.

'The akhara is a holy place. No one is allowed in unless he is pure in body. Now who are you and what do you want?'

'I am Panchapakesan, son of Sambu Sastry, grandson of Panchapakesa Sastry, great grandson of —'

'—Sambu Sastry.'

'You know my family, Aiya?'

'No, I just guessed that it was a tradition in your family to name children after their grandfathers.'

'Are you the owner of this place, Aiya?'

'Yes, I am Choturam Payilvan.'

'Sir, I came to develop my body and learn wrestling.'

The payilvan looked Panju up and down and burst out laughing.

'You,' he said, 'must be eight years old?'

'Nine,' said Panju, pride showing in his voice, 'and running ten.'

'And what caste are you?'

'Brahmin, Iyer.'

'Brahmin? You will be useless in any fight. Why don't you go home and recite mantras instead?'

'Aiya,' said Panju, 'I am determined to take up bodybuilding and wrestling seriously. I won't let you down.'

'Right, then. This is what I want you to do. Run around this akhara five times and come back here. No walking or sitting down anywhere in between. That will give me time to think about it.'

Panju's lungs were on fire when he completed the fifth round and stood in front of the payilvan. He was trembling and breathing heavily.

The payilvan looked at him. 'At least you have persistence. That's good. And you did the five rounds. I was counting. Joining the akhara for training means maintaining a strict discipline. You have to get up every day by 3.00 a.m., finish your bath and other ablutions and you will have to be here at 4.00 a.m. You cannot eat till you have finished practice. You have to follow the diet that I prescribe.'

'As long as it is vegetarian. I promise to do all of that, Aiya,' Panju had difficulty in forming the words as he was gasping for breath.

'Normally, I don't train children. You will be the first. I will see you tomorrow morning.'

It was so dark outside that Panju could hardly see his hand in front of him. There was the hint of a nip in the air that lifted his spirits and made him want to sing loudly. He ran almost all the way to the akhara, revelling in the feel of the breeze against his face. He arrived breathless. Two wrestlers were just getting ready to get into the pit. Panju watched, fascinated, as another young wrestler lay face down, palms flat on the ground directly beneath his shoulders. Then he lifted his buttocks high while touching the ground with his palms and the soles of his feet. He then bent his elbows and lunged forward, chest gliding between his palms and arching up as he straightened his arms, repeating the entire cycle in a fluid motion.

'That is called dandal,' said the payilvan from behind Panju. 'Would you like to try it?'

'Yes. Very much,' said Panju. The payilvan first made him wear the traditional langoti and asked him to pray to Hanuman before starting the exercise.

Panju closed his eyes and muttered a Hanuman sloka that he had learnt.

'Do five dandals,' said the payilvan.

After three, Panju's shoulders were on fire.

'I didn't realize this was so difficult,' said Panju.

'What you have to do,' said the payilvan, 'is to look ahead and above at a fixed point. This will help keep your head still. And the most important thing is to do the exercise with total awareness. If there is no concentration, you will not get the results.'

He then taught Panju baski, which involved squatting on the balls of his feet and standing up.

'How many dandals and baskis should I do in a day?' asked Panju.

'That depends on you. This one,' he said, indicating the wrestler whom Panju had seen earlier, 'does two thousand dandals and a thousand baskis a day, doing about fifty at a stretch.'

After an hour of strenuous working out, the payilvan called out to Panju. 'That is enough for today,' he said. 'You need to put on weight. Your daily diet should include a lot of ghee, milk and almonds. Tomorrow morning, when you get up, you will find your arms and legs stiff and they will be so for a couple of days. Just ignore that and come in the mornings.'

Sambu noticed that Panju was absent in the morning. He woke up earlier than usual the next day.

'Where are you off to, Panju?'

'Appa, I am doing exercises. Early morning is supposed to be the best time for doing that.'

'Why don't you do them here in our backyard?'

'These require a teacher. I am going to Choturam Payilvan.'

Sambu was immersed in thought.

'He is a Jat from the north, isn't he?'

Panju had already left. Sambu felt relieved that he didn't have to continue the conversation. For one he did not like the idea of confrontation, certainly not with his own son. For another, he was not sure if he wanted to pass on the biases of his generation regarding purity of caste, much less his own ambivalence in that regard.

He decided that he wouldn't quiz Panju anymore regarding his morning activities.

Bhavani was happy when Panju told her about his additional diet. Milk and ghee were no problem as they had three cows in their cattle shed. Almonds? They couldn't afford the almonds. Her brows furrowed in thought.

Kanakavalli.

Her brow cleared. Kanakavalli's husband had one of the largest grocery shops in Kumbakonam and he studied Sanskrit with Sambu. Her parents were among the biggest landlords of Tiruvaiyaru. At the moment, she was in Tiruvaiyaru. Bhavani set off to their house.

'The doctor has said that Sambu should have badam milk every day. Otherwise, he may lose his voice,' Bhavani told Kanakavalli, who consulted her husband. He was happy to be of some service to his teacher and agreed to provide her with a seer of almonds two to three times a year, whenever they came to Tiruvaiyaru.

Panju grew stronger and more muscular. Within a couple of months he could do a hundred dandals a day. He was also able to do, in a flowing sequence, the twelve poses of the surya namaskar, some fifty times consecutively, including the correct breathing, awareness and the mantras. His guru, happy with his progress, initiated him into the wrestling pit. At first, a lot of the older members of the akhara wrestled with him because they were supposed to start the day with a light wrestling load and gradually increase it. Within a couple of months, however, the same members didn't want to train with him first thing in the morning. Panju understood the implied compliment and was happy.

The payilvan taught him not just wrestling, exercises and how to swing Indian clubs, but also the arcane knowledge of marma points in the body. He also cautioned Panju that any strikes to these would immobilize, possibly even kill.

Panju nodded. He would be careful. He certainly did not intend to injure anyone badly, let alone kill.

Six

December 1899

It was the second of December 1899, a fact that Sambu noted as he came back from the temple later that evening. He had occasion to note the date as Janaki's face was tear-streaked and Bhavani's was wreathed in smiles. Bhavani's 'Your daughter has grown up,' was redundant as even Sambu had guessed as much.

When he consulted the ephemeris, he was shocked. Six planets were in conjunction in Scorpio, including the shadowy Rahu. This occurred in the seventh house from the ascendant, in the house of marriage and partnerships. Venus, the beneficent one, the significator for marriage who was outside the orbit of the planetary war, was afflicted by Saturn who was within a six-degree orb. This warned him of something dark and foreboding and at the same time noble and exalted: he couldn't quite figure it out.

Janaki did not understand why Bhavani asked her to sit apart from everyone. The Vedic and the traditional ceremonies went on for three days. The one thing that stuck in her memory was being drenched by potfuls of turmeric water in the presence of half the village.

Bhavani was conflicted. She was happy that her little girl had now come of age. She was worried about what the others in the agraharam would say about them keeping a grown-up girl at home without marrying her off.

'You are not going to school from tomorrow.' Sambu's words felt like iron spikes being driven into her head. Janaki consoled herself quickly. *This is not a battle I am going to lose.* She sat alone for a long time marshalling her thoughts. She looked for inspiration in the book that she was holding, but Noah Webster was unobliging. She gave herself an hour to consider her strategy before she approached her father.

'Appa, I want to know the purpose of human existence.'

Sambu was taken aback at this sudden question, but his face and the serious demeanour he always assumed while answering a question that excited him showed that he was pleased.

'I am sure you know the answer to the question. The objectives of human existence are dharma, artha or wealth, kama or passion and moksha—salvation.'

'The ultimate objective of human endeavour is then salvation, right?'

'Of course,' said Sambu with narrowed eyes, trying to guess what was coming next.

'Is it different for a woman? I am asking only because these are named purusharthas, indicating that these are male prerogatives.'

Now Sambu was animated. 'Not at all. Shakti or the female energy is subsumed in the form of the purusha. Have I not taught you all the pathikams of the saint Appar on Tiruvaiyaru? What does he say?' He cleared his throat and sang one of the verses without waiting for an answer.

'Does he not talk about the female energy being part of Siva? The ultimate goal of human existence is salvation—whether you are male or female.'

'And what does one need to do to attain salvation?' asked Janaki.

'Now you seem to be testing me. Anyway, our seers have said there are many ways to attain salvation. I firmly believe in the path of knowledge.'

'Is this path of knowledge denied to women by our shastras?'

'Not at all. Great women scholars are mentioned in the Vedas. Maitreyi, who was taught by Sage Yajnavalkya. Gargi, who confounded even the great Yajnavalkya with her knowledge, and many others.'

'And the knowledge is gained by…?'

'Learning at the feet of a guru.'

'Appa, is that what you want to deprive me of?'

'What do you mean? I want the best of everything for you. My daughter will be a Maitreyi, a Gargi.'

'So I can go to school,' said Janaki.

'Yes…no, what about your marriage? What will the agrahara folks say about my letting a grown daughter of mine go out of the house?'

'Appa, have you always acted according to what others say?'

'Me? No. I have always done what is right instead of convenient—the shreyas instead of the preyas. In fact, even against the wishes of my father, I—'

'—I am your daughter, Appa.'

Sambu was silent; the world was indeed changing.

The discussion had gone along expected lines for Janaki, even though the last bit was a fortuitous piece of serendipity. But Janaki did not want to tip her hand fully as yet by revealing her thoughts on marriage.

SEVEN

August 1901

She must have been thirteen.

Janaki read everything that used the English script. She read and reread *A Grammatical Institute of the English Language* by Noah Webster, of unknown provenance, but lying around at home for as long as she could remember. Her other favourite was his *Compendious Dictionary of the English Language*. Both tomes were dog-eared from long usage and constituted her primary reading material.

Janaki was busy thinking of imaginative variations she could introduce when they played paandi next when Sambu's voice, calling her, sliced through her musings. She ran to him even before she realized what she was doing and stood panting. Her father was seated on the ground on a mat. In front of him lay his accounts ledger in which he maintained a scrupulous account of his daily expenses and sporadic revenues. There was something new. A large pile of something tied up in red silk cloth.

'This is for you,' Sambu said, smiling.

'What is it, Appa?' Janaki couldn't imagine anything of that size and shape.

'Open it and see,' said Sambu.

Janaki put aside the book that she had in her hand and tried to undo the knots. Sambu had to help her. At last the knots were untied. Six vellum-bound books lay stacked, one atop the other. Janaki picked up a book from the top and turned to the title page. The verso had a frontispiece of an Englishman dressed in the height of conservative fashion of the late eighteenth century along with a small sketch of the Colosseum. The recto page proclaimed:

'The History of the Decline and Fall of the Roman Empire – by Edward Gibbon, Efq.' followed by 'Volume the first.'

Below this, someone had written in a dense but flowery hand, 'To my brilliant but opinionated teacher.' Even the signature was of uniformly slanted letters, the loops forming beautiful curlicues.

'What are these, Appa?' Janaki could not keep the excitement out of her voice.

'An Englishman whom I helped translate some Sanskrit works into English gifted them to me. I hope they satisfy your reading frenzy for a while. I would have given a few of them to Panju, but he is too young. Well, perhaps not too young, but he seems more interested in Sanskrit and Tamil.'

Sambu went back to his accounts and continued worrying about the quarter-anna difference between the balance on hand and the figure in the ledger.

Janaki was about to take the books away, two by two, when she hesitated.

'Appa...'

'Yes...' Sambu looked up from his ledger.

'Will you write something for me in the books the way your student has written?'

Sambu smiled at her and started writing in his copperplate hand on the flyleaf of one of the books. He finished writing in all the six volumes before he let her see what was written. The inscriptions read—'To my Maitreyi, a student of western culture.'

The books became Janaki's constant comrades over the next several years. She found it hard reading at first; but thanks to Noah Webster and a retired English teacher who lived next door, she found that the passages evoked fresher and deeper meanings every time she read them, even though the Greek and Latin gems that were interspersed through the books remained largely untranslated. Her appetite for learning only increased over time.

EIGHT

June 1904, Madras

Vichu entered the front porch of the house exhibiting the hurry of a sadir dancer changing for the next act during a brief intermission. He took off his turban and his coat and threw them on a chair. He removed his vest, dabbed at his armpits with it, rolled it into a ball and threw that also on the chair.

'Endee!' he shouted, sitting in the thinnai, resting his head against a pillar.

Bhagyam came out, bearing a lota of buttermilk. Her movements were quick, punctuated by pauses, during which her eyes darted to and fro. She gave the buttermilk to Vichu. She then occupied herself with fussing at the clothes on the chair.

'Are you waiting for an auspicious day to keep them away? Take them in.'

For a moment, she stared blankly at Vichu.

'This came in the post today,' she said, holding out a postcard.

Vichu glanced at it. It was a regular quarter-anna postcard closely filled with writing in Tamil.

'It's from my sister, Mangalam,' he said.

'Bhavani, you mean,' Bhagyam corrected gently.

'Of course I said Bhavani,' said Vichu, tossing the postcard unread on the chair.

'Why don't you read what is in there? It may be something important,' Bhagyam said.

'All right, give me the letter.'

Bhagyam abruptly put down the clothes she had picked up and handed Vichu the postcard again. He held it casually in his left hand while pouring the buttermilk into his mouth.

'The usual,' he said. 'Sambu seems to be in the best of health. Panju and Janaki are growing up well. What is this... she wants to visit us because it will provide Panju with a broad outlook? I will write to her and say there is plague in Madras, particularly in Triplicane.'

'Please don't do anything like that,' said Bhagyam. 'After all, she's your sister—'

'My sister is dead.'

'The other sister is still alive and she wants to come. I think you should invite her. After all, you are the only mama of her children. Otherwise people will say you are mean and ungenerous. All said and done, don't forget we, too, have a daughter. We might need the help of relatives in finding Vijaya a bridegroom. I have said whatever I wanted to say. Now it is your decision.' Before Vichu could answer, she grabbed his clothes and vanished.

Vichu was still staring at the postcard when six-year-old Vijaya came running up to him.

'Appa, did you call me? Amma said you did.'

'No, yes,' said Vichu. 'Go and bring me a blank postcard.'

'Where is it, Appa?' asked Vijaya.

'On my head,' snapped Vichu.

When Vijaya moved closer, perhaps to inspect his head, he said quietly, 'Ask your mother.'

'Is this what you wanted? Amma asked me to give this to you,' said Vijaya. She had a postcard in her hand.

Vichu started writing. He had to word his invitation carefully to preclude any possibility of Sambu coming along.

He wrote: '... Sambu is a busy man. He won't have the time to come up to Madras. It will also be difficult for him in this city to follow all those daily rituals that he has. The houses in Madras are not as big as the houses in Tiruvaiyaru. Our house is no exception. If you are worried about travelling alone, you can bring Panju along. You must stay for at least a couple of days.'

❖

Panju stared at the clock tower at the central station. 'Is Madras full of buildings like this?' was his first question. This was followed by a fusillade of questions. How big is Madras? Is it bigger than Kumbakonam? You told me it has a sea and a beach. Is the sea bigger than Mahamaham tank? Will there be a lot of white people there? He kept up the barrage until they arrived at Raja Street in the jatka that Vichu had hired for them.

It was late morning when they arrived and since it was a Sunday, Vichu was home.

'Come, come, Bhavani,' said Vichu and went back to his copy of the previous evening's *The Mail* that he had abstracted from the office.

'Mama,' said Panju in a high-pitched voice, 'Are there a lot of places to see in Madras?'

'Yes, yes,' said Vichu, irritation in his voice.

'Like, for instance?' Panju persisted.

'You have Seththa College, Uyir College, Marina, the lighthouse and many beautiful buildings. Many of them were designed by famous Englishmen like Mister Chisholm. Anyway, I have arranged for a jatka every day to take you and your mother around Madras.'

'How can a college be alive or dead, Mama? What is it?'

'That is the way the locals refer to the zoological gardens and the Madras government museum,' said Vichu.

'Why don't you also come with us, Anna,' asked Bhavani.

'I have no time at all. You see, those Englishmen simply depend on me for everything. If I am not there, not even a memo will go out of my office. I have in my custody so many important papers and documents. You see, there is a young Assistant Collector posted in my department. I have to train him. No doubt, he has the natural courage and leadership qualities of a Britisher. But you see, I still have to teach him government regulations and how to draft a memo to a superior officer. I would like to come. But I simply cannot.' Vichu kept shaking his head long after he had stopped speaking.

Vichu lived near the junction of Pycrofts Road and Big Street. Panju and Bhavani had to walk only for a few minutes along Pycrofts Road to reach the beach. Vijaya had joined them and she had Bhavani's forefinger firmly in her grasp all through the walk to the Marina. Panju loved the beach. He gawked momentarily at the magnificent buildings of the Presidency College but then went straight to the water and splashed around while Bhavani and Vijaya sat down on the sand, some distance from the water. Panju found the wet, coarse feel of the sand different from the drier, finer river sand. He found that he could float with little or no effort in the seawater. Bhavani had to drag him out of the water when it started getting dark.

Panju was too excited to sleep well that night.

'Let us go to the zoo first, Amma,' said Panju as they set out. Bhavani asked the jatka driver to take them to 'Uyir College'. Panju sat in the back, leaning out of the vehicle to take in the sights. He was mesmerized by the wide roads and the red-brick buildings built in a fusion of Indian and European styles. He loved the profusion of arches, roofs and gables. He was even more fascinated by the animals. He had never seen a tiger or a cheetah before, but what really took his breath away was the orangutan that stood at the back of the cage, massive arms reaching to the floor. He wondered what it would be like to wrestle with an orangutan. Not pleasant, he decided.

By the time they went to the 'Setha College', the museum, Bhavani was tired and wasn't too interested in looking at the 'dead' exhibits.

'I will be sitting down on one of the benches under a tree outside until you are ready to leave. See everything quickly and come,' said Bhavani and started walking back to the entrance. Panju hardly seemed to hear her as he was deeply absorbed in the array of stones that occupied the slanting display cases. He had to stand on tiptoe to look at them properly.

He was shocked at the size of the skeleton of a massive baleen whale. He tried to measure it and found that it was about twenty steps long.

'It is around forty feet long.' A new voice broke into his calculations. He turned around. A tall man stood in front of him. The most striking feature was his colour. It was a ruddy pink. He wore a dark grey coat and a waistcoat with trousers to match. A bowler adorned his head. He sported a well-trimmed beard.

The man put a hand to Panju's chin, turned it around a little and observed his face carefully.

'You are Brahmin, aren't you?' observed the man.

'That is not so hard to guess, after seeing the tuft of my hair and my poonal,' said Panju.

'I see that you are interested in measurements. I would like you to come along to my room. I just want to take some of your measurements.'

Panju did not completely understand what the man was saying. 'Are there other interesting things in your room?'

'Yes, well,' said the man, 'I have some equipment and stuff. Oh yes, I have a human skull.' The man's Tamil sounded strange. He seemed to speak in the formal way Tamil was written.

'Let's go,' said Panju.

'You must be an Iyer,' said the man as they started walking.

'Yes, how did you know?'

'Well, I have written what is considered the seminal book on the castes of southern India. I should think I should know an Iyer when I see one. Besides, the horizontal white stripes on your forehead are a dead giveaway. Anyway, what Iyer are you?'

'Vadama.'

'What Vadama are you?'

'Vadadesaththu Vadama.'

'How old are you?'

'Eleven.'

'Hmm... You are shorter than the median for Vadamas. But what really interests me is your musculature. It is so well defined. I must check your grip strength.'

'Can I ask you one thing?' asked Panju.

'Go on,' the man inclined his head.

'You are a white man, aren't you?'

'Yes, and so?' The man raised an eyebrow.

'How come you are pink and red and not white?'

The man did not reply. His eyes narrowed and he started walking faster.

The office was a potpourri of strange things. The mahogany desk that dominated the room was so cluttered with papers, files, ledgers bound in vellum, pieces of bone and stones of different sizes, shapes and colours that Panju could hardly see the surface. A human skull without a jawbone grinned from a corner. There were weighing scales and different kinds of instruments with dials around the room. A man in a black cap stood at attention when they entered.

'Of course, I will have your weight and other measurements taken. But first, I am curious about your grip strength. Hold this and squeeze,' he said, handing over a curiously shaped instrument with a dial. Panju took it in one hand and squeezed.

'Ninety pounds! Impossible,' said the man as he took the instrument back from Panju and tested it himself. Panju saw that the needle had not come anywhere near the mark that his grip had reached.

'That is truly remarkable. And only eleven,' the man murmured.

'What was that?' Panju asked.

'That's a Salter's dynamometer. It's an instrument to measure your strength.'

'You should have told me that before,' said Panju. 'I would have squeezed much harder.'

'All right, now take your veshti off and stand against the wall there,' said the man.

'No, no. I won't,' said Panju.

'Don't be silly, my boy. I am not going to harm you. Ahmed, hold this boy against the wall.'

'Just do what the sooppirandu dorai says. He won't harm you,' said Ahmed.

Panju quickly lifted the corners of his veshti and tucked the ends at his waist, winding them through his legs. Now he was ready. Ahmed moved in rather casually to hold him. Panju remembered the payilvan's words: 'If the opposition is stronger, there is no shame in running away to face them another day.' He lowered his head and butted Ahmed hard on his stomach. Ahmed sat down and unable to hold in his pain, toppled backwards. Panju was off in a flash, through the office and out through the entrance doors. He ran to his mother who was sitting on a bench in conversation with an old lady.

'Amma, let's go. Hurry!'

Bhavani looked perplexed at her son's hurry but followed him at a half-run into the jatka. With a cluck from the driver, the vehicle was away.

'So what was the hurry?' asked Bhavani.

'A white man took me to his office. He then asked his servant to hold me against the wall. I butted the servant in the stomach and ran back here.'

'Thank God,' said Bhavani. 'I think I will break some coconuts for Pillayar. You have escaped a horrible fate. The lady next to me on the bench was telling me—and I thought it was just a story—that the Britishers in the museum took good-looking boys and girls to have them stuffed and exhibited. Now we should not go anywhere near that place.'

After this, even the sight of the lighthouse inside the high court complex failed to excite Panju.

The week slid past quickly. Vichu was hardly to be seen. The only major embarrassment Panju suffered was when Vijaya shouted 'Athan!' and hugged him, saying 'Don't go back'.

The day of their departure was a Sunday too, and Vichu was home.

'Your stay has come to an end so quickly,' Vichu said. 'I can see that all your luggage has been loaded. Before I forget, make sure you pay the jatka karan three rupees when you get off at the station. I bargained hard with him till he agreed to the figure.'

'Yes, Anna,' said Bhavani.

'Thank God,' Vichu continued, 'if that miser Sambu had been there, he would have expected me to pay for it.'

Panju saw red. 'Don't talk about my father like that. You are the miser for not wanting to pay for your guests!' he shouted.

Vichu turned to face Panju. 'Stay out of what older people are discussing. Your father is not just a miser, he is a greedy one.'

Panju looked around for a suitable weapon. His eyes fell on a stout Malacca cane that Vichu had lovingly oiled and that he took out only on special occasions. It had a silver handle and a silver ferrule. He ran to it and grabbed it. He raised it but thought better of it. He put the cane across his knees and with a huge effort, broke the cane into two. He threw both pieces on the ground.

Bhavani assessed the situation quickly and rushed to Panju's side. She held his hand and literally ran out, muttering her goodbyes. Once they got into the jatka, Panju turned around and saw that Vichu was staring at him, his face contorted in fury.

Nine

A crude platform with a pandal around it had been constructed on the southern banks of the Cauvery at Tiruvaiyaru. The speaker who stood on the stage was young, perhaps in his twenties. He wore a jubba and a veshti made out of coarse handspun cotton.

He had a voice that carried clearly even to people who were seated on the ground twenty rows behind.

'Swadeshi is a word that now even a child of four knows. It stands for self-reliance. Why is it needed so urgently in our motherland today? The answer is simple. England has her large machines driven by steam that churn out goods at very low costs. If we do not protect our domestic manufacturing, our craftsmen and artisans will go hungry. Manufacturing itself will die out in our country. This will perfectly suit the British. More and more raw materials will be shipped out of India, either at throw-away prices or at rates that will benefit British traders and investors. This is particularly insidious because, when we were ruled by the Mohammedan emperors, even though wealth was concentrated in a few hands, it did not go out of India; they settled here. Not so the British.'

Panju was fascinated.

'A restricted meaning of Swadeshi is "buy Indian-made goods". To be effective, it has to be more than that. We have to use the powerful weapon of boycott.'

Suddenly he raised his voice. 'The veshti that is made by a weaver with his hands costs a rupee and three annas. The Manchester veshti is available for twelve annas. Which of you is ready to buy the one where the coarseness of the fabric has entwined in its very warp and woof the hard work of our Indian brothers rather than the fine steam-spewed veshtis of Manchester?'

Panju jumped up and shouted out, 'I will!' Many others also followed suit.

'As I said, the crucial way to succeed in our holy endeavour is to use the means of boycott too. At this juncture, I want to introduce to you—no, I want to re-introduce to you, someone whom you probably have met often. Arunachalam Chettiyar!'

Arunachalam Chettiyar, a small-made man dressed in a veshti and a shirt stepped forward quietly.

'You know him as the owner of the largest shop here selling textiles and cloth. He is going to initiate a yajna here that will reach to the very core of the British Empire and bring Manchester and Lancashire to their knees. He has something to say to you.'

Arunachalam Chettiyar spoke quietly. The crowd hushed to catch his words.

'I just received my stock of Manchester Mull veshtis last week. I offer it as an oblation for the great yajna. From now on, I am going to sell only Swadeshi cloth.'

Meanwhile, off to one side of the stage, a young man had lit a fire and got it going with some paper and kerosene.

Chettiyar stepped off the stage, carried a big bundle of veshtis with the help of his assistant and started feeding the fire, one-by-one initially. As the fire caught, he dumped the whole lot in the fire.

A murmur began in the crowd. Panju leapt up again and shouted 'VANDE MATARAM' at the top of his voice. The crowd took up the chant and soon the riverside reverberated with the call.

The young man on the stage tried to get the crowd to quieten down. At last he succeeded.

'Now,' he said, it is your turn. Bring your foreign cloth and goods and offer them to the fire god.'

Panju ran all the way home. The cupboard in his father's room was made of teak and had four doors. It had two drawers with brass knobs and a beautifully carved top railing, all polished a golden brown. The drawers and the bottom doors were locked. Panju opened the top doors. There was a faint smell of camphor and sandalwood. The shelf was stacked high with shawls, mostly silk with gold filigree on them, all of which had been presented to Sambu in honour of his scholarship. Below the shawls, something white peeped. He pulled it out. It was a veshti of fine cloth with no border. Manchester cloth! Panju grabbed the veshti.

'What are you doing in Appa's cupboard?' The question made him look around. Janaki stood there, hands folded, lips pursed, a question mark on her face.

'Nothing...' Panju closed the cupboard door and tried to slip out.

'I want to know what you are doing with Appa's veshti.'

Panju was silent until Janaki upped the stakes. 'I am going to tell Appa.'

'Hey, nothing, Janu. You know this is Manchester cloth.'

'And, so...'

'I am just taking it to the public meeting to have it burnt.'

'What?'

'Hold on. Let me explain.' Panju then explained the concept of Swadeshi and Swaraj and told her what the fiery man had said. 'Even Arunachalam Chettiyar is burning his foreign stock,' he concluded.

'You are going back to the meeting now, aren't you?'

'Yes,' said Panju.

'Then I am coming too.'

'No you are not,' started Panju. But on quick reflection, he realized that it would be better if they were to share the blame in case his father found out.

'All right. Come with me.'

By the time they reached the meeting venue, a big fire was blazing. People had started throwing various clothes into the fire and Sambu's prized veshti, too, went in.

They both watched in silence. In an hour or so the crowd was gone; still the dying embers of the fire cast a glow that was reflected by the Cauvery.

TEN

March 1906

'My early and invincible love of reading, I would not exchange for all the riches of India,' Janaki said, quoting Gibbon.

Janaki and Panju loved to have long conversations about life, death and everything in between. This continued and only became more intense as the years passed.

'I have missed you for the last month or so; you have been really busy,' said Panju.

'I know,' said Janaki. 'I have missed our conversations too. I couldn't help it. Ever since Amma has been more or less bedridden, I have had all the housework to do. I hope she gets better quickly. The doctor from Tanjore is with Appa and her. I hope he is able to cure her.'

'To get back to what you started with, don't forget,' said Panju, 'that the main riches of India are not the diamonds, emeralds, rubies and gold with its maharajas, but the incredibly rich literature, for instance in Sanskrit and Tamil.'

'It's hard to disagree with what you say. But don't you think, to gain perspective, you have to study a thing from afar? Look at people like Max Müller, Arthur Avalon and Monier-Williams, who have contributed to our rich literature. My contention is that they were able to do that only because of the geographical and psychological distance.'

'Ha, are you saying that Monier's translation of *Shakuntalam* is even one-tenth as good as the original by Kalidasa?'

'I have read neither. But that's not what I was talking about.'

'Then what are you talking about? Haven't you heard that the Motherland is loftier than heaven? *Breathes there a man with soul so dead,/ Who never to himself has said,/ This is my own, my native land?*'

'Panju, so you have read a few English poems as well. What I am trying to say is—do you realize that I will finish my First Arts this year?'

'Yes and we'll probably get you married to a nice Brahmin Iyer boy with a BA and a government job and you can cook, keep house and bear children for him and his parents—'

He stopped abruptly as he noticed the sadness that crept into Janaki's face.

'— I am sorry. What's wrong, Janaki?'

'I am pained, Panju. Do you think women are merely some kind of background support for men to do the real work? Apart from that, should women only be rearing babies, preferably male ones?'

'Janaki, I was only joking...'

'Panju, why is it that I don't find it funny? Do you think it is because I am only a woman? Look around you. I don't see the women here to be the force without which nothing in the universe can even move, as Sankara said. Have you read John Stuart Mill? Not his political philosophies, but his thoughts on women. He says that the principle that regulates the existing social relations between the two sexes—the legal subordination of one sex to the other—is wrong itself, and now one of the chief hindrances to human improvement; and that it ought to be replaced by a principle of perfect equality, admitting no power or privilege on the one side, nor disability on the other.'

'I think I can see what you are getting at. But the point is...?'

'I want to do my BA, Panju.'

'After you finish your BA, what kind of a job will you take up?'

'I want to teach, Panju. I want girls to have the independence of thought first. The right kind of education not only teaches that but also makes possible economic independence. That is the only way the lot of women in this country will improve. For now, the opportunities for women may be few; but the day is not far off when there will be women lawyers, administrators, doctors and even engineers. For now, once I finish my education, I will teach and prepare others for such a future.'

'But, Janaki, a girl... I am not saying girls shouldn't go to college, but I haven't heard of any college that accepts women or even of any women who have gone to college. In fact in your First Arts class, there were no other girls. You have already studied more than most girls in the district.'

'They will have to make an exception for me. I am going to ask Appa as soon as the doctor leaves.'

Panju stared long at her indigo-coloured pavadai that had faded in places. The half-sari she had draped around her was clean but crumpled and frayed at the edges.

'Janu!' Sambu's voice sounded feeble, even accounting for the distance. Janaki ignored it for the moment.

'Are you meditating? You seem to be thinking hard,' said Janaki. Panju sighed.

'In any case, whether you go to college or get married or take up a job, you will leave me. I will miss you.'

Janaki's heart melted at the sight of a teardrop making its way down Panju's cheek.

'You were always like this, even when a baby. Your tears fall directly from your eyes on to your cheek and roll down your cheek like pearls. I will never leave you, Panju. Even if we are physically separated, I will finish my college quickly and I will always be with you.'

'Appa is calling you,' said Panju.

'I know,' said Janaki. 'I wonder why he didn't call again.' She hurried to the mittam.

When Janaki saw Sambu, she pushed aside her concern about college, noticing that her father seemed unnaturally quiet.

'What's wrong, Appa?'

'Nothing.'

Janaki knew from experience that this was a preliminary pause and waited for him to continue.

'The doctor isn't happy about Amma's condition,' he continued. 'He has diagnosed it as rheumatism. He thinks it might get worse. He has a powder that's imported from Germany, I think he called it Aspirin. It has come into the market only recently. He hopes that will help cure her. He said he will measure out the correct dosages, fold them up in little squares of paper and send them across through his compounder tomorrow.'

'I hope it really does help Amma.'

'I am worried about you, Janaki. You are managing all the cooking and cleaning. It must be rather tough for you.'

'Don't worry, Appa,' said Janaki, trying hard not to let her disappointment show in her voice. 'I can take care of everything. Anyway, I don't think it will be for long.'

True to his word, the doctor sent a glass jar full of neatly packed paper envelopes containing a white powder. For a day or two, Bhavani seemed to be getting better. She certainly seemed more mobile. After a week or so, she complained of severe abdominal pain and nausea. She told Janaki in a shy whisper that her stools were black and occasionally tinged with red. When the doctor came to know of this in his subsequent visit, he asked for the dosage to be reduced, advising her to take the powder once a day instead of twice.

Bhavani took the powder for months and when it didn't help, stopped taking it and resigned herself to her fate. While Janaki got better at managing the household chores, she did not have time for anything else.

Eleven

December 1907

A dimly-lit hall. Sounds of busily scratching nibs on paper; the loud tick-tock of a clock. Panju tries to see the time. The clock is not visible. He tries to concentrate on the question paper. The writing on the paper seems to be in a strange language. As he looks at the paper, a sonorous voice reads it out for him.

'How much sand will be required to fill a pit two yards two feet three inches long, one yard one foot four-and-a-half inches wide and two yards three feet eleven inches deep (neglect your volume)?'

'Can you r-repeat the question, please?' Panju asks.

'All right. Listen carefully.' There seems to be a tinge of exasperation in the voice.

'Find by any method the value of 4,165 tons 17 hundredweights three quarters 21 pounds of wheat at rupees 107 and 14 annas 8 paisa per ton. Take an exchange of one shilling three and fifteen sixteenth pennies per rupee.'

'But that…that was not the q-question earlier,' Panju manages to stammer.

'Construct a polynomial entirely from parallelograms,' the voice continues after a pause. Now it is a chorus of voices. 'We can see that you do not know anything. By the power vested in us by Her Majesty, we the University of Madras, decree that S. Panchapakesan, alias Panju, has failed miserably in his FA first examinations. Not only has he failed, but he is also forever debarred from writing this exam. It is further decreed that he shall receive twenty-seven strokes of a cane two yards three inches long. Panchapakesan, compute and reflect on the total length of the punishment as you prepare for your caning.'

Panju woke up, sweating. He hurried to the back portion of the house and washed his face with water from the well.

Just three days left till the F.A. first examination!

Panju felt sad that he was probably visiting the akhara for the last time.

'I am proud of you,' said Choturam Payilvan. 'The only time you missed a day at the akhara was when *I* was sick. I must say you have been one of the best pupils I have had.'

'I will miss the akhara, Aiya,' said Panju.

'In the past five years I have taught you practically all that I know. You must continue the exercises even when you go away to do your higher studies. I wish you the best in your exams, Panju.'

The examination itself was not as traumatic as the precursor. When the results were announced, Panju found that he had secured a high second class, probably sufficient for him to get admission in the college of his choice—the same college in which he had written his FA first examinations. The Government Arts College at Kumbakonam was the nearest that offered science subjects.

Panju saw that his father looked tired. He had just returned from a trip to Needamangalam, a village situated where the river Vennar, a branch of the Cauvery, divides into three distributaries.

'We will have to do something about it,' said Sambu, addressing Panju. 'The lands at Needamangalam seem to be slipping out of my hands. I was hoping to sell them to pay for your BA education.'

Even though the news was bad, Panju felt a thrill, as it was the first time Sambu had treated him as an adult and shared his problems.

'What happened, Appa?'

'You know the tenant Dayalan? Until the year before last, he had been sending our share of the paddy regularly, even if not correctly accounted for. Last year, he told me there had been a death in his family. He also offered various other equally ridiculous excuses. He said he could not cultivate the land and didn't even send one padi of rice. I let him be because that was the first time he had defaulted and our kudir was nearly full.'

Panju was taking it all in, a serious expression on his face, nodding at appropriate times.

'I should have perhaps listened to the people who told me to convert the varam to kuthagai.'

Looking at Panju's blank face, he explained: 'Kuthagai is a fixed rent and varam is a portion of the produce that the cultivator keeps for himself. Some people even said that the one-fourth varam that I was paying was too much for these gold-yielding lands and suggested that I reduce it to one-fifth. Anyway, to cut a long story short, Dayalan claims that the lands are his. He has applied to the tahsildar with proof. I think he has paid the tahsildar off. There is only one thing to be done. We must petition the government. Apparently, the Collector is camping for a few days at Needamangalam. All said and done, the white man is fair in dispensing justice. I got the pleader to draft a petition and I have also given advance notice to the tahsildar. I want you to come with me.'

'Don't worry, Appa, we will fight it out,' said Panju, feeling rather self-important.

All through the journey to Needamangalam, Sambu was burdened with a cloth bag filled to bursting with documents and deeds and by Panju's incessant questions.

Sambu patiently answered the questions as well as he could.

At Needamangalam, they waited under the shade of a neem tree for hours. It was noon when a bullock cart arrived, bringing tent cloth and poles, a desk and some chairs. It took another half hour to set it all up. Finally, an Englishman came riding up, raising dust, along with three others.

'Collector dorai has come,' the tahsildar shouted to his assistants.

'That is not actually the Collector,' a bored-looking man, obviously a long-time petitioner, pointed out. 'That is the "Dipty" Collector of Mayavaram, Edmund Worthington. He is officiating for the Collector during his furlough.'

Panju wasn't surprised that Worthington's complexion was beet-red rather than the milk-white he had imagined once. He wore riding boots, a sola topi and light khaki coat. His moustache, which drooped slightly, was blond like his hair.

'Tell them,' Worthington said, 'not to waste their time and mine. I don't want to know how they are, whether they have eaten today and whether their daughters-in-law are pregnant. Let them just stick to the pertinent facts of their petition. I have read all the advance petitions and I hope to finish quickly here.' He added, 'Seekdam-seekdam, jaldi quick,' in a louder voice for the benefit of the gathered crowd.

He sat down on the chair, perched on its edge, as it was too high for the desk. Some seven or eight people stood around him, including a policeman and a man in the uniform of an orderly, a ceremonial sash encircling his body with a gleaming badge on it and another sash around his waist.

Edmund Worthington disposed of the petitions quickly, directing the tahsildar and often asking an assistant to note down certain things for follow-up action. By the time Sambu's petition came up, it was four in the afternoon and the Deputy Collector seemed to be tiring and becoming more and more irritable.

When his name was called, Sambu rose, folding his hands. Panju stood next to him, spine erect, arms akimbo. Before Sambu could even open his mouth, the Deputy Collector spoke:

'The petition is rejected. As per the noting of the tahsildar and the available evidence in the jamabandi records, I find no reason to believe that Sambasiva Iyer is the title-holder or for that matter has any rights in any form to the property under question. Next.'

'But, Sir,' Sambu remonstrated, 'I have all the title papers.' He kept a sheaf of papers on the desk in front of Worthington.

'Don't put anything on the table without my explicit permission,' Worthington snapped, making a dismissive gesture that sent the sheaf of documents flying.

'Sir—' Sambu started to say something.

'—Shut your mouth,' Worthington said in his queerly accented Tamil. He used the despective singular pronoun and verb forms rather than the plural honorific.

As Sambu bent down to retrieve the papers, a pulse began to beat at Panju's temples.

'Falling at my feet won't change my mind.' It was clear that Worthington meant what he said and it wasn't an attempt at humour.

As Sambu stood up, the Deputy Collector remarked, to the world at large, 'God, what a servile lot.'

Panju's fists began to clench.

Sambu tried again. 'Sir—'

'—Get out. Not one more word from you, you rascal. Another word and I will have you fined and arrested. You know, I am also the District Magistrate.' The Deputy Collector was shouting now.

Panju took a step forward and was about to raise his arm when he found it gripped by Sambu's hand. A few villagers who also knew Sambu, joined in and dragged Panju away from the Deputy Collector's presence as people dispersed.

'Let us rest a little beneath this tree,' said Sambu, indicating a large tamarind tree.

Panju sat down and closed his eyes, still thinking of the humiliation on his father's face.

'Why are you still here?' The voice sounded near.

'Dayalan,' whispered Sambu.

Panju opened his eyes. Dayalan stood before them, the tiger's claw that he wore around his neck swinging as he bent down. Panju got up. At a glance, he took in the two others who stood by Dayalan. Panju slowly and deliberately clasped his hands behind his neck, letting his biceps ripple as he noted the two men who stood behind Dayalan, stout sticks in their hands. One of them wore a turban and the other was bareheaded.

Dayalan took a step back. 'Leave now, both of you. Dorai has given his judgment. And don't bother to come back. That is, if you want your limbs and body to be healthy.' As he spoke, he looked significantly at the man in the turban, who skirted around Panju and approached Sambu with the stick raised.

Panju turned around and grabbed at the stick in the opponent's hand. The man tried to pull the stick back, but Panju held on. Panju let go of the stick suddenly and as the man staggered back, Panju leapt up in the air and kicked the man full in the face. The man dropped his stick, held his face and sat down, blood dripping between his fingers. The other man now came at him with his stick swinging. Dayalan was between the man and Panju. Panju grabbed Dayalan's arm at the elbow and applied pressure. Dayalan screamed in agony. Panju swung him around and the stick that came down met Dayalan's arm. Dayalan staggered against the tree trunk, clutching at his now useless arm. The second man hesitated a little before throwing down his stick and running away. Dayalan and the turbaned man followed him shortly afterwards, staggering a little.

'Are you all right, Appa?' Panju asked.

'I am fine. I suppose they deserved it.' Sambu very carefully tried to keep the pride from his voice.

'I wish it was the Englishman whose arm I broke,' said Panju.

Better news was to follow at home. When they returned, Panju found the postman at their doorstep. The old man was grinning as he handed over a letter and lingered on. Panju said 'Thank you' pointedly. The experienced postman merely grinned some more and said, 'Why don't you read it, Aiya? If there is some good news, I can also share in the good fortune.' The postman handed over a postcard addressed to Sambu and another envelope.

Panju gave the card to Sambu; he resisted reading it.

Panju noticed that the letter addressed to him was from the Government Arts College at Kumbakonam. He opened the letter and read it quickly. It was a letter of acceptance. Sambu, too, read the letter and gave the postman two annas. He then hurried inside to take out his ledger and make the entry—'Sundry charities: two annas.'

Panju went in and read the letter aloud to his mother and sister. He then went to his room and was reading it by himself for the fourth time to determine if there was a catch in it, when Sambu's voice sounded from the mittam.

'Panju, Janaki, come here. I want to discuss some good news with you.'

When Panju went out into the courtyard, Janaki was already there. Bhavani sat on the ground, some distance from Sambu, her sari hitched up to her knees, legs shiny with oil stretched out in front of her.

'Come on, Bhavani. I don't need to invite you separately with betel leaf and nuts,' Sambu continued. Panju wondered why his father was in such a jolly mood.

'Only my legs are frozen,' said Bhavani. 'My hearing is still fine. I can hear from where I am.'

'I have some great news.' Sambu stopped and looked at all of them in turn.

'Come on, Appa, out with it. The suspense is killing us.' Janaki's excitement reflected in her voice.

'I have settled all your marriages,' said Sambu dramatically and turning to Bhavani, 'No, no, not yours. You will have to be satisfied with me.' He was chastened by the absolute lack of laughter from anyone, even for politeness's sake; any urge to laugh was clearly trumped by curiosity.

'I was wondering what to do for money for Panju's education. My god hasn't let me down. You remember that mirasudar from Nannilam, who had asked for Panju's horoscope? He wants to settle the marriage of his daughter to Panju. They are willing to undertake all of Panju's education expenses.' He looked around triumphantly.

Bhavani was the first to react. 'Have you forgotten that we have a girl older to Panju, who ought to have been married off long ago? Already the people of the agraharam are saying a lot of things behind our backs. Now they will start saying things to our faces.'

Sambu looked at Panju.

'I have never thought of marriage. But if you want me to marry, I don't want them to send the girl to our home immediately after marriage, nor will I go and see her till I finish my BA. In any case, I can't marry till Akka's marriage is settled.'

'Anyway,' said Sambu, 'the girl is too young to be sent to the in-laws' place. In fact, they want to make sure that she comes into our home only when she is fourteen.' He then turned his full attention to Bhavani. 'I am not a fool,' he said, 'to have a grown-up daughter at home and look for a bride for her younger brother. They want to give a girl and take a girl. Their older son had so far been saying he didn't want to marry. Apparently he has now given his consent. He has finished his BA and he is a clerk at the revenue board office in Madras. They want Janaki for him. Apparently when the mirasudar was here, he liked the way Janaki was helping Bhavani in her domestic work and was able to convince his son.'

Panju was watching Janaki. A strange light had come into her eyes. She looked the way she had when she had attacked Kuppu, defending Panju.

'Appa, why don't you let Akka be. She knows what is good for her,' Panju said.

Janaki gave Panju a look which he interpreted to mean—'Don't worry, I can take care of myself.'

'Appa,' said Janaki, 'I have already said this before; I do not want to marry now. Perhaps this is the only thing in which I will disobey you. I have to finish my studies before marrying. I want to be the first woman in south India to get a college education—'

'—By then you will be an old woman. Who will marry you?' Bhavani interjected.

'Amma, I would rather be an educated old woman than an old woman who is worn out from cooking and cleaning and looking after children. Or maybe you can find a mappillai who will allow me to study?'

'I think your father has given you too much space and freedom and you have grown into a self-centred girl.'

'Amma, if I was self-centred, I wouldn't have wasted two years after finishing my F.A. I have not spoken about my education so far only because you have not been keeping too well. It would have been impossible for you to manage the household.'

'I know, Janu. I understand. You are anything but self-centred.' Tears were welling up in Bhavani's eyes. 'We are old. Brahma has written a sad script on my forehead. You are still young. You should look after yourself. We will manage somehow.'

'Amma, don't be ridiculous. In a few months, you will be perfectly healthy, jumping and skipping around like a gazelle. I am sure the ayurvedic treatment that Appa has arranged will help. Appa, please don't pressure me. I will not yield. Please let us go ahead with Panju's marriage. I am not getting married now. I am determined that Amma should get better and I will finish my education after that.'

Sambu said nothing. It is too late for him, Panju reflected, to start laying down the law and acting like an autocrat.

Twelve

December 1907

Vichu looked at the basket of fruits and flowers beside him in the ox cart. For a moment, he considered turning back. His wife's words came back to him. 'Your daughter is so dark. She is even two shades darker than Janaki. Who will marry her? After all, Panju is a moraippayyan, being your sister's son. He will be doing his BA. In any case, after he finishes, you will be able to use your influence to get him a job. At least for your daughter's happiness, you should do this. I don't know what you have against your brother-in-law. He seems to be such a timid and nice person. Now, don't go empty-handed to your sister's house. Take some fruits and flowers along. Don't forget our daughter's horoscope.'

Vichu had complied with extreme reluctance. He hated the idea of asking Sambu for anything, let alone for his son as a marriage match for his daughter. He, however, realized the truth in much of what Bhagyam had said in her staccato speech.

When he arrived at Sambu's house, both Bhavani and Sambu were at the doorstep to welcome him.

'Come in, Vichu, come in. At last you found the way to our place.'

'Don't say such things to my brother. You should be happy that he has come home after all these days,' said Bhavani.

'Oh,' said Sambu, looking at the basket of fruit and flowers, 'you must have come with some auspicious news. Please come in. We will talk inside.'

Sambu and Vichu sat on the swing.

'Yes,' said Vichu after a moment of uncomfortable silence. 'You see, I have come to ask that Panju be married to my daughter Vijaya.'

Sambu remained silent.

Vichu interpreted the silence as a form of assent and forged on. 'Of course, we will make sufficient jewellery. You know she is the only daughter. I have a house in Triplicane. I have fifteen velis of land in Thillaisthanam. After me, they will—'

'No, no Vichu. I am sorry it is not possible.'

'You know, I can give some three thousand rupees cash.'

'You are mistaking me, Vichu. I have already given my word. Panju's marriage is already fixed.'

Vichu's face was red. His breath came in spurts.

'To a rich mirasudar's daughter, I am sure,' he said.

'Well, a mirasudar from Nannilam, but—'

'Yes, yes,' said Vichu. 'And you have given your sacred word. You are Harishchandra incarnate. I know,' said Vichu as he walked out. He would have said even more, but thoughts of what Bhagyam would say stopped him.

Thirteen

January 1908

In 1908, one and a half years after the major split in the Congress at the Surat session, the revolutionary ideals, no longer mainstream, morphed, favouring radical individual action, particularly among the youth, rather than taking the shape of a mass movement. Panju, however, was anticipating a major union.

He awaited his marriage, not with excitement but with a resigned sense of forbearance, it being one of those normal vicissitudes of life that one had to endure. The girl, Meenakshi, was thirteen and had not attained puberty.

The wedding was a four-day affair, held at Thillaisthanam, the bride's village.

The janavasam—the procession of the bridegroom—was conducted with Panju sitting in something that resembled a chariot rather than a horse-drawn carriage, decorated with yards of white jasmine and yellow and white chrysanthemums, a few red roses peeking out from among the strings. Sambu's younger brother, who had come for the wedding all the way from Delhi, asked Panju to sit straight during the procession as befits a bridegroom and Panju strained his back attempting to do that. A heavy jasmine garland weighed his neck down. Panju also had the unwelcome company of a couple of young children at the peak of their mischievous years who simply loved the idea of jumping up and down on the leather seat, often treading heavily on the garland and yanking Panju's neck.

At the end of the day, Panju and Meenakshi had their photographs taken. The photographer had been specially brought from Madras.

The engagement ceremony was over and the drama of kasi yatra was enacted. The prospective son-in-law pretended to go off to Benares to lead an ascetic life, equipped with a hand fan, an umbrella and provisions of rice and pulses. The father-in-law persuaded him to return, promising his daughter to him.

Panju and Meenakshi exchanged garlands. They were supposed to sit astride the shoulders of their maternal uncles for the ceremony. Meenakshi's uncle, a hefty man, entered so far into the spirit of things that Meenakshi just managed to finish the final exchange by flinging the garland around Panju's neck. Vichu ought to have been the one carrying Panju, but he was nowhere to be found. A distant cousin, suitably strong, was cast for the role.

By tradition, there had to be someone from the bridegroom's side making things difficult for the bride's father. The role was played perfectly by Sambu's younger brother who complained that nobody thought it fit to offer him a beverage as soon as he arrived; he found fault with the fact that the leaf on which he was served food was torn in one corner, made snide comments about the jewellery the bride wore. He allegedly found two grains of stone, one of which was a small pebble rather than a grain, in the rice that he was served. He had kept them aside, obviously not wanting to start anything before he finished his food. He completed his meal by licking his hands free of any vestiges of food particles and was looking to escalate things to a full-fledged fight when Sambu took him aside and had a quiet word.

Panju went through all the formalities with patience. The highlight of the day was when, during the oonjal ceremony, Meenakshi slipped from the swing and fell down; her feet did not reach to the ground, the silk sari was slippery. Crushed balls of yellow and red rice clung to her sari. The womenfolk singing the oonjal song did not miss a beat and continued singing and extolling the grace with which the goddess sat in the swing and swayed.

Janaki was everywhere, a tornado of activity, now bringing

relatives and friends for Bhavani to meet while seated on a chair, now fetching the various items that the chief priest kept demanding and welcoming strangers, friends and relatives alike. The chief priest also kept hurrying up everybody lest the auspicious hour should be missed. He, however, had no compunction in delaying things by attempting to explain to Panju the meaning of the various mantras that he was uttering.

While Janaki assisted Panju in tying the three knots in Meenakshi's thali, Sambu and a host of others vigorously shook their forefingers, raising their hands high, indicating to the nadaswaram and the tavil players that they should increase the amplitude and the tempo for the auspicious moment. Janaki also managed to knot Panju's upper cloth with Meenakshi's sari, enjoying their discomfiture when they had to get up.

Panju felt unreal when, during kanyadanam, the giving away of the bride while she was seated on his lap, the bride's father said:

Desirous of reaching the abode of Brahma,
I give as kanyadanam the comely bride,
Bedecked with golden ornaments,
to you who is Vishnu incarnate.
I give her to you so that you may get children.
And perform all your prescribed religious duties.

Panju repeated the reply after the priest:

I accept her by the grace of the Sun who made this world
with my hands protected by the Aswini Devas.

Almost immediately Meenakshi's aunt burst into tears, perhaps trying to compensate for the absence of the mother, who, had she had been present in a material form, would certainly have done so. Panju was left wondering what he had said to provoke such a reaction. What he did not know was that it was customary for mothers to cry at that very moment. In fact, if he had looked, he would have seen Bhavani, too, wiping a tear or two and Sambu dabbing at his eyes with his upper cloth.

Panju took Meenakshi's right hand in his, all her fingers cupped together. They took seven steps around the fire, Panju leading, reciting the appropriate mantra for each.

Panju said:

With the first step: Let us nourish each other.
With the second step: may you provide us with the strength
in the marriage.
With the third step: may you increase our wealth.
With the fourth step: may you increase our happiness.
With the fifth step: may we have children.
With the sixth step: may we have pleasure in all seasons.
With the seventh step: our friendship has now become strong.
May our friendship last forever.

Meenakshi, too, had to recite her vows at each step, but for the most part, the priest recited the vow and when Meenakshi did not quite repeat it, he took it as said.

The wedded couple then went around the gathering to receive the blessings of all the older people, which in this case were most of the guests. This involved Panju having to prostrate himself several times with eight limbs—his arms, shoulders, legs, his chest and his forehead—touching the ground. For someone who could do fifty dandals at a stretch, this was not too arduous while, even though it was easier on Meenakshi since she had to only perform it with five of her limbs touching the ground, the number of repetitions did tire her.

Panju did not dwell too much on the meaning of the vows that he had uttered.

Fourteen

May 1908

Janaki looked at the letter that had been folded in four. Panju had sent it through a relative who had paid a visit to Kumbakonam, staying with him for a week, claiming a large share of his meagre accommodation for the price of a bunch of red bananas. Panju presumably hoped that the messenger services provided by the guest would even out the trade. Janaki wanted to read the letter in privacy and took it to the riverfront. She sat on the sand and opened the letter.

'*Dear Janu*, the letter began.

> *College is so different from school, you won't believe it. I have been exposed to so many ideas, not only from the teachers but also from the excellent library we have, that my head is reeling. While many students seem to regard college as an admission ticket to great job prospects, there are some who are genuinely interested in learning. To me, the greatest benefit of college education is that I am privileged to sit and discuss issues with great minds. It reminds me so much of the kind of discussions we used to have.*

Janaki looked at the Cauvery, the movement of the eddying and swirling water clearly visible. She went back to the letter.

> *I miss you very badly here. You would have loved the college atmosphere. During one of our discussions you mentioned John Stuart Mills. He has penned some deeply thought-provoking ideas on liberty and on representative government, even though I don't completely agree with him. He has written about extensive participation of citizens in the government. I totally concur with that. He has also discussed the enlightened competence of rulers, which is somewhat*

abhorrent to me as it seems to be a flimsy justification for the English to rule us.

But most of all, I enjoy our Tamil classes. Our Tamil pandit, Sri Vinayakam Pillai, constantly talks of U. Ve. Saminathaiyer and his mentor Meenakshi Sundaram Pillai. He says he wouldn't have been able to teach Silappadhikaram if it hadn't been for U. Ve. Sa. Our Tamil pandit makes the ancient cities of Puhar and Madurai come alive.

I have access to some magazines and newspapers here. This is absolutely amazing. I get to read regularly The Mail, which presents the British perspective, and The Hindu, which was started by, guess who, G. Subramania Iyer from our own Tiruvaiyaru! Swadesamitran is an interesting Tamil magazine whose editor until recently was Subramania Bharati! I wish I could discuss all I have read with you.

Now on to more mundane things. The place I stay in can just about be described as a room. The only merit it has is that it is cheap. I think I have said all I can say about it. The food is hardly edible. I don't know how they manage to get so many stones into the rice. I long for Amma's paruppusili and vattakkuzhambu. I presume that by now, you must also be quite good at cooking. I hope Amma gets better and you get to do what you want to do.

Give my namaskarams to Appa and Amma.

I wish we could just go back to those days when we played Paramapadam or Pallanguzhi.

Missing you deeply.
Panju

Janaki refolded the letter, got up, dusted the sand off her sari and made her way homewards.

1908–1909

KUMBAKONAM

*A*s the Cauvery reaches the head of the delta, she remembers that she is a gift to mankind. She decides to fan out into multiple distributaries—Kollidam, Vettar, Vennar, Vadavar, Kudamurutti and many, many more, criss-crossing the land, in order that the land can benefit the most. She gives of her munificence all through the delta, not just by depositing the rich alluvium, but also by leaving behind something of herself in the land. She fosters a culture that is replete with the finest of art, architecture, music, dance and literature. By the time she reaches her lover, however, she finds that she is a mere trickle, completely spent, having soaked her body and spirit into the delta, making the land incredibly rich and the people gloriously noble. She witnesses the transformation of her own obsession into something finer, self-sacrifice. This spirit too, she imparts to the people of the land.

Even so, she is certain she is not done as yet.

FIFTEEN

Even though U. Ve. Saminathaiyer, the 'grand old man of Tamil' had left the Government Arts College and Kumbakonam five years ago in 1903, his name was spoken in hushed tones in the corridors of the college. The pandit who taught Panju Tamil, the optional vernacular language that he had chosen over Sambu's advice of taking Sanskrit, was an unrelenting admirer of U. Ve. Sa. Panju's love for Tamil grew not just from the formal classroom sessions, but also from the gatherings at the pandit's house. Panju chose mathematics and natural philosophy, not because he was inspired by Ramanujan who had left the portals of the college scarcely three years before—Ramanujan was yet to achieve fame as a mathematician—but in a grudging accommodation of Sambu's desires. He had less choice with respect to English and mental philosophy, which were compulsory.

Panju was fascinated by the newness of college life and the big city of Kumbakonam. During his first year in college, he did not have any time for entertainment and spent most of the time in the library of the college and hardly any time in the portion of a slightly dilapidated house that he had rented from an old student of his father.

One day, when Sankaran, a year senior to him in college, insisted that he should come with him to attend a dance programme, Panju did not have a ready-made excuse and agreed.

The music was haunting. The stage was bare of any setting, but the actors! The heroine, Jaganmohini, was decked out in finery. She was dressed in a dark blue blouse and a blue silk wrap divided at the waist by an ornamented gold waist belt. She wore two heavy gold necklaces of different lengths, and a garland of gold coins. Panju watched, fascinated, until his eyes rested on the gypsy woman. The kurathi took his breath away. She wore a simple sari and large pieces of jewellery adorned her nose and ears. She held a gaily painted divining rod negligently in one hand, a large woven bamboo basket by her side and as she bent over Jaganmohini, her eyes wandered hither and thither, catching in their thrall Panju's eyes if not his entire soul. Her glances and the subtle position and movements of her body conveyed the pangs of separation, not just of the heroine but also of herself. *This is how Madhavi must have looked to Kovalan in the immortal epic* Silappadhikaram. *Not that she would have performed in the* Kumbeswar Kuravanji.

When the kuravan, the kurathi's consort, came on stage, Panju took part vicariously in the feisty, sexually loaded exchange and when finally the kuravan and the kurathi got together, waves of jealousy assailed him as he realized that he, Panju, was sitting only in the front row, whereas the kuravan had the best seat in the makeshift auditorium, by her side.

'She will be back,' his friend seated next to him whispered. 'There is going to be a full sadir kacheri by her.'

'My God, is she a nymph from heaven or what?' Panju did not realize that he had spoken aloud.

'That was Ranjitham, also called Nrityasaraswathi, a title that she was recently awarded. By the time the show is over, it will be rather late. Would you like to go back to the room?'

'No, no, I want to watch the whole programme: you carry on if it is getting late for you,' said Panju.

He was staring blankly at the empty stage, when the periya melam burst into a rendition of Thyagaraja's *nada thanumanisham sankaram* in the melodious Chittaranjani raga.

Then she made an entrance.

Panju's pulse was racing. He wanted to see and memorize every inch of the apparition before him.

She wore a dark blue blouse with a matching upper cloth, the shade of the night sky, almost completely hidden by the three rows of necklaces she wore. The arms of her blouse ended in V-shaped golden vangis that accentuated her slim arms. Her oddiyanam peeped through at her waist, showing off a slim figure. The head ornaments representing the sun and the moon coruscated in the uncertain light of the hurricane lamps. The nettichutti, hanging down from the thalai saman, a band of gold that encircled her forehead, swayed gently along with the jimikki at her ears with her confident swaggering gait. When she bent down to touch the feet of her guru at the beginning of the alarippu, the first item of her dance programme, her braided hair swung around and Panju could see her rakkodi perched gracefully atop her head, and the intricate ornamentation of her hair with circular gold pieces ending in a kunjalam of three fluffy cotton balls. Her legs were encased in heavily brocaded satin pantaloons ending at her ankles sporting belts of bells that jangled in rhythm with her steps.

Panju sat as though in a fugue through the varnam. He was jerked back into the land of the living when she began dancing a padam. Panju didn't understand the lyrics as they were in Telugu; but she seemed to be beckoning him. She was enticing her god-king-lover with her eyes, hands and her entire self. She sat down, folding the traditional betel leaf with come-hither glances, chewing it a little before feeding him, taking him off to bed after garlanding him.

Panju felt hot even though a breeze was blowing in from the river. He went out during the interval and in a dark corner adjusted his loincloth so that his erection would not be noticeable.

When he returned, the last part of the performance, a sloka, had already begun. He watched it till the end from the sidelines, not wanting to disturb the other viewers by attempting to get back to his seat. The crowd as a whole erupted as the performance ended. The dancer bowed to the crowd with folded hands. Panju wanted to go near her just to taste the joy of the proximity when he noticed a middle-aged man get up from the front row and make his way towards her. Two others, obvious hangers-on, had sprung up behind him. One of them spoke to Ranjitham.

'This is the Rajapuram zamindar. He likes your dance very much and wants to give a small token of his appreciation.'

Ranjitham's face lit up.

'Amma,' she called out for her mother. As though on cue, a middle-aged lady, wreathed in silks and gold, appeared.

'Zamindar, namaskaram. I am Parvatam. It is indeed a privilege that you have personally come,' said the mother, folding her hands together.

'I just wanted to show my appreciation for your daughter, I mean, her art,' said the zamindar as he handed over a gold necklace. Ranjitham's mother's quick eyes estimated it to weigh around five sovereigns. Her broad smile became broader.

'Zamindar, you must come home and have food with us sometime.' Parvatam's words were dipped in honey and coated with sugar.

'Sure, sure,' said the zamindar with a wave of indifference. 'Where do you live?'

'We live very near. You just have to go to Attakkaran Street and even a child there will point out Ranjitham's house.'

'I will see you later, then,' said the zamindar, looking Ranjitham up and down.

Panju did not sleep that night.

❖

Panju looked at the image in the cracked mirror. Time to go to the barber for a shave, he reflected. His gaze fell on his long hair gathered into a topknot. For a moment, he pictured himself with cropped hair. His head shook in denial. He would surely be excommunicated. More than that, long hair was the essential symbol of a Brahmin, the removal of which would negate, with one fell stroke, thousands of years of culture and civilization. His face looked too dark, he thought. He looked around and found the copper vibuthi container. He took some of the ash in his palm and rubbed in on his face, making his face look grey. Dismayed, he rubbed at it vigorously with his upper cloth. He gave an extra twist to his moustache so that it curled up at the ends. He hesitated for a moment and making up his mind, he took down from the wall the picture of Siva sitting on his bull. He removed his gold chain from behind the picture and wore it round his neck. He inspected the collar of the white full-sleeved shirt that hung on another nail, wore it, and rolled up his sleeves till they were over and beyond his muscular biceps. He took out a handkerchief, and after folding it diagonally once and refolding it several times, placed it under his collar. He undid the first button to let the chain show.

The morning sun poured its heat down the streets of Kumbakonam and Panju was glad of the kerchief under his collar. *Attakkaran Street. That branches from Ter Street.*

The street was short, lined with low, tiled houses with no gap between them, the wall of one house serving the neighbour as well. Except for a lone child who stood next to a tamarind tree, looking it up and down, presumably trying to decide whether it was worth climbing up, there was no one to be seen. Apparently, it wasn't the kind of street where the action peaked during the day. Panju remembered the words of Ranjitham's mother and approached the child.

'Which is Ranjitham's house?' Panju asked him.

The boy stared at Panju for a while, and hitching up his half pants that were a size too large for him, scampered off, stopped at a distance, made faces at Panju and ran away again. Panju looked around and saw an old lady sitting in the thinnai of one of the houses. She wore no blouse, one end of the sari indifferently covering her breasts. She paused to spit out the red betel juice before she answered his query, but Panju wasn't sure if it improved the clarity of her speech. He decoded her body language and went to the house a hundred feet away.

The house had been recently painted, certainly within the last year or so. The roof tiles that were visible still retained their colour and were unbroken. The thick front door had a cross-beam running through the middle with lotuses carved on it. In the front of the house was an elaborate kolam of seventeen by seventeen dots—Panju counted them—that had a strange symmetry that was obvious but could not really be pinned down.

The realization suddenly struck Panju that he was at Ranjitham's doorstep. He realized that he had not rehearsed what he would say to her. He brushed that thought aside as it might lead to his retreating.

'Amma…' he shouted from the doorstep.

He expected the graceful figure of Ranjitham and was disappointed when a large lady, almost as wide as she was tall, filled the doorway and came closer, swaying ponderously from side to side. She had a pottu on her forehead that was as big as a silver rupee. A large nose-stud with seven diamonds set in a hexagonal shape brought unfortunate attention to her short, amorphous nose. She held a silver box, almost certainly a betel leaf container, in one hand. He immediately recognized her as the lady he had seen at the dance—Ranjitham's mother.

'Parvatam Amma, namaskaram,' he said.

'Who is that? Is that minorvaal?' Parvatam asked, peering shortsightedly.

'No, no. You don't know me. My name is Panchapakesan. People call me Panju. I met Ranjitham at her dance last week.'

She noticed the chain around his neck and immediately her hand went to her sari border that she had wrapped around her shoulder and tucked in at her waist. 'Come in, come in. Why are we talking outside the house?' Her voice was now soft as a baby's bottom and a patently artificial smile lit up her face. As she wobbled in front of him, she kept up a barrage of small talk that Panju didn't fully hear. She led him to a small room.

She bade him sit on a brown three-seater sofa that had an antimacassar over it, embroidered with a simple floral pattern.

'Varadoo...' she shouted and soon a thin bare-chested man appeared, his veshti doubled at his knees, his posture bent slightly forward indicating an eagerness to please, hands folded across his chest.

The look that Parvatam gave him seemed to be designed to evoke a vague guilt of some unmentionable solecism. Varadu's neck craned forward even more under the stare. Finally, Parvatam spoke.

'Bring a glass of cool buttermilk for the guest. Also tell the child there is someone here to see her.'

'Child? I wanted to meet Ranjitham,' said Panju.

Parvatam turned to him. 'For a mother, a child is always a child.' She smiled, showing her betel-stained teeth and tongue. 'Anyway you have not told me where you are from.'

The entrance of Ranjitham saved Panju the necessity of answering the implied question. She looked like a goddess in a simple yellow organdie sari with a wide red border. The only ornament around her neck was a round gold pendant, slightly concave, worn on a yellow thread.

'Please come,' Ranjitham said, brows narrowing. 'Sorry to have kept you waiting and you must be...'

Suddenly her brow cleared. 'Oh yes, I saw you at the sadir performance last week. You were sitting in the first row. Suddenly you got up and left. You came back and stood next to one of the poles.'

Panju reddened but was euphoric. *She noticed me.*

'I am Panchapakesan. I am doing my BA at the Government Arts College. I think you were simply wonderful at the dance. I was wondering if one of the celestial nymphs, Ramba or Urvasi, had come down from the heavens. I just wanted to see you in person and tell you how much I liked the dance.'

'I suppose your father owns a lot of land around your place,' said Parvatam, somewhat inconsequentially.

Ranjitham turned towards her mother. The twin sparks that formed in her eyes gathered force till they were a wave of cascading lava. Where Parvatam stood, there was a handful of ashes. Well, it didn't happen quite the way Panju imagined, but Parvatam shut up, at least for the time being and Panju was again saved from the necessity of answering.

'And you particularly liked the padams, I suppose.' A smile lit up her face.

'Yes, for a moment I imagined that you were Madhavi at Puhar...'

'And, are you married too, like Kovalan?'

'Yes...but...' Panju stammered. He was astounded that Ranjitham had picked up the reference to *Silappadhikaram* so easily.

'You thought a devadasi like me won't understand your literary allusions? Let me tell you, Aiya, that we are the most educated—probably the only women to be educated—not just in dance and the arts but also in literature, language, etiquette, customs and traditions.'

'Look at this,' she said, pointing to a large oil painting that adorned the wall. The picture showed a young woman standing, dressed in heavy silks. The backdrop in the picture looked like a palace. 'That is my great grandmother, Ranjitham. Yes, I was named after her. She was in the court of the Sarfoji king. Nobles and princes from all over craved a side-glance from her. She knew how to read, write and speak six languages. She could compose poetry in three.'

'All this education hasn't been cheap either,' piped in Parvatam. 'For people who have to buy the rice, like us, it has been so difficult. Then there is milk, curd and ghee.' She looked at Panju significantly.

'Amma, will you keep quiet for some time?' said Ranjitham, without turning.

'No, no, I understand. It is difficult without a husband...'

'Who told you I am without a husband?' She took Panju by hand and led him to another room and pointed at the wall. 'There.'

A plain unornamented sword hung on the wall. A fresh garland of jasmine adorned it.

Panju looked at her without understanding.

'This is the symbol of Lord Kumbeswara, to whom I am wedded. Temple priests conducted the marriage ceremony when I was seven. You see, my husband can never die. He is immortal. I can never be a widow. I am a nityasumangali.'

NOVEMBER–DECEMBER 1909

TIRUVAIYARU, TANJORE

Sixteen

November 1909

Things had been settling into a kind of monotonous tranquillity in the Sambu household for more than a year, until Bhavani developed a fever and excruciating pains that galloped from joint to joint. She could no longer walk and could just about move by sitting down, legs stretched out and dragging herself along by using her hands. Sambu was desperate and wrote a letter to his friend who was a shirastedar to the Diwan in the princely state of Travancore. His friend promptly approached the ayurvedic physician who had cured him of a chronic backache. The physician agreed to go to Tiruvaiyaru along with his medicines and his wife, who would help him in the treatment. He said he would have to stay in Tiruvaiyaru for four weeks and attend to the treatment.

Janaki ran out to see who had come when the bells of a bullock cart sounded. The cart stopped in front of the house. The lady who got down wore a white sari that was also draped around her breasts. She wore no blouse. She sported earrings that looked like unusually large-sized clams, except they were in gold and they covered her lobes entirely. Janaki thought that if the lady nodded her head, her earrings would brush her bare shoulders. Her hair was long and the tip of her braid came down to her waist. She held her head high, quite unlike Janaki, who had always been told that it was unladylike to do so. The lady stood aside, making no effort to communicate with Janaki while a thin, short man alighted from the cart.

His long hair was white as bleached cotton. Unlike Sambu, he hadn't shaved the front portion of his scalp, and had tied his hair in a simple knot. His face was totally unwrinkled; all the wrinkles seemed to have been ironed out, leaving them accumulated in a profusion of folds at his neck. The sandalwood paste that he wore in the form of a crescent on his forehead had leached into his bushy eyebrows, which were black as a raven's wing, making them look as though they were knitted. His upper body, otherwise bare, boasted an angavastram that was made of a loosely woven cloth, folded and refolded till it was the size of a large pocket handkerchief. Janaki wondered how it stayed balanced on his shoulders. An indigo print peeped out from one corner in the shape of a filled 'W'. His wrists were unusually thick, veins radiating from them in unruly confusion.

The man looked up and down couple of times.

'Is this Sambu Iyer's house?' he asked in a Tamil that was saturated with Malayalam.

'Yes, yes, please come in,' said Janaki,' You must be the vaidyan.'

'Yes, I am the doctor, Narayana Tampuran,' the man said. 'There is a lot of luggage to be brought in.'

He hadn't exaggerated. There were baskets, a number of terracotta basins that were bundled in cloth, and large frying pans; bunches of green leaves that were tied in bundles and packed in large gunny bags, and all kinds of earthenware vessels, heavily lidded.

Sambu had gone to the temple. Panju was in Kumbakonam attending his college. So, the three of them had to make several trips, Tampuran only taking a small cast-iron mortar with a pestle in it during his first trip. Janaki looked strangely at him.

'This is very valuable to me,' Tampuran said. 'My great-great-grandfather, who was a vaidyan to the Travancore kings, used it.'

Tampuran held Bhavani's wrist delicately, turned away from her, staring up at the roof. After a while, he dropped her hand, made an indistinct noise at the back of his throat and fell silent.

Sambu waited for the vaidyan to continue and when it became clear that he wasn't going to, asked, with a touch of impatience:

'So, how is she? Can you treat her?'

'Yes. Vata,' said Narayana Tampuran, shaking his head, 'excess of vata.'

'What is vata?' Janaki asked, unable to check her curiosity. She also tried her best not to wrinkle her nose at the strong smell of coconut oil that emanated from his hair.

The vaidyan considered the question for a while. 'Excess of vata is excess of wind. Too much kapha is too much of phlegm and too much pitta is too much fire. She has amavata. Impurities or ama are distributed by vata to different parts of the body.'

'So, can you cure her? If so, how long will it take?' Sambu asked.

'In her case, it will take a very long time, but I can cure her,' said the vaidyan.

'How long?'

'I have to put her under intensive treatment for twenty-one days. She has to cooperate in the matter of patyam and apatyam.' Perhaps he saw the question forming on Janaki's face. 'Patyam is what she can eat and apatyam is what she cannot.'

'When can you start?'

'As soon as I set up my stove in the backyard. And I need a cot to be put there.'

In those three weeks, Bhavani's life altered dramatically. Balamba, the vaidyan's wife, was ever-smiling, unable to understand most of the things that were said to her, answering most questions with a smile that showed her teeth and her gums. In the morning she would bring Bhavani what the vaidyan euphemistically called snehapanam—a drink of love—a foul-smelling and worse tasting brew of the consistency of ghee. The vaidyan also seemed to have something constantly boiling on the stove. Bhavani had to drink the resulting concoction four times a day. There were also various powders, electuaries and liquids to be taken at different times.

The vaidyan took special care in prescribing a diet for Bhavani. No tamarind was to be used in cooking. No curd or ghee. Ginger, garlic, bitter gourd, drumsticks and rice were allowed.

This patyam was a challenge for Bhavani who loved her rasam and sambar, the principal constituent of which was tamarind. A meal was incomplete without curd. The one thing that she could not stand was garlic. For Bhavani, the food that she was forced to eat was only marginally better tasting than the medicines she had to ingest. All this was interspersed with enemas with herbal extracts and oils.

Every morning for a week, Balamba massaged her with warm oils. This was succeeded by kizhi, which involved hot fomentation with a cloth bag filled with herbs and dipped in warm medicated oils. During the next week, the massage was replaced by the smearing of warm oil all over her body, followed by hot fomentation with a cloth bag filled with cooked navara rice.

The effect on Bhavani's health was marked. She could get up and walk a little by the end of the first week. By the second week she told Janaki that her joint pains were almost completely gone. She would only limp a little while walking. By the fourth week she was back to her normal energy levels and all set to re-establish her sway over the kitchen.

The vaidyan said she would have to keep her patyam for at least another six months and also gave her a pasty concoction that was to be taken on an empty stomach and three large bottles full of oil for external application. He advised Bhavani to have an oil bath every week with a mixture of the oils—pinda, sahasradi and kottanchukkadi. He asked her to take two tablespoonfuls of dasamoolarishtam every day.

The happiest person, however, was Janaki. She was now free to pursue her plan of arm-twisting her father.

Seventeen

The education of women was a controversial subject even among Indians in the late nineteenth century. While the orthodoxy held that the woman's place was at home, and therefore, education was unnecessary and even harmful, thinkers like Gokhale and Ranade had other ideas. Even an enlightened person such as Tilak wrote:

'Every middle class man wants his wife to be literate and well-trained in household duties, to spend her leisure hours in reading religious texts in order to improve her mind, and to help him in domestic duties. Just as a trade is of primary importance to a craftsman and training is secondary, so are household duties generally primary for women and education incidental... By the age of 15–16 a woman should be well-trained in housework, and this training will never be available in school as much as at home. The marital home is the workshop of female education.'

Others, like Subramania Bharati in 1910, visualized the emancipation and rise of the modern woman as though it had already happened and celebrated it in his poems. For instance, in the poem 'Murasu', he exhorted people to dance and celebrate:

that those who believed that it was wrong for women to touch books,
that the weird men who wished to keep the women locked up,
have been made to bow their heads down in shame.

The British, however, only continued to pay lip service to the need for female education. By the turn of the century, only around one in two hundred Indian women were literate.

❖

December 1909

'They will have to make an exception for me,' Janaki told her father.

Sambu smiled, indulgence showing in the way his lips curled up and eyes crinkled.

'I don't think it's going to happen, Janaki. If you want, I will try,' said Sambu.

'Appa, I can stay with Chittappa and Chitti in Tanjore. They will be happy to have me.'

'I am just wondering if St Peter's college, Tanjore, will be happy to have you.'

'Appa, you said you knew the principal. What's his name?'

'John Russel Porter. Why do you want to know?'

'John Russel Porter! That's the name in the Gibbon books. Appa, you must know him very well indeed.'

Sambu squirmed but tried not to let his embarrassment show. He had helped John Porter translate works of grammar from Sanskrit to English, involving days and nights of discussions and clarifications and finally, when the Englishman offered to pay him, Sambu had refused to take money. He was a little ashamed to go back to him now for a favour.

When Sambu did meet John Porter, he seemed to be pleased to renew his acquaintance with Sambu. After an hour of conversation, John Porter finally asked him.

'Sambu, what brings you here? You have come to Tanjore for the express purpose of meeting me; yet you haven't told me the reason for your visit. Is it that you felt you had to see my face?'

'It is my daughter, Sir—'

'— John.'

For a moment Sambu looked nonplussed. He continued, thrusting forward a sheaf of papers containing the matriculation and FA results. 'My daughter wants to go to college. I was hoping your good self...'

Porter studied the papers in silence, shaking his head.

'Wait,' he said, 'she finished her exams nearly three years ago. And now she wants to do a BA?'

'John, my wife was not well. She was not even able to move around. During that time, Janaki took on all household work. But she always wanted to study and now that my wife is feeling much better...'

'Impossible, Sambu,' said Porter. 'This institution has never had a female student. Of course, if we were taking in girls, she would definitely have been accepted, considering her excellent performance in her matriculation and the First Arts examinations. We would even have considered her for one of the endowed scholarships.'

'I understand. I am sorry to have troubled you. I will take your leave.'

'However, impossible is not a word I should have used with someone to whom I owe so much. Everything is possible for the daughter of my teacher. Consider it done, Sambu. Including the scholarship.'

Sambu was speechless.

FEBRUARY–JUNE 1910
TANJORE

Eighteen

'Thank you very much, Appa,' said Janaki. 'I knew that your friend would agree to my joining the college.'

Before Sambu could reply, Bhavani intervened, 'Your father will say "yes" to anything from his favourite daughter. He doesn't care that you are still at home, unmarried. If your marriage has to be postponed by two more years, you will have to get married to an old man as a second or third wife. None of you give any weight to my words. Your father has spoilt you thoroughly.'

'Amma—'

'—I know, you want to study. How is that going to help you in cooking for your husband? Your father, of course, doesn't think of those things. He is up above the clouds, above anyone else with his Vedas. We are finding it difficult to have gruel twice a day. And you want to do BA? Who is going to pay for that?'

'Amma, I am getting a scholarship and I can use all of Panju's books for English, history and mental philosophy. I heard that the S.P.G. College has a good library. They also have an arrangement with the Royal Palace library. I can manage my moral philosophy by studying at the library. I will be staying with Chittappa; so there are no additional expenses.'

'Anyway,' said Bhavani, 'it is between you and him. In my days I just followed what my mother said without a word.'

Sambu was getting angrier and angrier through the exchange. 'Don't talk to me in the third person as though I am not there,' he burst out. 'I have made a decision. That's final.'

February 1910

It was still dark outside when Janaki and Sambu started for Tanjore. There was a chill in the air; just enough for her to wrap

the border of her sari tighter around herself. Murugan swished his
stick around, making clicking noises with his tongue and the oxen
soon found their rhythm. Though the covered cart swayed from
side to side, looking as though it would overturn at any moment,
the tinkling of the bells on the sure-footed oxen induced a sense
of safety in the passengers.

Janaki was not about to sleep; she was far too excited. Though
it was only around ten miles away, she had never been to Tanjore.
They crossed innumerable bridges over rivers. The only other trip
that she had taken—to Kumbakonam—did not involve crossing
so many rivers. Emerald green fields stretched as far as the eye
could see, relieved only by granaries and haystacks. She learnt
why Tiruvaiyaru—the land of the five rivers—was named so. They
had crossed all the five rivers—Cauvery, Kudamurutti, Vettar,
Vennar and Vadavar.

As they neared Tanjore, the first sight that greeted her eyes
was the magnificent principal tower of the Big Temple. Even from
a distance, it looked imposing. Janaki was sure then that the trip
marked an important beginning in her life.

Chittappa's house was large single-storey tiled house on East
Main Road, in the heart of Tanjore. When Janaki learnt that her
college was only a fifteen-minute walk away, she was very happy.
Not having seen such crowds under normal circumstances in
Tiruvaiyaru, the first thing she asked Chittappa was whether some
festival was going on.

If Chittappa seemed happy to see her, Chitti went a step farther.
She simply started treating Janaki as a member of the family
from the moment she stepped in. Janaki's seven-year-old cousin,
Saroja, whom she had never seen before, was the happiest about
her arrival. Saroja kept trying to show her where the bathroom

was, how the boiler worked and where she had drawn the lines for paandi, interspersing her conversation with at least three Akkas every minute. Sambu, realizing that his daughter was settling down quite well, left in two days.

Janaki's uncle accompanied her to the college on her first day. She was not overwhelmed by the college—or rather the school—as she found that the college department was a minuscule one with only around twenty students. The experience of finding herself to be the only girl was not a novel one; she had already experienced this at the high school at Tiruvaiyaru.

The tall figure with a well-cut beard and a moustache walked into the room. A clerical collar peeped out from underneath his coat and his boots shone.

'My name is John Russell Porter,' he said, gesturing at the dozen or so students to sit down. 'I have the unenviable task of teaching you English and mental philosophy and you have the onerous task of learning. Make no mistake; I will strive to make both things happen. I must warn you that I am also the principal of the school and the college and I do possess powers. I can cause a lot of discomfiture to you and your parents if I believe you are not putting in the requisite effort.'

'By the way,' he continued, looking around, 'I am "Sir" to you when you address me directly and Reverend Porter when writing or referring to me. At any rate do not call me "Father". Any questions?' Janaki and a couple of other students shook their heads; but he didn't wait for an answer and continued.

'We are going to learn mental philosophy. Before that, we need to be clear as to what constitutes the mind. Human knowledge falls under two great divisions—the mind and matter—'

'—The internal and the external.' Janaki didn't realize for a moment that she had said it aloud and bit her tongue when she became aware of it.

'As the young lady says, the internal and the external. At this point, I would like to make one thing clear,' said Reverend Porter, looking straight at Janaki. 'I do not mind questions, in fact, I invite them, provided they are at the end of my lecture. What I do object to strenuously are gratuitous interruptions in the form of statements. Do I make myself clear?'

'I…I am sorry, Sir,' Janaki flushed.

'In any case, I am happy to see that the daughter of my old friend is as sharp as he is,' said Porter. There was a hint of a smile behind the beard.

He continued for the next hour in his precise clipped English and concluded exactly at the bell. Janaki realized that he left no time for questions.

Nineteen

March 1910

Janaki enjoyed the privacy of having a room all to herself. This helped her to study—and there was a lot of it to be done—after she came back from college. Chitti had also asked her to look through various books her son had left behind on moving to Madras after getting an appointment in the revenue office. Janaki had rummaged through the lot and found one of the books prescribed in her syllabus. The title page read: M. Tully Cicero's five books of Tusculan Disputations Done into Englifh by a Gentleman of Chrift Church College, Oxford.

She was still getting used to the routine of waking up when it was dark outside—her mother had let her sleep till much later. She would finish her bath, dry her hair, bolt down her breakfast of cooked rice soaked overnight and laced generously with buttermilk, and get ready for college.

Janaki woke up early, went to the back of the house and cleaned her teeth with a chew stick made of a twig from a banyan tree, rubbing in with her forefinger a powder that her mother prepared from dried herbs and powdered charcoal. She wore a petticoat tied at the top of her breasts and had her bath, drawing water from the well into a large cylindrical brass container and pouring it over herself using a brass mug. She then washed her clothes on the granite stone near the well. She dried herself and tied a thin towel on her head and changed into a pavadai and a half-sari. She then went to the puja room and got the plate, water and the flowers for her Chittappa to perform his puja.

'You have woken up early even today?'

Chitti's words made her realize that it was Sunday and she didn't have to go to college.

'I didn't remember, Chitti,' said Janaki.

'Tell me,' asked Chitti, smiling, 'Do you always have a book in your hand? I have no problem with that. But didn't your mother complain? Especially if you brought a book when you were eating.'

'All the time, Chitti,' said Janaki, laughing. 'She has even threatened to fling my books into the stove.'

By then, Janaki had finished readying everything for the puja.

'Chitti, can I help you in the kitchen? Today is the one day when I have the time to do so.'

'I really don't need help in the kitchen. However, if you really want to help me, you can cut the vegetables for the drumstick sambar and raw banana curry.'

Janaki went into the kitchen and spotted the arivalmanai quite easily. It was slightly different in design from the one at home. This one had a vertical steel cutting surface that was fixed to a wooden base on its broader side. The other end was goose-necked and twisted through ninety degrees, ending in a round serrated blade for scraping coconuts.

She washed the drumsticks, sat down, pressed on the rectangular wooden base of the arivalmanai with one foot, held the drumsticks five in a bunch and with the dexterity born of practice, cut through them with bold quick movements of her hands. When she finished she had drumstick pieces that were neither so short that one found it difficult to get at the pithy insides with one's teeth nor so long that they tickled the throat. She then peeled the raw banana skin by slicing through it expertly, peeling the skin off the entire length in one fluid movement, and then cut the bananas first lengthwise and then breadthwise, producing small uniformly shaped slices.

'You are really good at this,' Chitti remarked. 'The one who is going to marry you is extremely lucky. I hope Saroja learns from you.'

Janaki beamed at the compliment. She wrapped a wet cloth over the cut pieces and got up.

'You have not gone out anywhere ever since you came. Why don't you wake Saroja up and when she is ready, take her out. You haven't even seen the Brahadeeswarar temple as yet. And it is so near. You can both go for a walk there.'

'All right,' said Janaki.

'Be a little careful with her. She tends to run off when not watched.'

When Janaki reached the small bridge in front of the Big Temple with Saroja in tow, it was a bright morning with the sun hanging low in the east in a cloudless sky.

'Now hold my forefinger tight,' Janaki told Saroja as they crossed the small bridge over the moat. The tower was not particularly impressive. The gopurams at Tiruvaiyaru were bigger. She was surprised to see a second gopuram behind the first. She wasn't that impressed with that either. Once she had passed through the entrance, the sight astounded her.

A large quadrangle paved with bricks and surrounded by cloisters stretched ahead, and looming above her was the vimanam—the edifice constructed above the sanctum sanctorum—that rose majestically into the sky and ended in a bulbous capstone that appeared huge even from that distance. The sight was magnificent; but unlike in most temples, she didn't get the feeling of being in a sacred space. When she lowered her eyes at last, she saw the Nandi Mandapam that housed an enormous stone bull in repose. In her excitement, she ran up the steps of the pillared pavilion to get a closer look at the huge Nandi. As she reached the top, she suddenly had the vague feeling that something was missing. She looked at her right hand. Cicero's book was there. She looked at the left hand that felt empty.

O God. Saroja. Where is she?

She looked back at the second entrance; no sign of her. She panicked and shouted out—'SAROJA, SARO!' Saroja was not to be seen or heard.

'Are you by any chance looking for a little girl?' a new voice from the bottom of the steps broke through her panic.

'Yes, yes.'

'About seven, wearing a green pavadai and a red top?'

'Yes, yes, that's her. Have you seen her?'

The stranger who had spoken softly seemed impossibly tall, at over six feet. He wore a white full-sleeved shirt that he had tucked into his black trousers. He was clean-shaven, his wide grin showing his white teeth that were even, but for a single incisor that overlapped its neighbours and protruded a little.

Janaki suppressed the thought that it was cute.

'Well,' said the stranger, 'If that girl who is crouched, hiding behind the steps is Saroja, I guess I have seen her.'

Saroja must have sensed that her game was up. She came running up the steps and hugged Janaki. Any transient thought of scolding her was gone, washed away in a flood of relief. Janaki hugged her back and smiled at the stranger.

'You must have thought me mad,' said Janaki, climbing down the steps.

'Not at all. In fact I have never seen a woman reading Cicero, much less taking him along for a stroll,' said the stranger.

Janaki laughed. 'I have Cicero with me because I am studying him for my BA.'

'Oh, no wonder, then. You are *that* girl.' Seeing the perplexed look on Janaki's face, he elaborated further. 'I heard at St Peter's that for the first time in the history of the college, a girl had joined for BA. You must be Janaki, then. I am Arul and I am afraid I am not that well known. I will be joining you in your English classes taken by Reverend Porter.'

'What a coincidence, bumping into you then. But I don't understand why you will be joining us only for the English classes.'

'Well, that wouldn't interest you all that much.'

'That's all right. I have all the time in the world.'

'No,' said Arul, 'you go ahead and see the main temple. I will wait for you here. Don't forget to look at the stone guards at the entrance. Try and imagine how big they were conceived to be in relation to the elephant in the panel.'

'Why don't you come with us?'

'I have already gone in once, along with a French priest who wanted to see the temple. But it is not an experience I would care to repeat.'

'I don't understand,' Janaki was genuinely perplexed.

'You see, I am a Christian. Though this temple is better than the others, in general, we seem to pollute sacred spaces with our presence.'

Janaki was embarrassed and did not know what to say. 'Fine, then,' she said finally. 'I will go in.'

She kept thinking about what Arul had said all the way to the main temple. In Tiruvaiyaru, there was no way anyone who was not a caste Hindu would be admitted into the temple. Then she realized with a shock that the Big Temple was more about the magnificence of its eleventh-century builder, Rajaraja Chola, than about the sanctity of the deity.

There was no priest in the sanctum sanctorum of the temple. But the stone linga was so large that she had to see it from two levels to take it in fully. While returning from the temple after performing the circumambulation of the deity, she fell in behind a group who had a guide with them. They were going around the main temple and Janaki followed them.

At one point, the guide stopped suddenly, threw his hands out in a dramatic gesture and said, 'Look,' pointing with an upward inclination of the head, 'can you see the four figures there one below the other? Can you see the warrior with the drawn sword? Above that there are three smaller figures, ending with a man with a beard wearing a bowler hat. These represented, at the time of the building in the eleventh century, the four dynasties that were to rule—the Cholas, followed by the Nayaks and the Marathas and finally the English. Can you see that the Englishman is King Edward?'

Janaki was startled, particularly at the distinctly foreign-looking figure on the tower. *There must be some other explanation.*

The guide wanted to get as much mileage as possible out of his story. 'This is clear proof of the prophetic powers of our ancestors.'

Janaki's mind had, however, wandered. She was wondering if Arul was still waiting. On one hand, she wanted him to be waiting; on the other, here she was, thinking about a stranger, that too a *man*. She shook her head to clear it, checked that Saroja was still attached to her and set off towards the Rajarajan gate. Even from a distance, she could see Arul, engrossed in a sculpture. As she came near, Arul turned around. His features broadened into a smile.

The crooked tooth again.

'Sorry, we got a little delayed. There was no reason for you to have waited for us.'

'Actually there is. I wanted to show you something else.'

Arul led them, following the high wall north and then west. They soon reached a reservoir with an old church in front. Arul took them around to the western end of the church.

'This is what I wanted to show you,' said Arul, indicating a group of carved marble figures. The group depicted a man lying down on a bed surrounded by three men and four boys.

'This is beautiful,' said Janaki and read the inscription aloud.

To the memory of the
Reverend Christian Frederic Schwartz
Born at Sonnenburg of Neumark in the Kingdom of
Prussia
The 26th of October 1726
and died at Tanjore the 13th of February 1798

'Read this,' Arul said, pointing to the lines further down:

His natural vivacity won the affection as his unspotted
probity and purity of life
Alike commanded the
Reverence of the Christian, Mahomedan and Hindu

'I am a Roman Catholic,' said Arul, 'but Reverend Schwartz is my hero.'

Janaki felt she had an open window into this smiling man's soul. She was also confused by strange feelings that she had never experienced before.

'I must be going,' she said, 'Saroja is tired.'

She did not wait for an answer. She set off homeward, virtually dragging Saroja along behind her.

She turned around after walking some distance and found that Arul was still staring at her.

Janaki was seated at a desk in the front row in the college classroom, waiting for Reverend Porter to arrive and commence his English lecture. She was busy reviewing the notes from the last class, when Reverend Porter entered. She stood up along with the other students.

'Sit down, sit down,' said Porter. 'In the last class we read the first scene in the first act of *Julius Caesar*. I am sure all of you must have reviewed it at home. What were the tribunes Flavius and Marullus worried about?' He paused.

'That was not a rhetorical question. Can someone answer?'

Janaki stood up. 'Unless public liberty is protected by intrepid and vigilant guardians, the authority of so formidable a magistrate will soon degenerate into despotism,' she said, and sat down.

'That quote,' Porter said, 'seems familiar. Who were you paraphrasing, young lady?'

'Gibbon,' said Janaki. 'I wasn't paraphrasing, Sir; that's an exact quote.'

Porter looked at her for a while and said, almost to himself: 'But other fell into good ground, and brought forth fruit, some an hundredfold, some sixtyfold, some thirtyfold.'

'Matthew 13:8,' she heard a familiar voice murmuring close to her.

She turned around. *Arul!*

She turned back quickly in her confusion, but not before Arul had flashed her a smile and a nod. She was disoriented throughout the lecture.

At the end of the lecture, she turned around to face Arul. 'When we met last,' she said, 'you didn't exactly tell me why we would be meeting again.'

'Mea culpa,' said Arul. 'I studied at the St Joseph's ecclesiastical seminary in Pondicherry thanks to my bishop at Kumbakonam. He is involved in translating the holy book into Tamil and I have been assisting him after I left the seminary. He wanted me to do some research here at S.P.G. College and also at the Royal Palace library. While here, he said I should attend the English BA classes by Reverend Porter and here I am.'

'If you have studied at a seminary, you must have studied a lot of Latin,' said Janaki.

'I have Latin and Greek pouring out of my ears,' said Arul.

'So you can help me,' said Janaki.

'Yes, of course, anything, if only you will tell me how I can help you.'

'You see,' said Janaki, I read Gibbon's *Rise and Fall of the Roman Empire—*'

'—Exactly what I expect every Brahmin girl to do.'

'You are making fun of me,' said Janaki.

'No, no. I meant just the opposite. It is one of those figures of speech.'

'Irony,' Janaki said. 'Anyway, I have made a note of the phrases I didn't understand. Most of them are in Latin. I was wondering if you could help me translate them. You can also help me with my Cicero.'

'Your merest desire is my command,' said Arul. 'I will be your Cicerone.'

They sat next to each other in every English class after that. They also took to meeting in the park near the palace whenever an opportunity presented itself.

Twenty

Arul was early to class. He squinted his eyes against the morning sun and walked with his head lowered.

He had missed Janaki desperately during the past week, while she was away attending a wedding. How could he, who aspired to be *In persona Christi*, even think about a woman this way? He remembered his somewhat naïve discussions with his spiritual advisor at the seminary.

'Father,' Arul had said, 'Sometimes I am strongly attracted to girls. I am afraid I may not be able to remain chaste.'

'My son,' the spiritual director had said, 'it is only natural; but you only have to ask God and he will give you abundant graces for a chaste life. If you keep practising, it will soon become a habit. Celibacy is truly a serious undertaking and you must consider it always in your discernment. It is indeed possible for those who are called.'

Arul thought he had the answers—until now.

He reached his classroom and sat down with his elbows on the desk and head between them. He did not know how long he was in that position, till the sound of anklets brought him back from his preoccupation. *Janaki*. A thrill shot through him.

Her large eyes looked more beautiful than ever.

'I met the office peon on the way. Apparently, Reverend Porter has been sick and won't be coming in today,' said Janaki.

'That's good. I mean…poor man,' said Arul.

'Let's take a walk along the banks of the Cauvery,' said Janaki.

'Good idea,' said Arul as he stood up and joined her.

They walked along for a while before Arul broke the silence. 'You must have had a great time at the wedding.'

'Oh yes. The food was fantastic; I met up with so many of my relatives. It was wonderful, except that I missed Panju who was busy with his studies at Kumbakonam.'

'Panju is your younger brother, right?'

Janaki nodded.

'And he is married?'

Janaki nodded again.

'Can I ask you something personal?' asked Arul and continued without waiting for an answer. 'How is it you are not married? I am only asking because I know that in Brahmin families, girls are married off very young.'

'Well, it's like this, Arul. I am determined to complete college, before even thinking of marriage. I am a little too strong-willed and my father a little too liberal-minded to impose his will on me. Marriage has been a frequent topic of conversation at home. Particularly with my mother. I have never yielded. Not that I don't want to marry at all. If there is someone who has no problems with my continuing my education for as long as I want, I don't see why not.'

Arul listened, his mind working more furiously than ever.

'And what about you?' asked Janaki, a twinkle in her eye. Before he could answer, her attention was distracted by something in the distance. A wild look came into her eye and she started running. Arul was shocked and turned around to see what she was running towards. He saw a young boy running and a dog scampering in the opposite direction in a three-legged limp. The boy had a long head start over Janaki and his movement was unimpeded by clothing. Soon Janaki gave up the chase.

Arul rushed to her and when he saw tears running down her cheeks, his heart melted.

'He hurt him…he hurt him,' she cried repeatedly, while Arul held her.

Arul was absolutely certain now that Janaki was the one who called to him; not the church.

'You asked me a question,' said Arul in a gentle tone. 'I was not sure of the answer until sometime ago. I am more than willing to be the husband who will let his wife study as much as she wants. What do you say?'

'Are you proposing to me?' asked Janaki, pulling herself away. 'That can't be. You want to be a priest. You are not allowed to marry.'

'I have chosen,' replied Arul. 'I know one thing for certain. My life will not be complete without you.'

'This is the most ridiculous thing I have ever heard,' said Janaki. After a small pause that seemed to last an eternity to Arul, she continued.

'It is also the most wonderful thing I have ever heard.'

Janaki allowed Arul to put his arm around her shoulders.

'Won't your father object to this?' Janaki asked.

'Which one,' asked Arul. Seeing the perplexed look on her face, he continued. 'Oh, I have many fathers.'

Janaki looked at him, a question still on her face.

'Let me explain,' said Arul. 'I too, like your brother, was a son born of a holy pilgrimage. My father was a carpenter in Kumbakonam and my parents were childless for a long time. They had prayed at the St Mary's cathedral, sorry, then a church, and offered votive candles. It did not help. Then someone told my mother about the shrine of St John Britto at Oriyur. John Britto was a Jesuit priest who was beheaded at Oriyur and attained his martyrdom. The earth around the place of execution is reputed to have turned red. He is a living presence and grants prayers. To cut a long story short, my parents walked the distance of over two hundred miles to Oriyur along with some other pilgrims, and prayed to St Britto in the traditional manner by carrying and planting coconut saplings. They returned after a month of arduous travel, vowing to return if their prayers were answered and apparently, I was born within a year. They named me Arul as John Britto was known as Arul Anandar.'

'That still doesn't explain why you talked of fathers,' said Janaki.

'I am coming to that,' said Arul. I was around five when my parents decided to return to Oriyur, leaving me with a friend. My father made a very small cradle as a votive offering to St Britto. It was exquisitely carved, and beautifully polished to a reddish-brown colour. I remember crying and insisting that I wanted it. My father consoled me by saying he would make another one for me. He never had a chance to make me one. The people with whom they had gone on the pilgrimage returned saying that my parents had left a couple of days earlier from Oriyur. My parents never returned from the trip and I never knew what really happened to them. The people who I was staying with were poor and it was a large family. They went to the priest, Reverend Francis, at the church. The priest, a Frenchman belonging to the Paris Foreign Missions Society, agreed to take care of me after hearing me sing.'

'I never knew you could sing,' said Janaki. 'You must sing for me sometime.'

'I will,' said Arul laughing, 'when I want you to run away from me. Anyway, my new father taught me to read and write. He travelled a lot and I was left in the care of different families in his parish. By the time I was eleven, he was going back to France and he thought I was ready for a seminary education. He sent me to the provincial seminary at Pondicherry. At Pondicherry I acquired more fathers—the Rector, my spiritual director and others. I still go to Kumbakonam for my holidays.'

'You have been through so much,' said Janaki. 'I can't imagine not having a father or a mother.'

As the love between Arul and Janaki ripened, he wanted more and more to be with her. On the other hand, he also wished, more than anything else, to be an ordained priest. Now that seemed impossible. He had to talk to someone to clear his mind. He wondered whether to talk to his bishop at Kumbakonam, the priest at Tanjore or his spiritual director at the seminary in Pondicherry. After much thought, he decided to travel to his seminary.

The old priest invited him to take a walk along the promenade. They made a spectacle on the beach—the short and wizened old priest and the tall Arul. They walked along silently for a while.

'Father, is it so wrong to love a woman?'

'It is not wrong for a layperson to do so. But as someone hoping to be ordained a priest, you must remember that it is impossible both theologically and canonically for priests to marry. You know a priest serves in place of Christ and, of course, he takes vows of celibacy.'

'Yes, Father, I know, but...'

'I understand. I just wanted that to be clear. Having said that, the proper way for us to live is to follow the holy will of God in this world. But, what is God's will? You can find that only through prayer. If your vocation is that of a married man, so be it. The council of Trent has declared: "If anyone says that marriage is not, truly and properly, one of the seven sacraments of the New Law, and that it does not confer grace, let him be anathema." St Paul has said: "If thou take a wife, thou has not sinned." The state of matrimony is, however, a common one. Of course, in episcopacy is the most perfect state. For that, a vow and practice of chastity are mandatory.'

'Father, my confusion is not over anything theological or canonical. My heart says I should marry the woman I love. I am confused as to whether I have discerned the will of God correctly.'

'Let me ask you quite bluntly. Have you sinned? Do you need to confess?'

'No, Father.'

'You must understand that as a spiritual director, if you have even a germ of longing for the perfect religious life, my duty is to encourage it, particularly when you have led a chaste life.'

'Yes, Father, I understand. I will simply have to trust my conscience, my heart, in order to discern God's will.'

'There are, of course, other Christian denominations that have no problems with a married priest—'

'—Father, are you suggesting that I join some other denomination, like the Church of England?' Arul looked intently at the old priest's face, but couldn't read anything in it.

'Certainly not, my son. I was just mentioning it to contrast with our Mother.'

'Father, I was baptized a Roman Catholic, and I will remain one. Orders or no orders.'

'And you must first intimate your bishop if you determine that your calling is a married life.'

'Yes, Father, I intend to see him.'

'So, your mind is made up.'

They started walking back, each in his cocoon of silence.

Twenty-one

June 1910

For the fourth time, Janaki scratched out what she had written and began afresh. It was a free period and she was determined to write to Panju, pouring out her heart. *Dear Panju*, she wrote again. *I have been meaning to write to you for a long time, to tell you about Tanjore and my feelings about the place and the people.* She dipped her pen in the inkwell and was about to scratch it out.

'Don't,' said Arul, who had been observing her from a few benches behind.

'Arul,' she said, without turning around, 'I am trying to write to Panju. I have just not been able to find the right words to describe my feelings. It will greatly help if you don't keep popping up to say "don't".'

'I was just trying to help you, Janu. Just do what I tell you and you will find that you will be able to write really fast.'

'All right, tell me your great method and be quick about it.'

'This is what you do. At the top of the letter, write "I AM NOT POSTING THIS". In capitals. Now go ahead. Write your letter.'

Janaki busied herself with the task. 'This seems to work,' she muttered as she continued writing her letter for another half hour. At last, she held the letter in front of her and blew on it.

'I told you it was easy,' said Arul. 'Now you have only one thing to do. Scratch out "I am not posting this".'

'No, I can't bring myself to post this. But it will serve another purpose.' She got up, turned around and held the letter out to Arul. 'I want you to read this.'

'Come on, I can't read a private letter that you have written to your brother,' said Arul.

'No, I definitely want you to read it,' said Janaki and stuffed the letter into his hands. Arul started reading the letter.

Dear Panju, the letter began.

I have so many things I want to share with you, about Tanjore, about the people here, the college. Most of all, I want to tell you something that I have not told ANYONE. I never knew I could care so much about a person. Don't get a swollen head, Panju. I am not talking about you now. I have met someone I really love. He is tall, not particularly good-looking, but when he smiles, all the world is gay. He is also such a beautiful person inside that you will really love him when you meet him. He also loves me and wants to marry me. I can't think of anyone who will make a better husband to me. There is one issue, however, which to my mind is not a problem. Arul is Christian. I know that Appa and Amma cannot accept this, but I know in my heart that you will understand me. I miss you very badly.

I haven't really opened my heart to Arul, but soon I will.

Lots of love.
Janaki.

Arul read it and was exhilarated.

JUNE 1910–MAY 1911
KUMBAKONAM

Twenty-two

June 1910

It was at one of the sadir performances of Ranjitham that Panju met Muthuswamy Mudaliar. By now, Panju was used to sitting in the front row. Muthuswamy was seated next to him, wearing a white turban. His forehead boasted clearly drawn horizontal stripes of vibhuti, adorned with a red kumkumam dot in the centre, straddling the lowermost and the middle stripes. He wore a black closed-neck coat that showed the merest hint of a collar and a white veshti with a filigreed border worn with the cloth taken through his legs and tucked neatly behind. The veshti was worn so well that, even while seated, only the barest hint of Mudaliar's ankles could be seen.

Panchapakesan BA. It did rather roll off the tongue smoothly when Panju first said it to himself. Sambu had been pestering him to go and meet Vichu, who was now a shirastedar in the Board of Revenue at Madras. He didn't want to meet Vichu for more than one reason. The only person, apart from Janaki, with whom he wanted to share the news of his successful graduation was Ranjitham.

She had merely looked at him and said, 'When are you leaving?' Panju wasn't sure, but he thought he had detected a hint of sadness in her voice. The BA seemed to lose its sheen.

He repeated it a couple of times and stopped short when he realized that he was now officially an unemployed graduate.

'You said something?' Muthuswamy's soft voice belied his bulk.

'I am sorry,' said Panju. 'I must have muttered something aloud.'

'You said "BA". I take it that you passed your BA exams recently.'

'Yes, that's true,' said Panju.

'In that case, may I congratulate you?'

'Thank you,' said Panju.

'Why don't we take a short walk? It will be a while before the dancer starts her next item,' said Muthuswamy, and without waiting for an answer, got up from his chair with an audible effort. Panju followed him.

'I suppose you know both Tamil and English rather well,' said Muthuswamy.

'I am good with all languages. Including Sanskrit.'

'You can read and write well in all these?'

'Yes, but I wonder why this is sounding like an interview or a proposal for marriage.'

'Well, it is an interview of sorts. You see, I have a printing press. I have a Stanhope that is capable of over two hundred impressions an hour. I am going to import an even more modern press. I need someone to manage it. I am thinking of printing some of the classical Tamil and Sanskrit works that have never been printed before. Hence the questions. However, a young man like you will probably want to go to Madras and work for the government.'

'No, never. Our country may be ruled by white men. I do not wish to subject myself to further slavery.'

'Lower your voice, young man. Sometimes it is better to keep your opinions to yourself. Anyway, what will you do otherwise? Eke out a living by teaching people the Vedas or old Tamil texts?'

'Sir, you know better than I do that Indians have even established shipping companies. I have heard that a bank is also being set up in Madras. I think there are enough things to do. You have yourself established a printing press.'

'Well, do you think I make money from the press? I certainly don't print currency notes there.' Mudaliar seemed so amused at his own witticism that he laughed uproariously for a full minute before continuing. 'If my great-grandfather had not been a noted dubashi with the British government, I would not have had the luxury… Anyway that is neither here nor there. I will see you tomorrow. Now let us go back to the programme.'

'You haven't told me how I can contact—'

'—I am sorry. My name is Muthuswamy Mudaliar. Surely you have seen the Velmurugan press. It is on—'

'—I know, Sir; I have seen the board. It is on Tanjore Road.'

'Good,' nodded Muthuswamy. 'Then I will see you tomorrow. Nine sharp.'

Panju was not sure, initially, if he had got the job. The moment he walked in, however, he was given errands to do and generally treated as though he was an employee. It was confirmed only when Mudaliar said, 'Come at 9:00 a.m. from tomorrow.' Panju was convinced that only his strong intent to stay close to Ranjitham had caused this serendipity.

Twenty-three

December 1910

The clap of the press, punctuated by silences, now familiar to Panju, induced in him a hypnagogic state. The press went: *Thai dit dit thai/ Thai thai dit dit thai/ Thai thai dit dit thai.*

Now Ranjitham faced him, her torso twisted, beckoning with her right hand, now receding, now beckoning with her left…

'Sir…'

'Who's that? Come in,' said Panju, his reverie shattered.

The man had hair that reached his shoulders, parted on the extreme right, the hair on the left swept up in a bouffant, a lock of hair curling on to his forehead. His glistening moustache ended in sharp points and had obviously been treated with ghee. When he smiled, as he did now, he displayed most of his pan-stained upper teeth and a generous expanse of gum. His eyes were deep-set, glinting from beneath bushy eyebrows. He was dressed in a white shirt and pyjamas. He carried a jute bag that must have sported legible printing at some point of time; now it was a jumble of faded blue characters. He wore slippers that curled up a little at the toe end.

'I would like to meet Mr Mudaliar.'

'He is not yet in. Can I help you?'

'Thank you very much, but I would like to see him.'

Panju was fascinated by the man's preaspirated 'v's and 'w's.

'I am in charge,' said Panju. 'Can I help you?'

'Oh, you are Panju, aren't you?'

'Yes, but how did you know?'

'Muthuswamy Mudaliar has talked about you.'

'Who is taking my name in vain?' asked Mudaliar as he walked in. 'Oh, I see that you two have already met. What do you think, Jatin?'

Jatin raised his eyebrows and stared at Panju. Panju thought he was being evaluated.

'We have just met. It's too early to form an opinion,' said Jatin.

'In that case, I'll leave you two to get to know each other. But I can assure you that he has the Cauvery water in his blood and the Cauvery soil on his hands and feet.'

'Is that better than the Ganges?' asked Jatin.

'Why don't you find out?' Mudaliar walked past them and disappeared into his cabin.

'Mr Jatin, I don't understand.'

'Jatin da to you, and let's talk a little more. Mudaliar said you were not interested in working for the British. Why is that?'

'It's simple really. I refuse to perpetuate the cause of slavery.'

'Do you mean to say that working for the Indian government is like being a slave?' Jatin had a trick of emphasizing his questions with his eyebrows.

'Well, at the moment, even the Indians who are not working for the British government in India are all slaves. But the people who actually work for the British government are worse, because they do so willingly and help continue that bondage.'

Jatin stared at Panju for a long time. He seemed to come to a decision.

'Are you willing to do something about this situation?'

Panju did not hesitate. 'I am willing to do anything in my power to help remedy that.'

'And you are not afraid?' asked Jatin, his brows furrowed and knit, making them even more conspicuous.

'Afraid? Of what? Once I was afraid that a boy who bullied me would strangle me to death. Since then I have thought a lot about fear. I have come to the conclusion that all fear is fear of death. If I am afraid to go to the bathroom in the dark, it is because I am afraid I might die. Sometimes I identify myself with an ideology so deeply that a threat to that is much worse than a death threat to my physical being.'

'So the problem then is with the process of identification?' asked Jatin.

'Forgive me for saying so, but this kind of thinking is absolute rubbish; someone who does not identify himself with something much larger than him is a complete wastrel, a burden on the earth. I choose to identify with Mother India.'

Panju was breathing hard. 'And don't ever call me a coward!'

'No, no, I didn't mean anything like that,' said Jatin. 'You said you identify yourself with Mother India. How do you handle the fear associated with the threat to her?'

'I don't know, but I would like to take it head-on rather than run away from it.'

'So, what do you think we should do?'

'There is a sloka in the *Kaivalya Upanishad* that my father quoted often,' said Panju, '*Not by performing Vedic rituals,/ Not through one's progeny,/ Nor through wealth;/ through sacrifice alone/ did they achieve immortality.*'

'And so?'

'We must act, prepared to risk everything. We cannot invoke the philosophy of our ancestors to justify inaction and to let things slide past.'

'It seems as though you are talking about someone in particular,' observed Jatin.

Panju almost said he was talking about his father.

'No,' he said instead, 'I have heard some older people say we must adjust to whatever fate has willed with forbearance. They even quote the Gita in their defence. Surely, that is not the message of the Gita. The Gita, to me, favours action to inaction.'

'Well said, Panju. We are a group of people who think like you. And we do have the means of doing something about it.' Jatin's features relaxed as though Panju had passed some unspecified test. 'We meet every Friday at the ruined Kali temple near the Mahamaham tank. Why don't you join us this Friday at seven in the evening? I will see you at quarter to seven at the Mukuntar Mandapam and I will take you to the meeting.'

'Fine, I'll be there,' said Panju.

The press clattered away as before. It was now a cacophonous intrusion.

When Panju stepped out of his house, the skies were two-toned. The west was thick with a morass of black clouds; the eastern skies were innocent of clouds of any description. A soar of low-flying kites glided in tight circles. Even though Panju was outside, he put out his hand to check if it was raining, and ashamed, withdrew it quickly. He made his way to the Mahamaham tank in brisk strides.

Jatin was already waiting for him at the Mukuntar Mandapam. He gave no indication of having seen Panju and started walking with short but quick steps. By the time Panju caught up with Jatin, he was panting a little. They walked in silence along a darkening mud road while the scent of fresh rain on earth carried across to them. After walking along for about half an hour, Jatin stopped suddenly. He cupped his hands together in front of his mouth and let out a shriek, an even-pitched trill descending into a shrill whinny.

'That was a screech owl,' he said, by way of explanation.

There was an answering shriek that seemed to satisfy Jatin.

'That means that there are no ghosts abroad,' he muttered, as he started walking again.

'You believe in ghosts, do you? In any case, what is the connection between—'

'—I am sorry, I should have explained. I have not told you

about the code words we use. "Ghosts" are the police and "sadhus" are people like you and me—fellow revolutionaries.'

What have I got myself into? The thought arose momentarily before being replaced by—*I am strong. I will do what I need to do.*

Jatin moved off the road and entered what seemed to be a thicket of trees and Panju followed. A few minutes later, the sight that greeted him made him gasp. It was quite dark; but moonlight revealed a temple that lay nestled in a clearing among a thick clump of trees. On a closer look, the cluster of trees resolved into a single banyan tree. The temple itself was in ruins; but a pillared pavilion made of granite stood intact in front. As Panju and Jatin walked towards the open pavilion, clouds obscured the moon and everything was dark except for a dull glow from inside the pavilion. They had to slow down to watch their steps.

The glow came from a single oil lamp atop an improvised wooden altar covered with a tablecloth. A framed picture of Kali, smeared generously with red ochre, was propped upright with some books. The edge of a long sword gleamed in the light of the lamp. The smell of sandalwood incense permeated the pavilion. It had started raining and there was the constant murmur of raindrops falling on leaves. The flame of the lamp, protected on three sides with makeshift partitions, held steady despite the wind.

Three men stood in an attitude of reverence, casting long shadows behind them. Panju thought that he recognized one of them, but wasn't sure.

'Bande Mataram,' said Jatin.

'Bande Mataram,' said two of them in unison. The third, Panju thought, said 'Vande Mataram'.

'Let us begin,' one of them said.

One of them began to sing. Panju identified the voice immediately as belonging to Mudaliar and the song as one written by Subramania Bharati:

When will this thirst for freedom be quenched?
When will our love of bondage die?
When will our Mother's manacles break?
When will our trials stop?

Mudaliar sang three more stanzas, in a clear voice, his Tamil accent precise and beautiful. When the song was finished, Jatin stepped forward to face everyone.

'Friends and fellow sadhus, today is a special day. I have brought with me a young man, in whose veins the warm blood of patriotism flows abundantly. He has come here today to take the irrevocable oath that already binds all of us.'

Irrevocable. Panju felt uneasy.

'May I now ask,' Jatin continued, 'Panchapakesan Iyer to come up here?'

Panju stepped forward, his heart now a buzzing sawmill.

Jatin read out the oath line by line and Panju repeated it:

'In the name of Bharat Mata,
In the name of all the martyrs that
have shed their blood for Bharat Mata,
By the Love, innate in all men and women,
that I bear for the land of my birth,
wherein lie the sacred ashes of my forefathers,
and which is the cradle of my children,
By the tears of Hindu mothers for their children
whom the Foreigner has enslaved, imprisoned, tortured
and killed,
I, Panchapakesan Iyer,
convinced that without absolute political independence or
Swarajya
my country can never rise to the exalted position
among the nations of the earth which is Her due,
And convinced also that that Swarajya can never be attained

except by
the waging of a bloody and relentless war against the Foreigner,
solemnly and sincerely swear that I shall from this moment
do everything in my power
to fight for Independence and place the Lotus Crown of
Swarajya on the head of my Mother;
and with this object, I join the Bharat Samman,
the revolutionary society of all Hindustan,
and swear that I shall ever be true and faithful to this my
solemn Oath,
and that I shall obey the orders of this body;
If I betray the whole or any part of this solemn Oath,
or if I betray this body or any other
body working with a similar object,
may I be doomed in this world and the next!'

Panju's voice grew stronger and stronger, ending with 'Vande Mataram!'

Jatin grabbed the long sword with his left hand. 'Can you affirm your oath by the blood of your ancestors that courses through you?'

Panju looked Jatin in the eye. 'Yes!'

Jatin grasped Panju's right thumb and ran it lightly along the edge of the sword. He then pressed the bloody thumb to Panju's forehead.

'Thus I anoint you a member of the Bharat Samman.'

'Bande Mataram!' The pavilion resounded with the joyous shout.

Outside, it continued raining heavily.

Twenty-four

January 1911

When Panju entered the by now familiar Attakkaran Street and stood in front of Ranjitham's house, the sky was ocean-blue spotted with flecks of foamy clouds. A sudden gust of wind stirred up dust. Panju closed his eyes momentarily.

'Panju, what's happened?' exclaimed Ranjitham.

'Some dust. Just got into my eyes,' he said.

'That's not what I mean. Why haven't you shaved? You haven't even shaved your forehead.'

'Oh, that,' said Panju, 'I thought somehow you had entered my mind also.'

'What do you mean "also"?'

'You have already entered my heart and have taken permanent residence there. I was wondering if you have entered my head also. Yes, something significant has happened. It's a long story.'

'You flatterer,' said Ranjitham. 'Anyway, tell me your long story.'

They sat in the thinnai. Panju rested his back against a pillar folding his legs. Ranjitham sat with her legs stretched, pointing towards the house.

'I have taken an oath not to talk about this to anyone. But I feel you are such an organic part of who I am that I won't be violating my oath in talking to you.'

He then described his meeting with Jatin and the oath that he had taken at the Kali temple.

As he related the events, Panju noticed the change in Ranjitham's expression, but could not read it.

'Jatin asked me not to shave. He explained that I would have to go around incognito and long hair would be necessary for me to be disguised in certain ways. I had to do it. I then realized how much a little thing like my hair meant to me.'

'I am glad that you have left your moustache intact, though you haven't spruced it up, like you usually do. I wanted to present you with a seer of ghee to groom it; now I will have to use that ghee for cooking.'

Panju laughed aloud. Something he had not done for several days, ever since he had been involved with Jatin. Ranjitham did not join him in his laughter.

'Let's talk about us, rather than my hair.'

'Fine then, how is your wife?'

'My wife? Of course. Ranju, you know very well that I have not lived with her since my wedding. Apparently, she is finally old enough and is going to be sent to my house at Tiruvaiyaru by the end of this week. You know it is a sham marriage. I have decided to tell her about my love for you.'

Panju reached for her hands. Ranjitham let him hold her hand.

'And then you will marry me?' asked Ranjitham, head cocked to one side, her sidelong glance taking him in.

'Why not? There is nothing—'

'It's an impossibility. As I told you earlier, I am already married.'

'What?'

'To the deity of Kumbakonam. Lord Kumbeswara. I have already told you that.'

'Are you saying it is impossible for us to be together?' There was anger in Panju's voice.

'I didn't say that. I only said we cannot marry.'

'What do you mean by that?' Panju didn't realize that he had shouted out the words.

'Panju, what do you think I am? Do you think it matters to me whether you are married or not? I can entertain you without worrying about it. I am a devadasi. This is what we do.' She had now let go of his hand and she kept pushing her bangles up and down her wrists. She remained silent for a while. Suddenly, in a burst she added, 'My mother wants me to stop meeting you. She wants me to be friendly with the Rajapuram zamindar, who apparently has met her. My mother says he will keep me like a queen.' She turned her face away from Panju and dabbed at her eyes with the edge of her sari.

'I don't care about what your mother wants. What is it that *you* want?' Panju's voice had risen further in volume.

A passer-by on the road driving a buffalo before him turned his head and stared.

'You have given me a lot to think about, Panju. Now I want to be left alone,' said Ranjitham, tears brimming in her eyes.

26 May 1911

The bullock cart rattled its way along the main road from Tanjore to Kumbakonam.

'Amma, will you please move back a little; there's too much weight in the front.'

Ranjitham was already at the back of the covered cart, drinking in the green expanse of billowing paddy fields on both sides, her legs swinging out over the edge of the cart. Parvatam ignored the cart driver's exhortations for the tenth time and did not budge. Varadu sat between them and every time the cart-driver asked them to move, he utilized his limited mobility of four inches to the utmost, moving back and forth within that narrow region.

'Ranju,' Parvatam called out, arranging her features into something that exhibited concern and love.

'Yes, Amma.' Ranjitham's voice sounded distant, as she hadn't turned around to speak to her mother.

'You know, Ranju, you know I am very ill. I cannot walk two paces without wheezing and gasping for breath.' Parvatam paused to see if there were encouraging sounds from Ranjitham. There weren't any. 'I am holding on to my life only to see that you are properly settled. Then I can close my eyes in peace.'

'Amma, please don't talk nonsense. Periya Patti—your grandmother—died only two years ago. You have many more years to live.'

'What do you know about how I feel? Every day, I have fever when I wake up. Every joint in my body aches. Even now I have fever.'

Ranjitham extended her hand briefly to touch her mother's neck.

'Amma, you are as cool as the underside of a water-kooja. You certainly do not have fever; nor do I remember you ever having one.'

'What do you know? I have internal fever. Anyway, that is neither here nor there. I will be happy if you are settled.'

'You mean—accept the offer of the Rajapuram zamindar? I have told you this before. My answer is still no. I don't want any more talk about this.'

'I don't want any more talk about this.' Parvatam mimicked Ranjitham. Her voice rose now. Her eyelids narrowed and her nostrils were flared. 'As if you can find someone more suitable than him. What is wrong with him? Do you know he owns a thousand acres of land? He will keep you in comfort for the rest of your life. If you are smart about it, he will even shower you with jewels. Don't you want to wear a real gold oddiyanam instead of all the fake dance saman? Are you waiting for the King of England to come and make you his Queen? I know what is in your mind. You are after that boy, Panchapakesan. Do you know he has virtually no land? Forget him if you know what is good for you. In our tradition, we cannot afford to fix our genuine affections on any one. Forget the drought-stricken foreigner. You cannot get anyone better than the zamindar.' Parvatam paused for breath.

'Amma. Don't waste your breath. My answer is still no. Anyway we have reached. I will speak to you later.'

The cart stopped in front of their house. Ranjitham jumped out and hurried into the house.

Varadu was about to follow.

'Wait,' said Parvatam. 'I need to speak to you.' She laid a restraining hand on Varadu's shoulder. 'We have to teach that Panju a lesson. Here's what you do. Every day, that boy seems to return late from the press. Go meet Vettiyan and Velan and ask them to make sure the boy doesn't trouble us again. Give them one rupee each and tell them I will give them two more rupees when they complete their job. Make sure that this is done by this week.'

The day was oppressively hot. The evening promised to be no better; the breeze that normally wafted across from the Cauvery was absent.

Panju was shutting the large double-hinged doors to the press prior to locking up when he saw the reflection in the glass of the front window. There were three men lounging around some distance away on the opposite side of the road, one of them pointing to him and saying something to the other two. Of the two, one was short and wiry, the other tall and hefty. He saw them nod briefly before the third man, who seemed familiar, disappeared from view.

Panju wrinkled his brow. *Of course! It is Varadu. The odd-job man at Ranjitham's house.* He was certain now that they were up to no good. He locked the door quickly, tugging sharply at the heavy padlock to ensure it was secured. He then tucked the bunch of keys at his waist and started walking fast towards home. He turned once, to see that Varadu had indeed disappeared, but the two men were following him and had cut down the distance between them. Panju felt an anticipatory thrill. He started curling and uncurling his fists. He slowed down further and when he estimated that his pursuers were close enough, whipped around.

'What do you want?' he asked. Panju's stance was low, his weight thrown slightly forward.

'We want to teach you a lesson so that you will stop troubling Parvatam Akka's daughter.'

Choturam Payilvan had repeatedly drummed it into Panju's head: 'When the odds are not in your favour, reduce them by attacking first.' He put the advice into action now. The smaller of the attackers was to his left and not quite facing him. Panju stiffened his hand and hit him between the collarbone and the neck, on the marma spot as the payilvan had taught him, concentrating on accuracy rather than power. The effect on the man was immediate, even though Panju's aim was a tad off. The man fell down heavily and lay on the road, groaning.

The larger man saw this, stepped back and charged at Panju, head lowered. Panju tried to move away; but the man caught him in a glancing blow to the chest, that all but knocked the breath from him. The man stumbled on for some distance from the momentum of his charge. Panju could feel the bruise forming on the side of his chest.

The man came at him more slowly now, his massive hands clasped together over his head, obviously intending to bring them down on Panju's head like a blacksmith's hammer blow.

Amateurish. He has left the apalapa marma points at his armpits exposed.

Panju crossed his hands in front of him, palms open, fingers stiffened, holding his upper arms almost parallel to the ground, inclined slightly downwards, and awaited his opponent's move. As the large man brought down his hands, Panju flared out his hands in a lightning move, his hands scissoring in a horizontal arc in front of his body, catching his adversary squarely in the armpits. His opponent's arms were weakened; still the downward blow caught Panju on the right eye and nose, bloodying both. Having done its work, his adversary's right arm hung limply at his side as he clutched it with his left arm, his face twisted in pain. Panju's eyes were burning, his nose was a mass of agony and his chest hurt.

Panju suddenly stumbled forward. The wiry man had crawled up to him from behind and tripped him simply by pulling at his legs. Panju took the fall on his shoulder, curling up as he fell to reduce the impact, and then sprang up. He lifted his extended right leg above his head as though he was wielding a sledge hammer, and brought it down on the back of the wiry man who was still down. The man stayed down with a short yelp. Panju then lifted his hands to deliver the coup de grace on the bigger man. The man made no move to block the attack, but was whimpering with a whispered 'no, no'. Panju drew his hands back in disgust.

Panju was a mass of bruises but took some pleasure in seeing that his opponents were in much worse shape. *These rowdies have been sent by Ranjitham.* His nostrils flared. His chest was thrust out. His breathing was heavier than his fight warranted. Instead of going home, his legs carried him in the direction of Attakkaran Street.

Attakkaran Street was dark. The sliver of moon in the sky didn't help.

'Ranjitham!' Panju shouted.

Ranjitham came running out from her house. 'What are you waking up the whole neighbourhood for?' she asked. When Panju came into the hemisphere of dim light cast by the oil lamp in a small niche in the wall, Ranjitham exclaimed, 'You are bleeding! Come in quickly. I will dress the wound.'

As he followed her, he felt a little faint. 'Huh,' he mumbled, 'you pinch the baby and then rock the cradle.'

Ranjitham didn't hear any of his mumblings. She made him sit. She then went in and returned with a brass basin of warm water. She dropped a few potassium permanganate crystals into the basin. The water turned a deep pink. She dipped the edge of her sari into the basin and washed the wounds he had received above his eyes and on his nose. Panju tried to say something. She shushed him, tore a strip of cloth from her sari and tied it over the main wound on his head.

'Now you tell me. What happened?' asked Ranjitham, her hand caressing his hair. She noticed that hair had just started sprouting on the area of his head above the forehead, which he had previously kept shaved.

Panju felt calmer now.

'Are you sure you don't know?' he asked, looking deep into her eyes as though he could detect if she was lying.

'Of course not. Don't be silly. How would I know?'

Panju continued staring at her.

'Oh my God,' said Ranjitham, 'you don't think *I* sent people to beat you up?'

'Well, I recognized Varadu pointing me out to them. Also one of them warned me to keep away from you.'

Ranjitham remained silent for a while. 'That means my mother...'

'Why would your mother want to get me beaten up?'

'I am really sorry, Panju. My mother has been against my meeting you. She has been telling me to accept the offer of the Rajapuram zamindar.'

'And you are all right with this idea?'

Ranjitham took Panju's hand in hers and placed it over her right cheek.

'Do you know what this means, Panju? I have never let a man touch my cheek. This is the holy space on my body that I have kept private.'

Panju felt wetness spreading from her cheeks on to his hands. He tried to remove his hand gently but found that he couldn't; Ranjitham held it against her cheek with immense force.

'I certainly don't want to be with the zamindar. He has the soul of a frog and a face to match.'

'That still doesn't answer my question. Do you want to keep seeing me?'

'Tell me,' said Ranjitham through her tears, 'how you have been with your second great love?'

'What do you mean?'

'I mean, the love for your country.'

'That, Ranjitham, is my first love. Mother India beckons to me in my every waking moment. I can't stand the sight of her tears; nor can I see her in shackles. I am just waiting for the day when I will be able to contribute to unshackling her. In fact, I am leaving for Pondicherry just for this.'

Ranjitham's expression became inscrutable.

Twenty-five

Panju took off his shirt and threw it at the nail in the wall and missed. He was too tired to care; he flung himself on the bed. 'I will just close my eyes for a bit,' he told himself.

It is dark everywhere. There are voices that are loud but indistinct, a depth of agony in them that Panju feels in his bones. He raises his hands and presses them hard against his ears. The noise is not shut out. There is now a growing sphere of light that is soon large enough to fill his visual field. He recognizes the female form within it. Four hands: one holding a human skull filled with blood, another a decapitated head, which is featureless, and the other two holding weapons—a curved sword and a long trident. Kali is standing atop a corpse, also with no features. But Kali's face! It is Ranjitham! He wants to shout 'Vande Mataram'. What comes out is 'I love you', in a voice surely not his own. It is high-pitched, like a child's. Now Kali raises the hand holding the head and blood starts pouring out of it.

Panju woke up sweating. He looked at the round alarm clock with serifed Arabic numerals. It showed 2:00 a.m. He wanted to go back to sleep immediately, but the kaleidoscope of disconnected impressions—the excitement of going to Pondicherry in two days' time, thoughts of who he would meet there combined with thoughts of Ranjitham—interfered. He was tossing about trying to sleep first in one position and then in another, when the sound of a knock at the door intruded. He got up groggily and opened the door to find Murugan outside.

'Periya Aiya wanted me to bring you home immediately. I started last night. Our specially bred Kangeyam bulls will have no problem in making the journey back quickly.'

'I cannot come now. I have to leave for Pondicherry the day after tomorrow. Anyway, what's the hurry?' asked Panju.

'Chinna Amma has come, Aiya.'

'Who is Chinna Amma?' Vestiges of sleep still hung heavy in Panju's eyes.

'That is Chinnamma, Aiya, Meenakshi Amma. Sambandi Aiya's brother came and left her at home yesterday.'

The mists of sleep roiled and evaporated.

This was a new complication.

'Why has she come now?' he said almost to himself.

'Some function, Aiya.'

Panju was puzzled as to why Murugan sounded coy.

Anyway, she needed to be told. It was going to be embarrassing, but he would face up to it. It was only fair and there was no point in postponing the inevitable. He would go to Tiruvaiyaru with Murugan.

'Feed the bulls some water and straw. I will come in half an hour.'

'Take your time, Aiya. We can reach by the time the sun is high in the sky. Especially if I use the goad.'

They reached Tiruvaiyaru's wide expanses of green before the sun attained its zenith. The green, stretching as far as the eye could see, served to calm Panju's mind a little.

Sambu was waiting at the doorstep to receive him.

'Panju, what is this? No letters at all. You have lost weight. You haven't even shaved. I will call the barber.' Sambu's voice greeted Panju even before he had alighted.

'Appa, I am in a rush. I have to leave tomorrow for Pondicherry. Why have you called me in such a hurry?'

'Calm down, Panju. I have called you for something auspicious. We will talk about that later. Why don't you eat first? Your mother has been waiting since morning without eating.'

Bhavani had made his favourite brinjal curry and morkuzhambu. He picked at his food and got up quickly when Bhavani offered a second serving.

'Can I help? Can I serve him?'

Panju looked up at the sound of the fresh voice. Meenakshi was standing behind his mother. For a moment, he could not take his eyes off her elongated eyes, slanting slightly upwards, her black irises sparkling, matching the kohl that she had applied on her eyelids.

'Go ahead. Serve your husband. I won't stand in the way.' Bhavani gave the vessel and the ladle to Meenakshi and retreated.

Before Panju could register his protest, Meenakshi had served him, the last bits falling on the back of his palms. Bhavani stood behind her, her lips curving up ever so slightly, obviously enjoying the bonding that she thought was taking place.

Panju looked at Meenakshi, this time no lust tainting his stare, and deliberately got up without eating what was put on his plate.

'What's happened to you, Panju?' asked Bhavani, trying to make light of the situation. 'Janaki was the one who never bothered about food. Give her a book in her hand and she would forget everything. You were different. You never stopped until I scraped the bottom of the dish. Even then you would ask if I had made only *that* much.'

Panju ignored her and addressed Meenakshi, not looking directly at her, eyes on the ceiling. 'I will talk to my father and come. Please wait in the room. Later, I have something important to tell you. Alone.'

Bhavani looked stricken but tried again, 'There will be a thousand things between a husband and wife. Go, Meena, go to your room.'

Panju washed his hands in silence and rushed to the thinnai where Sambu was sitting.

'Appa, you wanted to see me urgently.'

'Yes,' said Sambu, looking up from the Kumbakonam Mutt panchangam that he was immersed in. 'Tomorrow is a good day. We can have the shanti muhoortham.'

This threw Panju a little.

'Then you will have to have the nuptial night without me.'

Sambu didn't let the shock show on his face. He looked steadily at Panju for a while. 'What is wrong with Meenakshi? The child looks like a parrot.'

'I am involved with another woman, Appa.'

Sambu's eyebrows climbed high up his forehead and stayed there. A pause.

'So, this is what I have taught you.'

'The woman I allude to, Father, is Bharata Mata. I am committed to her service. I cannot describe in what way, partly because I myself do not know. Even if I did, my oath of secrecy would prevent my telling you.

'One thing I can say—my body is no longer mine. You, who taught me that the Motherland is loftier than heaven, you of all people should understand this.'

'What I have taught you is *mother* and the Motherland are loftier than heaven. Did you think about your mother too? Do you know you are a son born of our religious labours? A thavappudalvan. Isn't it enough that one person in this family has thrown away her life needlessly? Should you also do it?'

'It does not matter if it is useless, Appa. Gokhale said this a couple of years ago—"It will no doubt be given to our countrymen of future generations to serve India by their successes; we of the present generation must be content to serve her mainly by our failures. For, hard though it be, out of these failures the strength will come, which in the end will accomplish great tasks." Panju took a deep breath before he continued.

'Appa, I am sorry. My mind is made up. I did think of how my mother would react. But even as I did that, the plight of fifteen crore mothers rose up in my conscience. I am not even sure I will see you again. So, bless me, Appa, perhaps for one last time.'

Panju bowed his head, bent down from his waist and placing both hands on his ears, recited the traditional words seeking his father's blessing:

Belonging to the clan whose progenitor is Kaushika,
Whence came the sages Viswamitra, Agamarshana and Kaushika,
Follower of the rules of the Apastamba Sutra,
Learner of the branch of Yajur Veda,
I, Panchapakesa Sarma by name
Salute you.

Sambu could not vocalize the traditional benediction—'Be long-lived'; a lump had formed in his throat. He merely lifted his hands in a symbol of blessing and turned his head away lest his son, who was to have delivered him from puth, should see the tears welling in his eyes.

It was in a state of bewilderment that Panju entered the room. Meenakshi was waiting for him, a statue carved from stone. For a moment Panju was at a loss for words. She hadn't moved when he recovered.

Large expressive eyes, long, plaited hair that reached to her hips, a heady smell of kadambam and jasmine.

'I have something important to tell you.'

A lift of an eyebrow. Jangle of earrings.

'You have to forget about me. We cannot live together.'

Sudden confusion in the eyes. A silent tremulous question.

'I already love another woman.'

Panic. Who?

'Ranjitham.' Panju had meant to say Bharata Mata.

Blink. Tears. The kohl spreads.

'She is a dancer in Kumbakonam,' Panju says, still under a strange compulsion to tell the truth.

Flash floods. Meenakshi buries her face in her sari and runs away, lurching in synchronicity with muffled sobs.

Panju made no effort to follow her, his heart heavy.

Twenty-six

28 May 1911

Panju had a tiring day at work. He had to hand over everything to Mudaliar who appeared to hear him out with somnolent nods. At the end of it, he asked Panju, pointing to a set of papers on the desk, 'What do I do with these proofs?'

'That is what I have been telling you.' Panju allowed exasperation to leach into his voice, but couldn't get Mudaliar to concentrate.

'Don't worry, Panju, you take care of the important things like saving our nation and I will take care of the simple things like running a press. In fact, I might give it a rest as I want to go back to Madras for a couple of weeks.'

It was eight by the time he got back to his room. He remembered Jatin's caution to travel light. He packed a holdall that was really a canvas sleeping bag with leather straps. He managed to pack all his clothes and a jamakkalam with breadth-wise swathes of reds and blues. He also managed to cram into it a pillow, all the cotton stuffing of which had migrated in clumps to the sides, leaving a hollow in the middle that no amount of fluffing could entirely cure. A packet of sacred ash and a small faded picture of Ganesa in a dancing pose, framed in wood, carefully wrapped in a veshti to avoid breaking the glass, went in next. He looked for the paper on which the oath that he had taken was written, but couldn't find it.

It was now ten-thirty. His train was scheduled to be at the Kumbakonam station at eleven thirty-two. It would halt for only five minutes. He rushed to the well and washed his face. He ran back to the room. He remembered the instructions that Jatin had given him. *Don't wear a shirt. Wrap a thin red cloth round your shoulders. Remove your poonal. Don't wear any mark on the forehead.*

He rubbed out the sacred ash that he had already applied across his forehead as an automatic reflex, hesitated to remove his poonal, which was never supposed to be removed. After some thought, he said the mantra for changing the poonal, took it off and discarded it in a northerly direction. He then threw a red cloth across his bare shoulders, grasped the holdall in one hand and was off.

He lived on Mahamaham Tank North Street, quite close to the railway station, and was able to cover the distance in ten minutes by walking at a brisk pace. The train was late and he waited along with a man—Panju smelt him before he saw him. He squatted, smoking a beedi held between the left thumb and forefinger, a badly crinkled turban on his head, the folds of his veshti mirroring those of his turban. Skeletal legs protruded from his veshti. When he looked around in Panju's direction, his stare seemed to be completely unfocused. A man wearing a bush shirt and trousers but no footwear leaned towards the track, twisting and craning his neck to look up and down the rails, perhaps making sure that the train wouldn't catch him in an unguarded moment. Or did he want to relieve himself? A coolie squatted, pointedly facing away from the pell-mell of trunks, holdalls, bamboo baskets and knotted cloth bundles for which he was obviously the designated transporter.

At last the train came. Panju boarded it and tried to sleep but couldn't, despite the lulling rhythm. He reached Villuppuram at two in the morning. Pondicherry was only twenty miles away, but the connecting train was available only at nine. He decided to walk to a nearby choultry.

The huge hall was littered with over a dozen sleeping figures that he could just make out by the dim light of a couple of hurricane lamps. He chose a corner, opened out his holdall and using it as a mattress, went to sleep immediately. He was certain that he had slept for not more than five minutes when he was shaken to wakefulness. He could hear feverish whispers. He cracked his eyes open to see two figures bending over him. Even though he was completely awake, he did not want his interlocutors to know that. He sprang up suddenly and had the taller of the two on the ground. The other he held in a Half Nelson.

'Wait, wait,' the one he held in the lock cried out. 'We are friends. Fellow sadhus.'

Panju released his hold immediately on hearing the code word 'sadhu'.

The other on the ground seemed to have injured his back. Panju assisted him in getting up.

'We were waiting for you at Villuppuram station. The ghosts have spies everywhere. That is why we followed you at a respectable distance. They are watching the Pondicherry station very closely. That is why you can't take the onward train and must come with us by road to Pondicherry. You are Panchapakesan, aren't you?'

'Will I get some sleep?' asked Panju.

'I doubt if you will get any sleep on the bullock cart. Also, at the French border, we must get off and make our way through the fields.'

After what seemed to be hours of being jostled about in the cart and then walking interminably, during which the tall man introduced himself as Gopal and the short man as Aloke, they reached the outskirts of the city.

'I wish I were a horse,' said Panju.

'Huh?' Gopal exclaimed.

'Horses can sleep standing up. I wish I could do that,' said Panju. 'Anyway, how much longer?'

'An hour or two at the outside,' answered Gopal.

To Panju, it seemed that they walked for another three hours.

'This is Easwara Dharmaraja Koil Street,' said Gopal finally. 'This is where you will be staying.' He pointed to an old shingle-roofed house, built in the Tamil style. 'Don't worry, you will have company. You are staying with me. You can go in and refresh yourself. We will be back soon with some food.'

MAY 1911
TIRUVAIYARU, KUMBAKONAM

Twenty-seven

29 May 1911

Throughout the way from Tanjore to Tiruvaiyaru, the sky was covered with clouds the colour of dull silver, tarnished here and there with black oxide. The still air contributed to the mugginess, which the slow movement of the cart did nothing to improve. Janaki got down from the cart. The normal sight of her father in the thinnai didn't greet her. Nor was her mother at the doorway, smiling broadly at her. The window that faced the road was also closed. The front door, instead of being open, was only slightly ajar.

She pushed the heavy door open and walked in. She heard his low 'Come in, Janu', before she saw him. He was seated on a chair, his back bent. The *Viveka Chudamani* of Sankara that he read whenever he felt the need for solace lay closed on his lap.

'Panju was here,' he said. 'He left for Pondicherry on urgent work. Not his regular work, but for something that will help Bharata Mata.' His voice reflected the bitterness he felt.

'You should be proud of him, Appa, instead of getting depressed about it.' Janaki recalled the many discussions she had had with Panju on patriotism and the duty of the individual to the Motherland. While she had always argued that the first priority was to ensure that Indians were educated enough to be able to demand their place as global citizens, Panju had always held that India must first be freed of the foreign yoke.

'That is not all, Janu. Your sister-in-law has been crying incessantly ever since Panju left. She has also not eaten all day. God knows what he has told that child. I would have sent for you if you hadn't come today. Please find out what the problem is. She won't talk to me or your mother.'

'I will find out, Appa,' said Janu. As she entered Meenakshi's room, she saw her seated, head on her knees. Her hair was disordered; her pottu had spread on her forehead, her sari was crushed. As she looked up, Janaki saw that the black colyrium had spread to her cheeks and stained her sari. On seeing Janaki, Meenakshi started sobbing, hugging her. Janaki sat next to her and put her head on her lap and stroked her hair till the sobs quietened.

'What happened, kanne?' Janaki asked.

'He doesn't want me.'

'Who?' For a moment Janaki was nonplussed.

'He...your brother.'

'What did Panju say to you? I will set him straight.'

'No, no. Don't say anything to him. It is my bad luck that I am all alone. My mother died even before my marriage, and my father is bedridden, looked after by his widowed sister. I don't know why I have no one.'

Janaki turned Meenakshi's face with a hand on her chin till she was looking straight into her eyes. 'Don't feel sorry for yourself. If you do, no one else will. Now just tell me what my brother told you.'

'He said he doesn't want to live with me.'

'Why? Has he gone mad? You are like a beautiful doll. What's wrong with him? Did he say why?'

Meenakshi was beginning to sob again. 'He is in love with someone else.'

'Who is that?' asked Janaki. 'I will catch her by her hair and tweak her ears till she says sorry and lets Panju go.'

Meenakshi smiled through her tears. 'She is a dancing girl in Kumbakonam. She has a stupid name like a man's. Ranjitham.'

'When is Panju back?'

'I don't know, Akka. He said he is going to be away for more than a month.'

'All right. I will take care of everything. I will go and talk to this Ranjitham. I was originally planning to leave for Tanjore tomorrow. Now I will go right back and go to Kumbakonam tomorrow itself. I will make that man-named female understand what an evil sister-in-law she will have if she tries to live with my brother. Then I will be back next weekend to see a permanent smile on your face. Let me see a sample now.'

A tentative smile lit up Meenakshi's face.

'Now come with me and have lunch.'

'Wait, Akka,' said Meenakshi, 'I will wash my face, comb my hair, change into a fresh sari and come with you.'

'Wash your face quickly, I will comb and plait your hair for you.'

There was a spring in Meenakshi's steps as she ran to wash her face.

Now that she had given the girl so much hope, Janaki was a little unsure as to how she was going to fulfil her promise. She had only a name, an occupation and the name of the town. Even if she were to find Ranjitham, she had no idea how she would react. She vowed to herself that she would do whatever was necessary to get Panju back.

Twenty-eight

30 May 1911

Janaki had never been on a train before and everything was a new experience. Arul had helped her to book the ticket. When he further offered to accompany her to Kumbakonam, she declined saying that she was going there to attend to a private matter. Janaki was fascinated by the railway platform, the coolies, the compartment, the bustle when the train arrived, the steam whistle, and the way the stationmaster waved the green flag to set the train in motion. She loved the slice of humanity represented by the passengers, the people who came to send them off and the coolies who scurried to and fro carrying, at times, impossible burdens.

She shared her compartment with four others. An old lady had placed a large basket on the floor, the mouth covered with gunny sacking, only half-hidden under the seat. She had a proprietary foot over it, the other tucked underneath her. Janaki fancied she saw the hessian cloth move. Had the ticket examiner seen it, she would have had to pay at least double the 'dog rate'. The kindly old ticket examiner hadn't and he confined his attentions primarily to Janaki and why she was travelling alone when the times were not good, not good at all.

The journey lasted only an hour; but for the entire duration another lady seated in front of her kept raining questions and advice in equal measure on Janaki.

'How many children do you have?'

'None.'

'Then you must go and pray to Garbarakshambika at Mullaivanam.'

'But I am not married.'

'Oh, oh. Then you must pray to Kalyana Sundarar at Tirumananjeri. You will get married in no time. From your speech it is clear you are a Brahmin. What sub-caste are you?'

'These days all that is not important, Patti.'

'No, no. That is very important. If people do not follow all the caste rules, they will go to hell. Actually the reason I was asking is—I have a nephew, perfect for a bridegroom. Poor chap. His first wife died in childbirth. Luckily, the baby also died. It was a female baby, you know. The second wife died within six months of marriage in a kitchen fire.'

'Must be a singularly unlucky man.'

'Maybe. But look how lucky it has been for the wives. They all died with flowers in their hair and pottu on their foreheads.'

Janaki reflected on the lady's notion of luck, but didn't say anything.

'Do you have a Mars defect in your horoscope? Don't worry, my nephew also has the same problem. He has Mars in the seventh house. At such a young age, the poor boy has no one to cook for him, no one to wash his clothes.'

Janaki was morbidly curious. 'How old is your nephew, Patti?'

'He must be only forty-five. At any rate, not more than fifty.'

Janaki wanted to laugh. At the same time, she also wanted to push the lady off the train. She decided she had had enough.

'But, Patti,' Janaki said, her voice turning dulcet, 'if he has Mars in the seventh house, it is very bad for him. He will die of fire or water before he turns fifty if he marries a third time. I know this because my father is an astrologer.'

'Fire or water!' exclaimed the old lady.

'Or he may die scalded by boiling water,' Janaki said with a deadpan face.

The lady looked at her suspiciously and turned her head away.

She no longer pestered Janaki and kept her eyes closed till the train reached Kumbakonam station.

❖

Janaki had already devised a plan. She found her way to the Kumbeswara temple, asking people for directions. She prayed to Lord Kumbeswara. When she went into the enclosure containing the sanctum sanctorum of Mangalambika, the deity was just being shown the lamp and a flower fell from the garland around the deity's neck. Janaki took it as a positive omen. She decided to circumambulate the outer enclosure when she saw a group of musicians and dancers leaving the temple. She hurried to one of the women dancers, who was lagging behind the group. 'Do you know where Ranjitham lives? She is a sadir dancer here.'

'Ooh, so you are missing your husband, are you?'

Janaki improvised. 'No, it's my brother actually. My father is sick and I have to get the message to him.'

'I know where she lives. You go to Attakkaran Street. The house is the only one that is freshly painted.'

'Thank you, is it very far from here?'

'No, just follow this road and take a turn to your food-eating hand side. Ask around there.'

It wasn't too difficult to locate Ranjitham's house. She found the door open. She shouted 'Amma!' a couple of times. No one appeared. She heard a faint tinkling, as of bells. After hesitating at the doorstep, she decided to go in. She was at the mittam of the house, which was spread with a generous layer of fine sand. A woman clad in a plain blue sari danced on it, facing away from her. The sand muffled the sound of the ankle bells to some extent. Janaki was so captivated by the precision of the moves and the faint smell of incense that hung in the air that she stood still. The dancer, as a part of the adavu, twisted around, saw her and stopped dancing. 'Who are you? What do you want?' the woman asked, her eyebrows crinkled.

'You must be Ranjitham. I am Janaki, Panju's sister.'

The expression on Ranjitham's face changed to one of pleasure.

'Please come. Panju has talked so much about you. You are so beautiful. Panju never mentioned that. He only talked about how smart you were and how courageous. You seem to have walked a long distance in the sun. Come into my room and sit down. I will get you something to drink.'

'Don't bother,' said Janaki as she followed Ranjitham to her room. 'I have something important to ask of you.'

'I insist that you have something to drink first.' Ranjitham went into the kitchen. Her ankle bells sounded all the way to the kitchen and back. She returned with a tall tumbler of buttermilk.

Janaki took a mouthful tentatively at first and finding it cool and refreshing, she emptied the tumbler, much against her will, pouring it into her mouth without the tumbler touching her lips.

'Now you can ask me whatever you want to ask,' said Ranjitham.

'I have come to ask you to let go of my brother.'

'Your brother is not here. I am not holding him prisoner.'

'Did you know he is married?'

'I do.'

'Still you have no problem casting your net for him?'

Ranjitham's back stiffened just a bit.

'Listen. I know he is married. In fact among us, we prefer married men. It gives them a standard to measure against. Often, entirely in our favour.'

Janaki went on. 'He has a young innocent wife who is practically an orphan. Her mother is dead and her father is ill. She depends entirely on her husband. Doesn't her plight move you?'

'Frankly, no. If you knew in detail about the lives that we devadasis lead, you would be convinced that our lot is far worse.'

'You will then hold on to Panju?'

'Get one thing clear, we don't cast nets for poor Brahmins who don't own even a cent of land. I come from a long line of devadasis who worked only with gods and kings. I have already decided to turn him away. In fact—' she moved to the sword on the wall and said, touching the handle with her right hand, 'I promise by my husband Kumbeswara that I will do so.'

'You will?' asked an astonished Janaki.

'Yes, and not because I have suddenly realized that he is poor. I am not sure whether this will help his young wife. He probably will not go back to her. He has a higher calling. His love for his Motherland is far greater. By way of my small contribution to my Motherland as well, I will not stand in his way.'

For a moment Janaki felt a deep pang of jealousy. *I have been with Panju ever since his birth. This woman talks as though she knows him better.* It lasted only for a moment. Then the jealousy vanished, replaced by admiration.

'I must thank you,' said Janaki.

'I must thank *you*,' said Ranjitham. 'Talking to you has clarified and strengthened my convictions.'

'I never knew—'

'—that prostitutes have such fine sensibilities? I am not attracted to him professionally. You see, I love him.'

Janaki did not trust herself to speak. For a moment, she fancied she heard the gurgle of the Cauvery nearby. She wanted to prostrate herself at Ranjitham's feet. But Ranjitham moved away and she left without a word.

Twenty-nine

Sambu was concerned. His daughter-in-law was still given to bouts of uncontrollable sobbing since Panju had left. Janaki's visit had helped. Still, Meenakshi showed signs of depression. He decided to try and console her.

Meenakshi lay curled up on a mat. Her knees were drawn up against her chin. For a moment he panicked. Then he saw the gentle heaving of her bosom and knew that she was merely sleeping. He averted his face immediately. A small booklet that lay on the floor caught his attention. It must have been blown on to the floor from the table. He picked it up automatically. The cover page of the pamphlet, which had been facing the floor, depicted a shaded line drawing of the goddess Kali in her ferocious aspect. She stood with one foot on Siva's chest. She wore a garland of skulls and held in one of her hands a decapitated head, the features of which were contorted, presumably in the last spasm of death. The head, complete with a bowler hat, was unmistakably European.

Sambu read the text with increasing unease.

'… The time has come. The golden age of Kali, as foretold by Lord Krishna, is beginning. The time has come for Sanatana Dharma to rule again. To make it really happen, drive out the foreigner from this sacred space that is India. If he does not run, kill him where he stands. Even if one in two thousand among us kills just one white man, India will be rid of all white men.'

I used to be so proud of him. What a travesty of Sanatana Dharma, the way of living prescribed by our ancestors. What has happened to all the world being one family?

Sambu's normal inclination was to let things be to take their natural course.

But I can't let this be. My son is not joining a national movement; he is getting into the worst company possible.

Bhavani's voice from the kitchen interrupted his thoughts.

'My brother Vichu has sent word that he will be in Tiruvaiyaru for a day or two. He has come on government work. We have not seen him for ages.'

Vichu! Why didn't I think of him before? He is a man of the world and being from Madras and working for the government, he will be the right person to ask for advice.

'Enna, did you hear me?' Bhavani's voice sounded, this time a little louder.

'Yes, yes,' said Sambu. 'In fact I will go the taluk office and bring him over for dinner.

Vichu was short, definitely under five feet, Sambu thought. His forehead was completely covered with white vibhuti, which had a large dot of kumkumam in the middle. He wore a black coat closed at the neck. The solitaire diamonds that he wore in his ears shone bright, just below his well-oiled kudumi. There was a cloyingly sweet smell about him that Sambu could not identify. A cane with an ornamented silver handle was balanced against his chair.

Vichu continued writing at his desk and didn't seem to have noticed him even after Sambu cleared his throat.

After a couple of minutes, Vichu looked up suddenly: 'Athimber, very good of you to come. I haven't met you since my sister Mangalam's unfortunate death, have I?' Vichu was loud, held his cane in his hand and waved it around as he spoke.

'We also met during my wedding,' said Sambu.

'Of course, of course. You are our mappillai—actually son-in-law twice over.'

Sambu thought of Mangalam and it was clear that Vichu bore no resemblance whatsoever to his twin sister.

'You are looking good and smelling good too, if I may say so,' said Sambu for want of an opening gambit.

'It must be the Rowland's Macassar oil that I use. You know, it costs nearly eleven shillings even in London. I don't like all these posh things.' At this point he lowered his voice. 'If you deal with the British, you have to be like them, you know.'

Sambu didn't know, but was saved from further speech by Vichu's continuing.

'You must have come to take me to your place for dinner. But I have a lot of work to do. You see, I have to work twice as hard as the Englishman; otherwise he won't have the same level of respect for me as he does now.'

'Then you are the right person to advise me,' said Sambu, finding the opening.

'Yes, yes, a lot of people come to me for advice. Why, even the Inspector General of Police in Madras comes to me for advice. I cannot talk about it because it is a personal matter, you see.'

Sambu again did not see but nodded his head and plunged ahead.

'I am worried about Panju. He seems to be involved in some dangerous activities.'

Vichu did not interrupt even though Sambu paused.

'I found this in his room.' He handed over the leaflet that he was carrying.

As Vichu went through it, the lines on his forehead became more pronounced and his lips pursed.

'Hmmm... Not good at all, you know. Do you know what this is?'

'There must be something wrong in the way I have brought him up. I used to be so proud of him. He could recite the entire *Ashtavakra Gita* and explain the meaning. I thought then that he would bring honour to all of us through his mastery of Sanskrit. I wanted him to specialize in Vedic prosody and Sanskrit grammar. He had taken Tamil in college, studying some obscure literature written by Jains and Buddhists.'

'Athimber, I am sure you have committed a lot of mistakes including bringing him up badly. But that's not what I am asking. Do you realize what this is?' Vichu's face was creased into an expression of disgust as he brandished the leaflet in front of Sambu's face.

'This is obviously a pamphlet put forth by some misguided—'

'—No, Sambu, it is sedition, pure and simple. Do you know the punishment?'

Sambu's agitation was such that he missed the fact that his brother-in-law, younger to him, had called him by name instead of the more traditional athimber.

'Death,' Vichu hissed. 'Death by hanging.'

Sambu froze.

Vichu's tone suddenly changed to a more conciliatory one. 'But don't worry, what is family for? I will take care of everything.'

Sambu felt a burden being lifted from him.

'Thank you, Vichu. I knew I could depend on you.'

'I heard that Panju has finished his BA. What is he doing now?' Vichu asked.

'He is in Kumbakonam, working at a printing press.'

'Press? What is he earning? Forty rupees per month? What are his job prospects? You know, you made a big mistake. You didn't want me as sambandhi. Anyway, you should have at least brought him to see me in Madras. I would have made sure that he didn't go astray. I would have recommended him for a steady government job. He could even have become a shirastedar like me, you know. Anyway, where is he working? I may go and see him.'

'He works at the Velmurugan press. He told me he was going away for a month or so to Pondicherry.'

'Why Pondicherry? Where is he staying in Pondicherry?'

'I don't know. He didn't tell me. He said his duty to the nation called him.'

'Don't worry, athimber. Now that you have told me, you can go home and forget about this matter completely. I will just keep this leaflet, you know.'

Sambu returned home feeling very much easier in his mind, though he was sweating, felt tired and thought his body weighed a ton.

THIRTY

The agraharam was quiet, stewing in the afternoon sun. As Janaki got down from the cart, a cloud of dust rose—rendered powder-dry by the onslaught of the sun. The kolam in front of the house was not the usual elaborate pattern bordered with red, but a simple five-pointed star that could be drawn with rice powder without lifting the hand. A small dot in the centre was the only embellishment. Her mother stood leaning against a pillar in the mittam.

'Come,' said Bhavani. Her voice seemed lifeless. 'Go and see your father. He has not been well for a week.'

Janaki ran to the well behind the house and washed her feet, hitching up her sari carefully, taking care to pour water over her heels and the backs of her ankles, letting it flow to her toes. She then rushed to Sambu's room.

Sambu was lying down on the bed, something unusual in itself, particularly during the day.

'Come, Janu,' he said, sitting up with some effort.

'What's wrong, Appa?' Janaki asked, sitting next to him.

'I have had a headache for the past week and I am feeling a little tired. That's all. Now that I have seen you, I will be fine in no time.' Sambu stood up and as he retied his veshti, turning his back to Janaki, he lost his balance and nearly fell down. He sat heavily on the bed again. Janaki put a hand on his forehead. It was warm.

'You have fever, Appa,' she said.

'Yes, yes. I've been getting this low-grade fever. I have asked Bhavani to prepare trikaduga kashayam. I should be all right after drinking that.'

'What's trikaduga kashayam, Appa?'

'It's a concoction made from dried ginger, pepper and thippili. It's a cure-all for everything.'

'Appa, this doesn't seem like something that home remedies will cure. You need to see a doctor. I will ask Murugan to go fetch the ayurvedic doctor.'

She then stepped out and gave Murugan instructions to bring the doctor back with him. As she came back into the house, she realized that she hadn't given Meenakshi the news. Meenakshi's door was shut. She knocked.

'Come in, Akka,' Meenakshi's voice sounded from inside.

'You rascal,' said Janaki, feigning anger, 'you knew all the while that I had come. You didn't come to meet me.'

'Akka, I was nervous. Just tell me quickly please. Did you go to Kumbakonam? Did you meet the rakshasi? What happened?'

'Don't jump to conclusions, Meenu. Ranjitham is a fine, sensitive human being. Not a demon.'

'Let me judge that, Akka. Has she agreed to let go of my husband?'

'Yes, unconditionally.'

Janaki had never seen such a wide grin on Meenakshi's face. Meenakshi jumped up and hugged her hard.

'Don't break my bones in return for the favour I did,' said Janaki, laughing.

'Akka, I agree with you now. She is an angel. For you, of course, I have no words.'

The talk then turned to what Panju was like, what he liked. Meenakshi began an elaborate interrogation of Janaki regarding what Panju liked to eat, the colours he liked and sundry other things, to which Janaki gave enthusiastic answers.

The ayurvedic vaidyan, a short, mournful-looking man of indeterminate age, held Sambu's wrist for a while. 'Pitta jwara,' he pronounced solemnly. 'Take this powder three times a day, before food and the lehyam first thing in the morning.'

'He has lost his appetite. He hardly eats,' Bhavani chimed in.

'Yes, yes. Pitta jwara. No curd, no buttermilk or tamarind,' said the physician. 'I will see him three days later when his fever goes up.'

'Is his fever expected to go up?' asked Janaki, anxiety in her voice.

'Pitta jwara,' said the physician as he left.

The 'big doctor' from Tanjore was visiting Tiruvaiyaru the next day, a Sunday, and Janaki persuaded him to come and take a look at Sambu. He heard Janaki out carefully as she listed the symptoms. He listened to the sounds within Sambu's body through a long tube. He then proceeded to poke Sambu in the abdomen. Sambu cried out when he prodded him in the lower abdomen. He then took his temperature with a long thermometer.

'A hundred and three degrees,' he said, shaking the thermometer to get the mercury back down into the bulb. 'Typhoid. There is a system of treatment with cold baths. I am not too familiar with it although one of my colleagues from Madras has had some success with that. But I don't think the patient can travel. So that will not be possible. I will ask my compounder to prepare a mixture of salol and beta naphthol. Give it to him twice a day before food.'

'Will he be all right, doctor?' asked Bhavani.

'Make sure he rests a lot. Keep the fever down by sponging him and let us see,' said the doctor.

It was getting late for Janaki. 'I will see you next week, Appa. Just send for me, Amma, if he becomes worse.'

'You should be concentrating on your studies, Janu,' said Sambu. 'I will be all right soon enough.'

'I wish we knew where Panju is,' said Janaki.

MAY 1911
PONDICHERRY

THIRTY-ONE

29 May 1911

Panju got ready quickly as Gopal had said, 'I will show you around Pondicherry. We are meeting Iyer at 10.00 a.m.'

The sun was not yet up; the land was bathed in an ethereal half-light as they stepped out. Gopal pointed out Subramania Bharati's house.

'Such a simple house,' remarked Panju. Whenever I read his poems, I imagine him to be living in a magnificent palace.'

'It's a pity,' said Gopal gravely, 'that the circumstances of poets are often not as lofty as their thoughts.'

Panju was impressed with the way he had put it and looked at him with newfound respect. Gopal noticed that Panju was looking at him curiously and continued. 'I know that to be true since I too, am a poet in a small way. Of course, though occasionally my thoughts may be as lofty as Bharati's, my words are nowhere near his.'

He then pointed to a man squatting opposite Bharati's house, obviously asleep, a black shawl wrapped around his body. 'That,' he said, 'is one of the ghosts. He is supposed to note down the movements of all the people who come to Bharati's or Iyer's house.'

'Why is the French government spying on you? I thought the reason you are here is that they treat you well.'

'He's hired by the British CID—Criminal Investigation Department. You can imagine how effective they are merely by looking at this specimen.'

They walked along till they came to the Grand Canal and Gopal guided him to the quayside road, Quai d'Ambour, which led to the 'White Town'.

Panju loved the grid layout of the avenues and marvelled at the beautiful buildings stuccoed and lime-washed to a brilliant white or beige, with arcades and colonnades, and on their terraces, parapets with terracotta balusters and brick loopholes.

'No wonder it's called the "White Town", remarked Panju. He was enchanted by Promenade Beach and Goubert Avenue.

Panju gawked at the statue of Dupleix, his right hand holding the plans for Pondicherry and the left hand resting on the hilt of his sword.

'Look at the base!' Panju exclaimed suddenly. 'It looks like our temple architecture.'

'Well, it is from one of our temples,' said Gopal, his tone carefully neutral.

By the time they returned, Pondicherry's sweltering heat had created islands of wet patches on Panju's shirt. He desperately needed a wash.

A beard, moustache and long hair covered V.V.S. Iyer's face but couldn't hide the intense eyes below a pair of bushy eyebrows. Nor could they completely obscure the pugnacious lift of the chin. His forehead sported a perfectly marked half-crescent of sandalwood paste that came down to below his eyebrows. Panju folded his hands in a namaskaram.

'So you are the young man Jatin has been writing to me about. What do you know about the foreign devils in India?' Iyer asked.

'Just enough to know that they need to be driven out of this country, Sir,' said Panju.

'Not enough,' said Iyer. 'You need to understand the duplicity of the Englishman to a much greater extent. We are united by a single vision—that of Bharata Mata, an aspect of Shakti. This unity is what the British rulers are trying to break. They have wreaked horror over horror upon us. They have brought famines, plagues and abject poverty to India. They are determined to let

Indians remain ignorant by controlling access to the right kind of education. You have done your BA. Did you read in your history books about Shivaji? About the great Cholas? Oh yes, you probably know all about Roman emperors and English kings.'

Panju kept silent as Iyer continued.

'The English want us to believe that Indians are incapable of self-rule. They think they have done us a huge favour by giving us the railways, which developed because of many other reasons. With their experience in the Boer War and the scare they got from the mutiny—rather the First War of Independence of 1857, as my friend and mentor Savarkar rightly calls it—the English realized they needed the railway to move troops quickly in wartime. They also created a profitable outlet for British investment, and a means to move raw materials out of India and import finished goods into India. They intend giving us a "modern education" that is completely irrelevant to us. They want us to believe that they are ruling over us for our own good.'

Panju nodded, taking it all in.

'Do you know what Curzon said? Wait, I have the exact quote somewhere here.' Iyer paused to examine some papers and took out one of them and started reading aloud.

'The highest ranks of civil employment in India must as a general rule be held by Englishmen, for the reason that they possess, partly by heredity, partly by upbringing, partly by education, the knowledge of the principles of government, the habits of mind, the vigour of character, which are essential for the task, and that, the rule of India being a British rule, and every other rule being in the circumstances of the case impossible, the tone and standard should be set by those who have created and are responsible...'

'Do you know what he is saying,' continued Iyer, 'He is saying that in essence, our ancestors were useless, our upbringing faulty and our character not worth speaking about.'

A vein began to throb at Panju's temples.

'You won't believe it if I tell you what some Indians want to do about it. They want to send more petitions, more representations. When will they ever learn? Do you think this will work?'

'Petition the British? You might as well squeeze oil out of stone,' Panju remembered, and spoke louder than he intended to.

'Absolutely. We sent dozens of petitions to prevent the partition of Bengal. They went through with the partition anyway. Do you know the reasons why the British were so keen on splitting Bengal into East and West?'

'Yes, I have read the leaflets. They wanted to halt the rise and spread of nationalism from Bengal by driving a wedge between the Hindus and Muslims and ensuring that even in the newly created Bengal, there were more Hindi- and Oriya-speaking people than the Bengalis.'

'Not just this. The main organ through which the ideas of boycott of foreign goods and Swadeshi can be spread is our vernacular press. They have enacted various repressive laws to curb our press. I want you to read these pamphlets about how the British are systematically destroying domestic industry, inducing famine and worsening the poverty of our people. The situation is actually much worse than in the days of the earlier rajas. They no longer rule through tributes, looting, plunder and sporadic violence. They do it through carefully calibrated restrictive laws, a prejudiced judiciary and a ruthlessly repressive administration. For the common man, the violence is no longer occasional and directed at his back. He lives in a continuous state of violence directed at his belly.'

Panju did not trust himself to speak. He nodded.

'One last thing for the day before you leave. I also want you to think about how we can solve this problem.'

❖

30 May 1911

Panju read all evening and late into the night in the dim light of an oil lamp. As he read, he became more and more incensed.

'Let's go for a walk,' said Iyer.

Panju tightened the upper cloth around his body against the morning chill.

They walked in silence for some time.

'So, you have done your homework?' Iyer asked.

'Well, I have read all the material you have given me.'

'Have you thought about the solution?'

'Boycott of foreign goods, Swadeshi and demand for Swaraj are some of the solutions that we seem to have adopted.'

'Let's take all these things one by one. By boycotting Manchester cloth and Liverpool salt, do you think the British will go away? They are here to stay. Certainly, it helps in dealing a blow to Britain where it hurts—to their trade. But, they will merely increase the taxes on finished cloth produced here and continue exporting cotton. We will be worse off than before. The use of indigenous products also helps, but suffers from the same problem. Swaraj is something that different people interpret in different ways. Some moderates seem to think that Swaraj means begging the government for greater representation. To me and many of our friends, Swaraj means complete freedom. Freedom from the yoke of the British. Swaraj is not a solution; it's an end; nor is a petition for Swaraj helping.'

They walked in quietude for a few minutes. A bulbul flew overhead, the splash of red along its vent clearly visible. Somewhere in the distance, Panju heard a cawing match between crows. There was not much traffic on the roads. Panju saw a curiously shaped vehicle, four-wheeled, the front wheels smaller than the back ones, with a canopy covering two seats, headed in their direction.

'What's that?' Panju exclaimed.

'Oh, that is a pousse-pousse. A favourite mode of transport for the Pondicherrians,' Iyer answered.

As it neared, it suddenly went out of control, careening to one side. The two ladies seated in it started screaming. The man pushing it had stumbled and fallen. Panju acted reflexively. He jumped in front of the vehicle and stopped it. The man soon got up, hitched up his veshti and smiled, showing betel-stained teeth. He appeared none the worse for the fall. He looked at Panju, said, 'Romba thanks monsieur,' and went on his way, pushing the vehicle.

'That is typical Pondicherry for you, 'Iyer said, 'in one sentence of three words, he has managed to combine Tamil, English and French. Coming back to our question, what is the solution? All right. You don't have to answer that now—'

Something had disturbed Iyer's concentration. Panju twisted around to look in the direction Iyer was looking. He saw a young man in a colourful lungi limping past them on the other side of the road.

'Who was that?' asked Panju.

'Bad news. Murugesan. He's *un coquin*. A bad sort, I mean. He is a local. He was a paid informer for the British CID, until the CID realized that he was absolutely unreliable. But I am not happy that he has seen us together. He will now probably try and collect a couple of annas from one of the CID men by informing on us. I think you should make your way back on your own. Spend some time with Gopal today. He will tell you more about our movement. Come tomorrow night at ten to my place. That's when the CID shift ends. Meanwhile, here is another question for you. Think about it and tell me when we meet tomorrow. How far are you willing to go in driving out the British? You can—'

'—I can tell you that right now,' answered Panju. 'I am ready to die, if required for the cause.'

Iyer then turned and walked away, muttering something.

Did he smile? Did he say something? Did he just say, 'But that's not enough...? How can sacrificing one's life not be enough?

He could sense that Iyer was leading him somewhere through his Socratic questioning. He suddenly thought of Janaki. What a huge source of strength she would be if she were here. His mind was a jumble of thoughts as he walked homewards. It was worse when he tried to sleep.

31 May 1911

'You said that you are ready to die; do you think it is enough?'

Panju paused a little to collect his thoughts before attempting to answer Iyer.

'Namaskaram, namaskaram,' a cheery voice interrupted his thoughts.

A luxurious, deliberately turned-up moustache, a turban worn almost in the style of the sardars, a closed-neck coat, a vertical stripe of vermillion on the forehead. *Bharati! Subramania Bharati.* The poet he worshipped.

'So who is this young boy?' asked Bharati.

'Vango, vango. Please sit down, and let me quote your own poem to you as an answer.'

Iyer cleared his throat and began to sing in Tamil. Panju recognized the raga as Ranjani.

I put in the hollow of a tree,
a young spark I found.
The forest turned to ashes;
in valour, are there the young and the old?

Iyer stopped singing and looked at Bharati. 'Is the poem in the right context?'

'Well,' said Bharati with a smile, 'a poet's work always has multiple meanings and layers. But you have forgotten the last line of the poem.'

Iyer appeared bewildered. Only for a moment. 'I was hoping that you could demonstrate it. You know I am more familiar with western dance than sadir.'

'All right. Here goes,' said Bharati, and adjusting his turban tighter around his head, he sang the entire song over again, ending with: *Thath-tharikita thath-tharikita thith-thom/ Thaka thath-tharikita thath-tharikita thith-thom*. As he sang, he danced, showing the steps and hand movements.

Iyer broke into applause.

'Thank you, thank you,' said Bharati, bowing in an exaggerated fashion. 'Now I must be going. I wanted to read out one of my new Kannan poems, but you seem to be busy doing something that's far more important. Some other time then.' He looked at Panju and said, 'Vande Mataram.'

Panju managed to whisper, 'Vande Mataram.'

With a wave of his hand, Bharati was off.

'When I close my eyes,' said Panju, 'he is over a hundred feet tall and is bathed in brilliant light.'

'He is that, and much more. Now coming back to where we were, is it enough to die? Everyone dies at some time or the other.'

'No, one must also die in such a way that his death benefits others.'

'Panju, do you remember, you said you were ready to die.'

'Yes, I do. I still—'

'—Are you prepared to kill?'

Panju did not answer.

'Are you prepared to take another's life for the cause?' Iyer's voice was now more insistent.

Panju took some time to compose himself.

'My father explained to me why we draw a kolam outside our houses with rice powder. It is not merely for decoration. It is so that even the smallest beings of God's creation are benefited. I remember swatting an ant when I was a child. My father got really angry.'

'You cannot compare an ant with a venomous viper that has bitten many and is likely to harm many more. Your duty may be unpleasant; but you have to do it. Would you rather take the life of a single person painlessly or witness three hundred million people in everlasting torment? Krishna tells Arjuna in the Gita—"If you die, you will reach heaven and if you win you will be the ruler of the earth." I cannot promise such rewards either in this world or the next. But I can assure you of this: whether you win or not, whether you like it or not, thousands of people will regard you as a hero. They will be inspired to do the right thing by their Motherland.'

'I will do it,' said Panju, deciding, his mind still in turmoil.

'It is all right to be afraid—'

'I am not afraid,' Panju snapped back.

'Then we begin the training. Meet me at the Puliyanthope at seven in the morning tomorrow. Gopal will tell you how to get there. Give yourself at least an hour and a half to get there.'

THIRTY-TWO

1 June 1911

When Panju reached the tamarind grove, he saw an iron gate resting on one hinge and propped up by an enormous boulder. Rough-hewn granite posts, some of them broken, lay strewn around. Iyer was already waiting for him. They entered the forested land. Iyer led Panju deeper and deeper into the grove till they came to a small clearing. Half a dozen tin cans, large and small, were arranged on the stump of a tree. Some of them were crushed and had small holes through them. A piece of paper on which a series of concentric circles had been drawn was pinned to another tree.

Iyer stopped and addressed Panju.

'I have to tell you a story. Once Arjuna performed a severe penance for obtaining divine weapons. Siva appeared but—'

'—I know,' said Panju. 'I know this story from the Mahabharata. I have also read the *Kiratarjuneeya* by Bharavi. Arjuna is finally granted a boon by Lord Siva.'

'Siva gave him the divine weapon Pasupatha, but do you know the condition that came with it?'

'No, please tell me,' Panju said.

'Siva said that the Pasupatha astra should be used only against a superior foe. Not against the weak.'

Panju remained quiet, guessing there was more to come.

'I give you this,' said Iyer and with a dramatic flourish pulled out an object from his coat pocket.

Panju's eyes widened.

'This is a semi-automatic Browning FN 1900 pistol. You will learn to maintain and use it.'

Panju thrust his hand forward to receive it. But Iyer still held on to it. 'You should use it only against our common enemy. Promise me.'

'I promise,' said Panju as he received the pistol. 'This is so small,' he said, turning it around and holding it by its knurled grip.

'We chose this precisely because it is small and can be easily hidden. It chambers .32 bullets.' Iyer took the pistol back and showed him how to cock it and load and unload the magazine. He made Panju repeat the action several times. He then taught Panju the two-handed grip with the unloaded pistol.

'This is a single-action semi-automatic. What it means is you need to cock the pistol only once for the first bullet to align with the bore. After that, to fire the other six rounds, you simply have to keep squeezing the trigger. The blowback will ensure that the next round is in the chamber.'

Panju closed one eye and bringing the pistol close to his open eye, pointed the pistol at Iyer's chest.

Iyer reacted instantaneously. His hand swept out, knocking the pistol from Panju's grip.

'But,' said the enraged Panju, picking up the pistol, 'the pistol is empty.'

'There are many things wrong with what you did. Never point the pistol at anyone unless you intend wounding or killing that person. Even if you know the pistol to be empty of bullets, even if the safety is on. For instance, there may be a bullet in the chamber though the magazine is empty.'

'I am sorry,' said Panju.

'And if you intend to kill someone at this close a range, aim for the head and the face—not the chest.'

'Can I start to practise shooting?'

'We have done enough for the day. Practise cocking, loading and unloading and the operation of the safety in your room, till it becomes second nature to you. Also, I want the carrying of a pistol to seem natural to you. But right now, I am not giving you bullets. We will come back to this range and practise firing at the target for at least three weeks.'

As they were returning, Panju thought he saw some bushes at a distance move. He hurried to the spot and saw a limping form, half running. He returned to Iyer and told him.

'Murugesan,' said Iyer, a frown on his face. 'This may mean trouble. Not from the French authorities, who let us be with a nod and a wink, but from the British CID. We don't have the luxury of time. You should be ready in two weeks' time.'

'And who will be my ultimate target?'

'Almost any white man will do. But we do have someone specific in our minds. We will discuss that later.'

'Do you know what the twenty-second of June is?' asked Iyer as soon as they met.

'Let me see,' said Panju. He thought for a while and said, 'It ought to be a Thursday.'

'You are right. But, I was asking if you knew the significance of the day.'

'I can't guess.'

'It falls in the middle of the waning moon. A day of waning of the moon of the British Empire. The sun, too, will start setting on the British Empire and eventually, hardly ever rise.'

'Are you making an astrological prediction?'

'No, I am making a promise, although the ten-thousand-year golden period in the era of Kali as foretold by Krishna in *Brahma Vaivarta Purana* has already begun.'

'I did read about the old prediction of Vyasa in one of the pamphlets about the destruction of the white empire between the Nandana and the Ananda years.'

'Yes, that too fits in. The white empire will be destroyed between 1892 and 1915.'

'I am sorry, I still don't understand the significance of the date.'

'Let me explain. The coronation ceremony of King George V will be held in London on the twenty-second of June. He will be visiting India later on, along with Queen Mary, to attend the Delhi Durbar.'

Iyer poured water into a brass tumbler from a flask and took a couple of draughts from it before continuing.

'That is the day on which you will be inspiring three thousand south Indians to contribute to the struggle in a decisive way. That is going to be the symbolic day on which the assassination will take place; one that will start the downfall of the British Empire.'

'Three thousand south Indians?'

'Yes. The British have always thought that the south Indian is timid in comparison to the more ebullient north Indian or the Bengali. This will prove that the south Indian is no less in bravery. Three thousand youth from the Madras Presidency have already signed the pledge. Now your act will be as a beacon to them. Everyone will hail you as a hero.'

'Please, Sir, I respect you like a father. Please don't glorify this act any more than it deserves. A killing is a killing—'

'Don't you remember what Krishna said to Arjuna in the Gita—'

'Sir, please remember that I can recite the entire Gita by heart. Still, as I said, a killing is a killing. Nothing will change that. I will, however, do it, as did Arjuna. That is not going to make it any easier for me. I doubt if I will ever find redemption. I have to do it in the cause of Bharata Mata and Sanatana Dharma. Please leave me to fight my own inner battles.'

For once, Iyer was speechless.

'Tell me, who is this white man I have to kill?' Panju asked.

'He was the Collector of Tirunelveli a couple of years back. He ordered the firing on unarmed striking workers in Tuticorin and was the one who got V.O. Chidambaram Pillai arrested, almost nipping the Swadeshi movement in the bud, at least in the south. He immediately proceeded on leave to England and is back now, posted as the Collector of Tanjore.'

'And what is his name?'

Panju's eyes went wide as he heard the name—'Edmund Worthington.'

JUNE 1911

MADRAS

THIRTY-THREE

6 June 1911

Edmund Worthington and his wife Mary sat sipping tea in the verandah of a spacious house at Esplanade in Madras. They were both seated on rattan cane chairs. A plate of biscuits lay on the table between them. Mary looked longingly at a biscuit before she bit into it.

'I know you miss England,' said Worthington. He had a curious lisp as result of speaking with his tongue in contact with his lower teeth, something he had been advised to do to cure a childhood stammering problem. 'I guess our provisions of McVites & Price should last us another three months.'

'Well,' said Mary, 'if you must know, I will miss Sarah more than the biscuits.'

'Of course,' said Edmund. They fell silent.

Worthington had left India on furlough a year ago, taking Mary and his daughter Sarah with him, intending to leave Sarah with Mary's father, who was the headmaster of a boy's school in Cheltenham; he had promised to look after Sarah's education.

Edmund Worthington was the son of a clergyman. While his father led a nondescript life, his father's more illustrious elder brother, Uncle John as he was known to Edmund, had far more clout, at least in holding a £20-share in a school at Greenwich that allowed him the nomination of a student. He used it in favour of Edmund, preferring to send his own sons to Eton. The school was known for its reasonably good standards in education. Edmund was pitchforked into the school, which was known more for football than for cricket, his passion in life. In Form Six he made it to the first eleven with his slow left-arm spin and the occasional chinaman. He even took nine wickets in an innings against a village team, thanks to a pitch soaking wet with rain, even though he got them at the expense of sixty-two runs, twenty of which had come in a single over in which a burly left-hander had carted him repeatedly over mid-wicket. In his studies, to his credit, he tried hard to be taught and to learn—as his school motto, *docendum et discendum,* advised him.

The school specialized in preparing students for the competitive exams, more particularly for the Indian Civil Service, and when Edmund sat for the examination at Burlington House in Piccadilly, he chose as many subjects as possible and managed to scrape through. He had to choose the province in India where he wished to be posted. He was left with little choice in this, as pupils normally chose the northern provinces, northwest provinces, Bengal, the Bombay Presidency and the Madras Presidency—in that order. He had scored a low rank and was assigned to the Madras Presidency by default. It didn't bother him that he was now destined to become a mulligatawny-soup-drinking 'mull', as he was not too interested in hunting and shooting; nor did he wish his limitations to be under close scrutiny by being posted in Bengal, which was the seat of British power in India.

He was excited to receive a personal letter from the head of Balliol College at Oxford asking him to enrol there. He did not know then that the headmaster routinely wrote to every successful student asking him to join. He joined at the earliest opportunity, Uncle John again coming good for the price of his clothes. The curriculum included languages of the students' chosen province, Tamil and Telugu in his case, and he tried very hard to learn them without too much success. The Oxford dons and other students there just about tolerated the ICS boys as there was very little possibility of their winning either sporting laurels or academic distinctions. The ICS boys stuck together, but Edmund was excluded from many club and social activities as he was painfully shy. Frequent trips to Lord's kept him happy where he could heckle even the incomparable W.G. Grace.

It was bad form to talk about India, but in moments of occasional drunken conviviality, the ICS boys would promise to meet once a year in India. Edmund Worthington did not get such a promise. He could have stayed for one more year over the two probationary years and got himself an Oxford degree as well. But his father wanted him to start earning as early as possible and the extra year would also cost him a year of seniority at the ICS.

At nineteen, he set sail for India and arrived in a little over three weeks, enjoying the leisurely passage through the Suez. His superior officer gave him the first piece of useful advice he received as a Griffin, as a new recruit into the ICS was called. 'Don't marry in the first five years. It will simply ruin your career.' He followed this advice scrupulously and didn't get hooked until his first furlough, even though he had ample opportunity to meet quite a few ladies and their wards looking for husbands, commonly referred to as 'fishing fleets'. He also learnt to overcome his shyness by adopting a patronizing condescension unlike the sneering haughtiness a few of his friends developed, particularly in their dealings with natives.

His superior, an old Haileybury hand, made fun of the utterly prosaic and unromantic way in which he set about finding a wife. Edmund did not intend to fall in love; he wanted a wife who would run his house for him and worry about orders of precedence at the dinner parties he might have to throw. He was quite a catch for Mary; she hadn't heard of the hours of solitude and loneliness Indian memsahibs had to endure. Mary accompanied him back to India after his leave of absence, stardust in her eyes and a hideous collection of 'what a memsahib should wear' in her trunks.

Sarah was born in 1901, when Edmund was an assistant to a secretary in the Revenue Board at Madras. Sarah proved lucky for him. Soon after that, he was made a Deputy Collector, a vacancy having arisen in the Tanjore district.

A civilian had to be thoroughly incompetent *and* outrageously insubordinate for his promotion to be blocked. He was certainly not insubordinate and not incompetent enough to be nudged on to the 'judgey' side of things. So, in two years' time, when the Collector went on leave, he was acting for him, taking on both his administrative and magisterial roles. He was then transferred as Collector to Tirunelveli district, where he had to face the first industrial strike ever organized in India—surprisingly by an Indian entrepreneur, who had started the Swadeshi Shipping Company in competition with the British India Steam Navigation Company. V.O. Chidambaram Pillai was motivated more by his unyielding nationalism than by entrepreneurial avarice. The District Magistrate actually ordered the shooting against the striking workers; but the vernacular press ascribed it to Worthington. A settlement was reached between the workers and the management and subsequently, V.O. Chidambaram Pillai was arrested and sentenced to prison—again Worthington had no hand in this, but he did not bother to dismiss the rumours, which he thought lent him an aura of authority.

In any case, soon after the affair, he went with Mary on his second furlough to England, eighteen years after he came to India. He met his mother who was living with his sister and visited his father's grave with a heavy heart; there was much he had left unsaid. He also visited Lord's as many times as he wished and was a witness to the inglorious loss to the Australians in the summer of 1909, joined fans in the round condemnation of the Selection Committee—going so far as to even question the sanity of A.C. McLauren, one of the selectors—and repeated the phrase 'we will never see the likes of him' whenever W.G. Grace was mentioned.

Towards the end of his furlough, he dropped Sarah off at his father-in-law's, thanking him profusely, if in trite phrases.

Now, he was back. Mary accompanied him dutifully, even

though she would have preferred to remain in England with her daughter. He wanted to reconnect with the powers that be in Madras and returned a week before the joining date as Collector of Tanjore. A friend of his, who as part of the summer migration of the government of Madras had headed for the cooler climes of Ooty, allowed him the use of his bungalow in Madras for the duration. He also found a native who offered himself for service, and finding his references excellent, though none of which could be immediately verified, hired him as his general factotum. At least the man could communicate in English, though he had a rather distressing habit of shaking his head and splaying out his hands whenever he spoke, as though it took a huge effort to bring the words out of his gullet.

'We should be all packed in a couple of days,' said Mary. 'In any case, I haven't unpacked most of our things.'

'That reminds me,' said Worthington. 'I must change our train tickets to Tanjore. I have just received information that our bungalow won't be ready until the twenty-fourth. Apparently, the Collector in charge got so busy arranging the various events for the coronation that he won't be able to move out in time.'

'This is the same bungalow the Collector was living in when we were there? At Vallam. The house with the large garden in front?'

'Yes, the same.'

'I wish,' said Mary, 'we had been able to postpone our return by a month. I would have given anything to be at Westminster Abbey for the coronation.'

'I wish you wouldn't interrupt me and take the conversation in diverse random directions. You almost made me forget about our change in schedule,' said Worthington.

'Moonswamy!' he shouted out for his factotum, who appeared almost immediately.

'Go to the railway station and get our tickets changed to the twenty-fourth from the twenty-second of June.'

'Yes, Sir,' said Munuswamy, 'twenty-fourth June 1911 AD.'

'What the devil is that AD for?'

'AD. After Death, Sir. Of Yesu Christu. Our history teacher always taught us to put BC or AD after the year, Sir.'

For once, Worthington thought of a clever remark to make, but thinking his man may not be able to handle sarcasm, merely said, 'Just go to it, will you?'

'Yes, Sir.' There was a firm shake of the head, but Munuswamy remained where he was.

'What are you waiting for?'

'Sir, cancellation charges as applicable on the date of the journey, Sir. Also, the travelling and conveyance expenses for engaging a jatka to get to the station, Sir.'

'All right, take this,' he said handing over twenty rupees to Munuswamy. 'This should cover it.'

'Yes, Sir. This will also cover the cost of the telegram.'

'Telegram? Whatever for?'

For a moment Munuswamy appeared to be at a loss for words. 'For informing the stationmaster at Tanjore that you are coming, Sir,' he managed to say finally.

'Do whatever is required, but go quickly.'

'Yes, Sir,' said Munuswamy. He walked all the way to the central railway station, pausing only to send a telegram to Pondicherry.

MARRIAGE DELAYED BY TWO DAYS STOP ALTER TRAVEL
PLANS ACCORDINGLY STOP

Thirty-four

The acting Deputy Inspector General of Police, Robert Hall, was hot under the collar even though there was a long rectangular strip of stiff cloth fixed to a pole that hung from the ceiling swaying to and fro and creating a reasonable breeze. The pole itself hung from a rope attached to the ceiling. Another rope attached to the pole passed through an opening in the wall. The invisible hand of a punkha-wallah pulled and loosed the rope alternately. Hall's desk was spotlessly clean, thanks to his insistence that whoever placed a file there, left the room with the file after obtaining instructions. No one suspected that he read and wrote only with difficulty.

His education was bequeathed to him not from the hallowed portals of Oxford or Cambridge, but from the shadier streets of East End, London. Born in a small village in Durham to miner Charles Hall and Mary née Hardy, he ran away from home to London before he turned twelve, before he could be forced to work in the coal mines. He found himself in the hands of a printer, who was the nearest person to a father that he could clearly remember. He was lucky that he was, in a manner of speaking, adopted by a printer as other people paid money to learn the trade.

The printer didn't take the boy into his home, but kept him well fed and warm by allowing him to sleep in the office. He also made sure that the boy could read and write.

Robert was tall even as a child and as he grew into manhood, his shoulders and his chest broadened, and he managed to keep fit through street fights and brawls, most of which he won.

The printing press, in due course, ran into debt, partly because of the owner's soft-hearted nature and largely due to Robert, who often collected the money owed to the owner and neglected to inform him. In the five years he was with the press, he also collected a passable Oxford accent from his employer—one that he could produce on demand.

When the owner of the press hanged himself, Robert paused only to steal his clothes and offered himself up for recruitment in the British army. The recruiting officer took one look at the towering six-foot physique, much in excess of the required five-foot-three and obviously in excellent health—unlike most of his other compatriots who offered themselves for recruitment. Soon, Robert took the Queen's shilling. He then indulged in a carefully calculated orgy of borrowing, collecting a handsome nest egg in the bargain; he did not spend his ill-gotten money unwisely, nor did he plan to return any of it.

He was packed off to South Africa, to participate in the Second Boer War under Lord Roberts—much to the detriment of his creditors, who were annoyed at his mysterious disappearance and only consoled themselves by speculating that he must have been bumped off by one of the fellow-creditors.

He showed great enthusiasm in South Africa for burning farms, sometimes with the inhabitants still inside them, and rounding up women and children for the concentration camps and worse. The horrified commanding officer gave him the option of an honourable discharge without pension on request, or court martial. He chose the former; he at least had a free passage back to London.

He did not intend to stay within the reach of his creditors and didn't linger in London for long.

He booked a passage to India and arrived in Bombay three weeks later instead of the six months it would have taken him before the Suez was opened. On board, he befriended a Superintendent of Police from the Madras Presidency by uncorking his accent. The Superintendent, son of a vicar and from one of the lesser-known grammar schools in England, on learning that his co-passenger served in the army, offered him a position immediately as an Inspector with the Madras police with prospects of making Superintendent in three years.

Robert jumped at it. Not before long, he arrived in Madras only to be posted to Tanjore. His superior officers loathed him for the unrestrained zeal he showed in bringing the errant natives to book. The people he arrested always confessed, even in court, fear often palpable in their eyes. He was reprimanded several times. Since he was a British officer, none of that entered the official records. Thus he got his promotions automatically and when the Criminal Investigation Department was formed, Robert's superior officer, the Deputy Inspector General of Police, was happy to be rid of him by recommending the suitability of his services to the CID rather extravagantly, without a trace of the British understatement.

Robert Hall had success in breaking up some insurance frauds and an opium trade network—thanks in part to his able Sub-inspector, Chanduru. After the assassinations in 1908 and 1909 of Kennedy and Jackson in India, and Curzon Wylie in London, the focus of the CID shifted to preventing revolutionary activities. It was then, for the first time in south India that some of the revolutionaries had taken shelter in French Pondicherry. The Foreign Affairs and Political Department gave Robert a free hand in transferring and deputing more personnel to the CID in general, and more particularly for keeping tabs on the Pondicherry revolutionaries. He drew resources of Sub-inspectors that a reluctant Inspector General of Police provided from the districts.

'Shandroo,' Hall shouted. Chanduru appeared in front of him instantly like a genie from a bottle and saluted smartly, placing all the papers and files he held on his superior officer's desk. Chanduru was a thin man whose face seemed to mainly consist of a sharp nose. He was in mufti in a veshti and a coat. The Sub-inspector had a reputation as a brilliant investigator and even his friends called him 'CID Chanduru'.

'Sit, sit.' Hall said. Chanduru was one of the few subordinates he allowed to sit in front of him.

'Should I call the Inspector, Sir?' Chanduru asked.

'No, I want to review the Pondicherry situation. Give me the latest intelligence. I am meeting the Inspector General to apprise him of the situation.'

'Over the last two weeks,' Chanduru began, 'revolutionary activity has gone up. There are more frequent meetings. Our men there have reported that someone new has joined the revolutionaries. The man is not from Pondicherry. They have seen him in the company of Iyer who, as you know, is the noted revolutionary hiding in Pondicherry. Our informers have even seen them in the tamarind grove that they have used in the past as a shooting range.'

'Shandroo, just breathe a little between your sentences. So there is a stranger in their midst. Do we know his name and where he is from?'

'We managed to plant a cook at Iyer's house. Our operatives were able to scare off the previous ones. He has so far been able to learn only the name of the new person. It is Panchapakesan. Called Panju. Apparently, Iyer and his guests stop talking whenever the cook goes anywhere near them, even to serve them coffee. So we have been unable to learn anything else. Yes, there is this other thing. He seems to be from Tanjore district.'

'How did they get that?'

'His way of speaking indicates that. And this came in yesterday, Sir,' said Chanduru, offering a piece of paper to Hall.

'This is a cable from Paris. Just read it.'

'This is from the British Special Branch in Paris, Sir... THIS

IS AN EXTRACT FROM MADAME CAMAS BANDE MATARAM
STOP QUOTE IN A MEETING OR IN A BUNGALOW ON THE
RAILWAY OR IN A CARRIAGE IN A SHOP OR IN A CHURCH
IN A GARDEN OR AT A FAIR WHEREVER AN OPPORTUNITY
COMES ENGLISHMEN OUGHT TO BE KILLED STOP NO
DISTINCTION SHOULD BE MADE BETWEEN OFFICERS AND
PRIVATE PEOPLE END QUOTE STOP TAKE ALL POSSIBLE
PRECAUTIONS IN INDIA STOP'

Chanduru read the cable actually saying STOP instead of
pausing.

'So, something's up certainly. We have found before that
Madame Cama's newspaper predicts revolutionary events
accurately even before they happen in India. So what do you
make of it?'

'I am sure an assassination is being planned in Pondicherry,
Sir.'

Robert Hall saw him before he heard him. A pair of feet hesitated
a full minute under the half-partition of frosted glass that spanned
his door before the 'Sir, may I come in?' was tentatively spoken.

'Come in, goddammit. Stop hovering like a half-witted
butterfly, whoever you are,' Hall shouted.

'Thank you very much, Sir,' said the man as he entered.

Hall merely stared at him.

'I am Viswanatha Iyer, BA,' he said. 'People call me Vichu. I
am a shirastedar in the revenue department. I am the right hand
of Mr Cotton. I deal with very confidential matters also.'

'What do you want?'

'I don't want anything, Sir. I am the government's humblest
and most obedient and most loyal servant.' Suddenly, he struck at
his head with his palm, pulled out a pocket watch and looked at
it. 'Oh my God, it is already late. I hope you have eaten, Sir. You

must be finding Madras food very spicy but tasty. I also don't eat much spice, you know. I am developing an ulcer, you see.'

'I don't care if you have ulcers or the clap. Just tell me why you are here. Or get out.'

'Sir, don't dismiss me lightly. I bear very important news, you know. Something that affects the entire nation.'

'If you don't tell me in the next one minute, I am going to affect you personally by kicking you out.'

'Sir, don't do that, Sir. I am a loyal subject of His Majesty. I wanted to talk to you about a conspiracy.'

He looked around him and said in a whisper: 'And treason, Sir.'

'Go on,' said Hall, now interested.

'My own sister's son, Sir. As the bard said, you know, how sharper than a serpent's tooth it is to have a thankless child—'

'Who the devil is Thebard? Talk sense, man.'

'The bard, Sir, of Avon.' Vichu saw the expression on Hall's face and continued in a hurry. 'This is a pamphlet we found in his possession, actually in his room, Sir.' He extracted the document from his shirt pocket. He had to stand up and undo several buttons of his coat to do that.

Hall took a quick look at it. *Sedition.*

'My sister's son, Sir. Panchapakesan. We used to call him Panju for short—'

Now Hall became animated. '—Son of a prostitute, mother fucker!'

Vichu was taken aback at this outburst in Tamil. 'Sir, don't say that, Sir. He is my own sister's son and you are casting aspersions—'

'—You said Panju? And is he from Tanjore?'

'Yes, well he is from the district, actually from Tiruvaiyaru, which I am sure you guessed from his name itself. He—'

'—Just answer my questions,' Hall snapped. 'What does he do?'

'My brother-in-law said he works at a printing press at

Kumbakonam. You see, he has done his BA at the Government College there.'

'Do you have an address?'

'It's called the Velmurugan press. That's what Sambu told me.'

'Do you have his home address in Kumbakonam?'

'No, but you see, you can always find out from his place of work. You police have a way of asking—'

'—Where is he now?'

'I am not sure, but my brother-in-law said he has gone to Pondicherry, you know. He has gone there and will be returning in a month's time. Wait,' he stopped and made some mental calculations accompanied by a lot of finger movements. 'Since I met him a week ago, I suppose he may be back in three weeks.'

'Now, write down your current house as well as office address. You should be ready to come to this office at any time or be prepared to testify when required.'

Vichu finished writing on the piece of paper provided, using the pen on the DIG's desk, dipping it into an inkwell on the desk.

'Sir, myself and my sister are completely innocent. I am not so sure about my brother-in-law. I hope you will be taking appropriate action against Panju.'

'Bugger off,' said Hall, drying the paper on a blotter.

Vichu left in a hurry.

'Shandroo!' Hall shouted as soon as Vichu was out of sight.

Chanduru came rushing in and saluted.

Hall showed the revolutionary leaflet to Chanduru and told him the story that Vichu had related.

'We are going to Kumbakonam in a week's time. Make the arrangements. I will be personally in charge of this investigation. Tell our people in Pondicherry to make sure that they don't miss anyone leaving Pondicherry, least of all that son of a bitch, Panju. The moment he steps into British territory, I want him arrested.'

Hall began to feel the thrill of the hunt.

JUNE 1911
KUMBAKONAM

THIRTY-FIVE

10 June 1911

The inspection bungalow in Kumbakonam must have been built quite some time ago, but it had been whitewashed and maintained well. For some reason, the main gate into the premises was missing, the gateposts painted in dual tones of cream and white. Robert Hall strode through them. The clerk at the reception desk took him to his allotted room. He had a quick wash, changed into a bush shirt, khaki drill trousers and riding boots. He washed down a packet of Huntley and Palmer biscuits with his tea, which a native bearer brought in a faux-silver tea set.

'Has Shandroo come?' he asked the bearer.

The bearer guessed correctly that he must be referring to his assistant and said he was waiting outside with the horses.

Neither Hall's childhood nor his stint in the Transvaal had included riding lessons. He had found it difficult in India in the beginning, needing two servants by the side of the horse at all times, much to the open mirth and veiled ridicule of his Superintendent. Now he was far more comfortable on horseback while far from being a master equestrian.

They reached the Velmurugan press inside of an hour. It was hot and Hall's sola topi seemed to be filling with sweat.

'You go in first,' Hall directed Chanduru.

The press was silent and there seemed to be no one around. Chanduru finally found a thin man, perhaps in his forties, sleeping in a corner, on the floor. He was bare-chested, ribs showing through, his vest bundled under his head providing a pillow.

'*Yov,*' Chanduru called out, nudging him in his ribs.

The man woke up with a start.

'Where is the owner?' Chanduru asked.

'He is out of town,' said the man and attempted to go back to sleep.

'What's your name?'

'Manickam. I compose here. I told you the owner is not there. He has gone to Madras and I don't know when he'll be back.'

'Who else works here?'

Manickam stood up. 'I am not supposed to answer any questions. Who are you, coming here and asking questions? You are not in uniform. You are not even the police.'

'We are far worse,' said Hall as he came in. 'We are the CID.'

Hall walked slowly till he came close to Manickam. His right foot suddenly shot out and his boot caught the man on the shin. It was hard to tell whether the crack heard came from the boot hitting the shin or the man's head hitting the floor. The man cried out and started sobbing.

Hall placed his foot on the man's neck and pressed.

'You will learn to answer questions the moment I ask.' Hall's Tamil was strangely inflected but comprehensible.

'…I am…choking. Please don't do anything to me, Aiya.'

'Oh no,' said Hall, 'you are not choking to death. As yet.' Without turning, he commanded Chanduru, 'Search the place. Literature. Guns, bombs, anything.'

Chanduru said nothing, but he couldn't keep the horror from his face. He busied himself searching, upturning crates and opening the gunny bags that lay around.

When he came back, Hall's boot was still on Manickam's neck. His eyes were rolling and there was a track of spittle from his mouth that had dribbled on to the floor.

'Nothing incriminating, Sir. A whole lot of devotional books. Nothing being printed now.' Chanduru's voice was pitched a little low.

'Don't worry about it,' said Hall. 'We can always plant some, if necessary.'

'Now tell me, Manickam,' said Hall, switching back to Tamil, 'Who else works here?'

Manickam's answer came in halting words; yet his eagerness to talk quickly was manifest.

'Muthuswamy Mudaliar is the owner, Aiya. He lives in Madras and doesn't come here often. We don't have any printing jobs right now. Panchapakesan was working here as the manager. He is not in town—'

'—Where is he?'

'I heard Pondicherry, Aiya, to get us some orders.'

'Where does Panju live?'

'18, Mahamaham Kulam Tank North Street, Aiya. You go east on Mahamaham Kulam Street, it is about fifteen to twenty houses down the road on the eating-hand side. It's an old house, Aiya, with tiles falling off. In front of the house, there is no thinnai and there is a window looking into the street. You can't miss it. It has iron bars, Aiya.'

Hall took his foot off his neck, but brought it down immediately on Manickam's hand. Chanduru saw it. He heard the crunch of breaking fingers and winced.

'This is for taking your time answering us. Don't even think of going to the police. We are the police's father.'

Even as they left, Chanduru could hear the low keening sound from Manickam.

Thirty-six

'This must be Panju's house,' said Chanduru, pointing.

It was a dilapidated single-storey house, some of the tiles having fallen off and exposing the rafters on one side. The remaining tiles were a faded brown, tending to black at the edges. There was no sign of anyone. On the right was a window set in the wall, barred with heavy vertical iron rods, making it look more like a cage than a human dwelling.

Hall withdrew his heavy Webley revolver from his pocket, and went in holding it muzzle down, with both arms extended in front of him. Chanduru followed. There were three doors. The doors in front and to the left were locked with heavy Aligarh padlocks. The door on the right had two locks hanging from it. One of the locks was attached to the fixed bracket on the door and the other went through the first lock and the latch on the bolt so that the key to either lock could open the door.

'This is it,' breathed Hall, looked around and saw that there wasn't enough room to use his body to break open the door. Chanduru said, 'Let me try,' and fished out a small iron tool from his pocket. He inserted it into the lighter of the two locks. He bent down and listened intently as he twisted the slender tool inside the lock. He had the padlock open in a few minutes.

'You seem to have learnt some useful trades,' Hall remarked as he put his revolver back into the holster and entered the room.

There was nothing much to see. A cot occupied half the room and gave the appearance of being stored there rather than for anyone's use. A couple of pictures and a mirror with a crack in the form of an arc around one edge, a ledge with a small copper vessel, a fine-toothed comb and a copy of the Bhagavad Gita. Chanduru bent down and pulled out a wooden steamer trunk from underneath the cot. The box contained only a few clothes and notebooks that contained Panju's class notes.

'Got something here,' he eventually said.' A photograph. Obviously taken during the wedding.'

Hall made Chanduru remove the pictures from the wall. He found a small gold chain behind one of the pictures. Hall took it from Chanduru and put it in one of the pockets of his bush shirt.

Chanduru took the copy of the Bhagavad Gita in his hands and started to turn the pages. A piece of paper that had been folded and refolded fell out of the book. Hall pounced on it. Meanwhile Chanduru stared at the book. It was open on chapter 3 verse 9.

The English translation of the verse read:

'O Arjuna, the whole world is bound by actions except for actions sacrificed into the supreme Lord; being free from all other actions, engage perfectly in actions for the purposes of sacrifice.'

Meanwhile, Hall unfolded the piece of paper. It took him a while to read through the first couple of sentences penned on it.

'Blimey, that's the ticket!'

'Ticket, Sir?' said the bewildered Chanduru.

'See this,' Hall handed the paper to him.

He studied it intently.

'This seems to be an oath of admission to a secret society, Sir. Called Bharat Samman. Sounds like an extremist society, Sir.'

'Bet your boots on it,' said Hall. 'Now take your diary out and start writing.'

Hall waited for Chanduru to fish out his diary and start writing with a pencil so short that it disappeared entirely into his hand.

Hall studied the photograph he had found earlier. 'Take it down. Description of suspect: short, around five feet, wiry, no, scratch that. The buggers probably won't understand. Thin, but muscular. Large separated ear lobes. Ha, what do I see here? Right, mole on cheek below the left eye.'

'Sir,' said Chanduru. He sounded diffident. 'That is not a mole. That's a drishtippottu.'

'A what? Can't you see the mole, large as life?'

'No, Sir, that is a black spot that is painted on the cheek to ward off the evil eye. This is normally done for marriages and other occasions.'

'So, scratch that. I want our people in all railway stations from Pondicherry to Kumbakonam. How many stations are there?'

'Let me see, Sir,' answered Chanduru as he started making notes in his diary. 'From Pondicherry, you have to change at Villuppuram. The stations are Cuddalore, Chidambaram, Cheerkali, Mayavaram, Kumbakonam.'

'Make sure we have two people during the day and two people at night at Villuppuram and three in each shift at Kumbakonam. Two people will also travel every day from Villuppuram to Kumbakonam and check all suspicious passengers. All Sub-inspectors and head constables. No constables. Circulate the description of Panju immediately to everyone in the field. Meanwhile, get a current description from our Pondicherry people.'

'Sir, but we don't have enough people in the field for all this.'

'Just get the men from the district police. The Inspector General has given me carte blanche in this matter. Actually, the Foreign Secretary did the arm-twisting. Get some men from the railway police as well. Am I not also the head of the railway police? Go. Get moving.'

'I have a problem, Sir. I am just a Sub-inspector and...'

'I am taking care of that. For the duration, you will have the powers of a Superintendent. I am also making sure that you are promoted to Inspector with immediate effect.'

'Thank you, Sir.'

Thirty-seven

11 June 1911

Hall paced up and down in the garden of the bungalow. For a minute or so he didn't recognize Chanduru, who saluted and stood quietly. At last, he looked up at Chanduru, a question on his face.

'We have the required number of people in place, Sir,' said Chanduru. 'I have sent out the description of Panju. I sent it by telegram through the railway police who will hand-deliver it to our field agents. By now, they should have received it.'

Hall continued pacing. 'We know a crime is going to be committed. We are not sure what the crime is going to be. In all probability, a murder. We even know the perpetrator. We don't know who the victim or victims are going to be. We don't know when it's going to be committed. We need answers to all these questions.' Hall paused for a breath. 'The only way we can be somewhat sure of preventing this is to arrest this Panju and take him into custody. Right now, he is beyond our jurisdiction. This is what I want you to do.'

He continued pacing for a while before he spoke. 'We have to intercept all communication from Pondicherry to Kumbakonam. All cables, letters, parcels, railway consignments—everything.'

'Letters and cables from outside British territory are already being monitored, Sir. Consignments and parcels are also tracked by customs since they would be imports into the country.'

'I am not happy with that. I want my man monitoring letters and cables to Kumbakonam specifically originating in French Pondicherry. I want a good man on that.'

'I could do that, Sir,' Chanduru volunteered.

'No, I want you to be with me most of the time. Remember that young man from Kumbakonam who came to see us in Madras? He gave us some important leads on the insurance fraud case.'

'I think you are talking about Tulasingam. He is with Superintendent Meyer. He won't release Tulasi that easily, Sir.'

'He won't, won't he? I will see to it that he is on this job by this evening. Brief him on what we are doing and let him go directly to the post and telegraph office. Let him work with our person there, concentrating on communications from Pondicherry. I want a copy of every suspicious piece of communication on my desk first thing in the morning along with an oral report.'

He was still upwind of his quarry, but he was certain it wouldn't be long before he got a whiff.

Thirty-eight

'Give me just the gist of your reports,' said Hall, looking at Chanduru and Tulasingam in turn.

Tulasingam was short and wiry with a moustache that was much broader at the ends than in the middle, ending upon his cheeks like a fast-spreading moss, and a sharp hooked nose that jutted out from between his eyebrows, looking like an eagle chick peering down from its eyrie. He wore khaki shorts that were so well starched that he could have taken a couple of steps inside them without encountering cloth.

'We don't wear uniforms here,' continued Hall, looking at Tulasingam.

'I am not wearing uniform, Sir,' said Tulasingam, 'I am in mufti.'

Hall rolled his eyes and before he could say anything, Chanduru spoke up.

'We have some information from Iyer's cook and we have a current description of Panju from Pondicherry, Sir.'

'We will look at it later. Anything to report, Tul...Tul...'

'Tulasingam, Sir. Tulasi for short.'

Tulasi placed a postcard on the table.

Hall glanced at it. The Pondicherry postmark was prominent on it. He turned the card around and found that the writing was in Tamil.

'So what does that say?' asked Hall.

Tulasi placed another piece of paper with English writing on it upon the desk.

'I have prepared a translation for you, Sir.'

'Just read it, dammit.'

Tulasi stroked his moustache lovingly once, took the piece of paper in his hand and began to read in a sing-song voice.

Many namaskarams to the beloved aunt,

I hope everything is fine with you. We are all fine here. I will send the cook this month. He should be there exactly two days before the grand marriage. He will be bringing the vessel required for making idli. Please meet him at the station and provide whatever help he needs. You should have no difficulty recognizing him as you have seen him before.

Affectionately yours,
Shanbagam.

'So what do you find so suspicious about this?' growled Hall.

'Our agent at the post office did not find anything suspicious about it either. In reality, everything about it is fake, Sir. It is not the marriage season now and there are no auspicious days left in the month. I checked with an astrologer to make doubly sure, Sir. Secondly, no one in their right minds would hire a cook from Pondicherry, especially to go to Kumbakonam, which is full of them. He doesn't need to bring the vessel needed to make idlies. Kumbakonam is virtually the birthplace of the idli.'

'So you think this letter is in code. By the way, what the hell is an idli?'

'An idli is a dish that is soft and white—'

'—White? That could mean a white man.'

'Also, Sir, the term he has used in Tamil to denote "making an idli" can also mean "shooting".'

'You are saying this is a plot to assassinate a white man. "Vessel" could mean a gun of sorts here.' Hall was getting excited.

'Yes, Sir,' Tulasi nodded.

'Marriage must be a code word. This refers to an event or a date. Here's what we do. Have the postcard delivered. Both of you will go to the address on the card and arrest anyone who's there. Bring them to me. I still haven't lost my interrogation skills.'

Hall was immersed in thought as Tulasi and Chanduru left.

It was nine when they arrived at the house and the occasional oil-fed street lights provided only enough illumination for them to see the lamp posts and not much farther. It was a small tiled house, typical of Tamilian houses. Chanduru felt around and touched the lock that was hanging on the front door.

'It's locked. There's probably no one at home.'

'Do we break in?' asked Tulasi.

'No,' said Chanduru. 'We don't have a warrant—'

Tulasi started laughing. It was a series of rhythmic coughs ending with a suppressed plosive.

'All right. That shouldn't really stop us. But if someone does come back during the night or by morning, we don't want them scared off by the broken lock.' Chanduru then went down on his knees at the door, placing his cheek on the floor.

'What are you doing?'

Chanduru answered as he got up, straightening his clothes.

'I was just looking under the door to see if there was any sign of light. It's an old trick that criminals use, to be locked in by an accomplice so that people think they are not in. But I see no signs of a light.'

'What do we do?' asked Tulasi. 'Do we wait all night?'

'No,' said the superior officer. 'We leave now and come back here tomorrow morning, say by ten. When I say we, I actually mean you. If the occupant of the house hasn't returned, you make enquiries with the neighbours. Let's go. I am feeling sleepy already.'

13 June 1911

Hall came into the room that had been designated as the 'Head Office, Camp' at noon. His eyes were bloodshot. He had met up with an old soldier at the Kumbakonam club and they had been drinking for the most part of the previous evening and late into the night and had killed a bottle of Glenlivet whisky together. Hall had woken up so late that his breakfast had turned into a breakfast-cum-lunch.

Both Chanduru and Tulasi were waiting for him. Chanduru indicated with his eyes and a tilt of the head at Tulasi to begin the report.

'It was eight o'clock when Inspector Chanduru and I reached the alleged perpetrator's house—'

'—Just get to the point,' Hall mumbled, head between his hands.

'The house was locked,' said Chanduru. 'We waited till late and when no one turned up, we decided to come back in the morning.' He again inclined his head at Tulasi, who took out his notebook, moistened his finger with saliva and began to turn the pages furiously.

'Just give me the gist,' growled Hall.

'Yes, Sir. We went again this morning and the door was just bolted from outside and was not locked. We checked with the neighbours and located the house owner who said the occupant had left early in the morning after settling the rent.'

'So you let him go. Did you search the house? Do you know where he has gone?'

'We searched the house and found nothing, Sir, except for some blackened bits of paper and ash in one of the rooms. No one seems to know where he has gone.'

Hall exploded. 'Get the hell out of here, you buffoons.'

Tulasi took a step back, but Chanduru remained where he was

and spoke. 'We have further information from Pondicherry, Sir, from the cook at Iyer's house.'

Hall was calmer now. 'So, out with it.'

'Apparently, Panju and Iyer had some altercation and the cook was able to listen in. It involved a woman called Ranjitham, who is said to be Panju's kept woman. She is a temple dancer in Kumbakonam.'

'So, bring the woman in. I will interrogate her.'

'We also now have a clear description of Panju, Sir. Apparently he has long hair and a stubbly growth of beard.'

'Circulate the additional description to our people. And bring in the floozy.'

'Yes, Sir. And I have already circulated the description, Sir,' said Chanduru. He then saluted and left with Tulasi.

THIRTY-NINE

13 June 1911

Ranjitham read and reread the letter from Panju in the streaming light, her right shoulder resting on the wall next to the window.

> *Love of my life,*
>
> *The day that I will meet you again is near. Memories of your beautiful form torment me constantly. Anything that I see in Pondicherry reminds me of you. I cannot tell you anything more, but I am going to perform the most important action of my life. Perhaps the last thing that I will ever do. But I need to be with you, for one evening at least. I will see you soon.*
>
> *Your lover,*
> *Panju.*

Tears streaked down her cheeks of their own volition. She stopped reading, looked at the vertical bars of the window. She twisted around. Even her shadow on the ground seemed imprisoned. She looked again through the window and saw two men walking down the street, stopping once or twice to ask for directions. She knew instinctively that they were bound for her home. She tucked the letter between her breasts and adjusted her sari around it. She wiped her eyes with the edge of her sari and walked towards the main door that was usually left open.

'What do you want?' she asked them.

'Is this Ranjitham's house?' the older one asked.

She nodded.

'You need to come with us.'

'Who are you?'

'We are the police,' said Tulasi.

'We are the CID,' said Chanduru.

'Are you arresting me?'

'No,' said Chanduru, 'we want you for questioning.' He waited a while and in response to the question in Ranjitham's eyes, said, 'In connection with a sedition case.'

'Why not here?'

'Our boss, the dorai, wants to question you,' said Tulasi. We are taking you to him.'

'Do you know Panju?' asked Chanduru.

'Do you want to question me here?'

'No.'

They walked in silence, one on either side of Ranjitham.

Panju is in trouble. I have to give the best performance of my career. I may have to use all the navarasas.

She repeated the names of the rasas and their meanings to herself.

Sringaram—love. Hasyam—mirth. Raudram—fury.
Karunyam—compassion. Bibhatsam—disgust.
Bhayanakam—terror. Viram—heroism. Adbhutam—
wonder.
Lord Kumbeswara, help me.

When they arrived at his makeshift office, Hall didn't get up from the chair or even look up.

'Your name?' asked Hall in his accented Tamil.

'Ranjitham.'

'Father's name?'

Silence.

Hall looked up. Turned to Tulasi. 'Write, "doesn't know".'

'Mother?'

'Parvatam.'

'Occupation? Oh don't bother, write "prostitute".'

'No, I am not a common prostitute. I am a devadasi dedicated to Lord Kumbeswara.'

'And you live at…'

'11, Attakkaran Street.'

'Who else lives there?'

'My mother, Varadu, a distant relative, a maid servant and myself.'

'Do you know a Panju, Pancha…Pancha…'

'Panchapakesan, Sir,' Chanduru intervenes.

They already know. Stick to the truth as much as possible. There will be a time for outright lying.

'Yes.'

'You meet him often?'

'He has come home a couple of times. He has come to some of my performances.'

'You are intimate with him?'

Silence.

'What does he do?'

'He is a Brahmin boy who was studying in Kumbakonam and now has a job.'

'Where?'

'Some press. I don't remember the name.'

'Where is he now?'

A beat. 'I haven't seen him for some time. I don't know.'

'He is in serious trouble,' said Chanduru. 'He is plotting trouble against His Majesty's government. Tell us all you know about him. Otherwise you will be held for aiding him in a serious crime.'

Hall shot him a look that said 'You're talking too much'.

Bhayanakam. Ranjitham cowered. 'I really don't know anything.'

'How much does he pay you every month?'

Hasyam. 'Nothing now. He will have to start shortly.'

'Why do you say that?'

'He has fought with his father and run away from home.'
Adbhutam. Stardust glittered in her eyes. 'His father is a wealthy
mirasudar in the Tiruvaiyaru area with over a thousand acres
of land. He will soon be reconciled with his father—I will see to
that—then I will be showered with gold.'

Hall started laughing. 'Tell her, Chanduru.'

'He is the son of a poor Brahmin who does not own any land.
His father makes his living teaching the Vedas and other shastras
to children in Tiruvaiyaru.'

Raudram. Her brows knit, eyes widened. Chest heaved. 'What,
the son of a whore has been lying to me?'

Hall still had the vestiges of an amused look on his face. He
got up. Took a step nearer. Switched to English. 'Now my pet.' He
switched back to Tamil. 'What will you do?'

'Well, my mother has been negotiating with a zamindar—'
She stopped abruptly and looked at Hall who was now just a foot
away from her. *Sringaram.* Her eyelashes fluttered rapidly. 'You
like me. You want me?' Her lips pouted.

Hall's eyes blazed suddenly. His fists bunched up and he lashed
out hard and hit Ranjitham on the side of her head.

'You fucking bitch. You think I want to get clap—'

He stopped suddenly. As Ranjitham fell down, her sari slipped
from her shoulders and a folded piece of paper fluttered to the
ground.

'Aiya, she is—' Tulasi said, pleading in his voice as he picked
up the fallen letter.

'—Read it,' Hall commanded.

Tulasi read the letter as Ranjitham, still on the ground, looked
on with increasing horror.

Hall walked up to her calmly. With no change in his expression,
he kicked Ranjitham, his heavy boot thudding into her cheek
instead of full on her face as she managed to turn her head a little.

'That was for lying to me that you didn't know where he was. Now get out.'

As she got up, blood running down her cheek and from the corner of her mouth, bibatsam, viram and raudram came unbidden until raudram dominated. She was Kannagi about to reduce Madurai to ashes; she was Kali about to perform a death dance. Her eyes were embers of coal as she slowly and deliberately clasped her hands together, fingers entwined, extended them till they pointed to Hall's knees and muttered a curse. She then clapped her hands once.

'Sir,' said an obviously agitated Tulasi, 'that is a terrible curse. The curse of a Nityasumangali.'

Even as Ranjitham left the office, unmindful of her disarrayed sari, Hall's laughter resonated in her ears.

FORTY

The letters on the arch—'Kumbakonam United Services Club'—were freshly painted, but the tin sheet itself showed signs of its age. A small board by the side proclaimed 'Members Only'.

Robert Hall walked along the verandah and through the curtained entrance. He wanted to avoid company and steered his way to a small table for two. He had just seated himself when a cheery 'Good day to you, Sir', made him look up. It was the soldier friend with whom he had spent the previous evening drinking.

'And good day to you, my friend,' he replied, trying to remember the man's name.

'Well, I thought I would have only the company of this,' the soldier said, brandishing a bottle. 'Now I see I may be privileged to have your company too. If I am not intruding, I propose that you and I toast to our health with the help of my companion.'

Hall inclined his head to ask the soldier to be seated.

'Let me introduce you,' the visitor said, 'to this excellent bottle of a genuine Imperial Highland whisky.'

He asked the waiter for ice, glasses and the soda siphon. Robert was morose and monosyllabic, but his friend didn't seem to notice. He prattled on.

'…Two weeks from now, it will be all fun and frolic in England. I'd love to be at Westminster Abbey then. Not that our George has invited me. But it should be a great occasion—just like these big native weddings, but on a much grander scale.'

Robert was suddenly interested. He had just had an epiphany.

Two days before the marriage.

'Why, the coronation is on the twenty-second of this month, right?'

'Yes…'

Hall's mind was racing. He didn't hear any more of what his friend said.

FORTY-ONE

14 June 1911

Hall went for a walk just as the sun came up. He wanted to clear his head. By the time he returned, it had turned hot and uncomfortably muggy. He had a bath in the cold water that had already been drawn for him and finished a breakfast of toast and eggs with coffee. He was relaxed and as he walked into the office, Chanduru and Tulasi were already waiting.

'Let's summarize what we know. Chanduru, go ahead, start.'

'The individual called Panju is probably being trained in shooting by Iyer and other conspirators to carry out an assassination of a white man, presumably at the Kumbakonam railway station. We do not know, as yet, when he is coming in or when the assassination is planned. We—'

'—I have figured out the code in the letter from Pondicherry,' Hall said. '"Marriage" probably refers to the coronation of His Majesty, King George. The assassination is planned for that day. The twenty-second of June—that is this month. The assassin will probably come in from Pondicherry two days before that, that is, on the twentieth.'

'That was really clever of you, Sir,' said Tulasi.

'When you have been in this business for as long as I have, and have a naturally analytical mind… Never mind, continue.' Both Tulasi and Chanduru had spent a considerably longer time in the police force, unless one counted the time Hall spent on the other side of the business. They forbore to mention their length in the service.

'We have to find out who the intended victim is. Tulasi, get the list of British officials who will be passing through or alighting at Kumbakonam station on the twenty-second of June from the stationmaster. Continue your summation, Chanduru.'

'We have no idea who the intended victim is,' Chanduru said. 'We have a complete description of Panju that has since been circulated. We also know that he has an accomplice in Kumbakonam, who has slipped through our net.'

'I have a problem with all this,' said Hall. There are too many "probablys" involved. We have so far been on the defensive. Now we have to take the fight to the enemy territory.'

'Sir,' Chanduru said, 'won't anything we do on French soil create an international incident?'

'So, we hire a local to do the deed. That will give us sufficient deniability. Do we know the bugger's habits?'

'Every evening, he meets Iyer at a desolate spot that they use as a shooting range. They arrive and leave separately.'

'Do we have him killed or something, Sir?' asked Tulasi, anxiety showing on his face.

'No, I want him alive.'

'Chanduru, take out a warrant for his arrest on charges of sedition so that he can be arrested as soon as he enters British territory. I will speak to the District Magistrate about this.'

'What exactly are we going to do, Sir?'

'Kidnap him,' said Hall.

FORTY-TWO

17 June 1911, Pondicherry

It was Panju's idea that they start the shooting practice an hour later. This also meant that they finished much later than usual. Iyer was pleased with his shooting. Panju had scored three bullseyes in seven shots and the grouping was good despite the poor visibility. The moon had taken to hiding behind clouds and only occasionally peeped through.

'You are almost as good a shot as me,' said Iyer.

'Is that a compliment?' Panju retorted and they both laughed.

When they finished, Iyer stretched out his hand for the magazine, but Panju loaded a full magazine into the pistol and tucked it in at his waist.

Iyer retracted his hand. 'I almost forgot. I like your *en passant*. It is bold, imaginative and perhaps a little sneaky.'

'I am sorry. In my month or so here, I haven't learnt much French beyond *comment allez-vous* and *très bien merci*.'

'*En passant* is French, but it's more a chess term. It refers to the play in which you wait for the opponent to make a pawn move two spaces across a square guarded by your own pawn, and gobble up the opponent's pawn.'

'I see,' said Panju in a distracted tone.

'Are you sure you don't want me to come with you?' Iyer asked, concern showing in his eyes.

'I am certain I want to stick with my original plan. I don't want to make anyone suspicious. I think it is already late,' said Panju.

Iyer looked up at the sky. 'Yes,' he said, 'it is close to 8.00 p.m.'

'You haven't looked at your watch. How do you know that is the correct time?'

In answer, Iyer pulled out his pocket watch and showed it to Panju. It was eight o'clock.

'How did you do that?'

'You know my interest in astronomy. I look for the pole star, Dhruva. The seven sapta rishis go around Dhruva. Based on the relative position of the sapta rishis around Dhruva and knowing the month, I can tell the time. And since I know the position of the zodiac constellations, I can tell the time even when Dhruva is not visible. Anyway, it is getting late. You should be on your way. Be careful.'

As Panju walked along the rapidly darkening road, he kept his head straight, but his eyes darted to and fro to take in as much as possible with his peripheral vision. The road was deserted, and the sound of his own footsteps was so amplified and distorted that he had the constant feeling that someone was following him. Then he saw what he was looking out for.

Two figures that moved a little behind a tamarind tree. He walked past the tree affecting a nonchalance he didn't feel. His senses were now on a hair-trigger. He walked a dozen steps before he heard it. A rustle. A scrape. He counted slowly to five and turned around abruptly.

He easily recognized Murugesan lagging behind the huge man who was now sauntering towards him. He wore a half-vest tucked into a pair of faded trousers with no belt. His biceps were defined clearly in the moonlight as were his grinning teeth.

'Stop right there,' Panju shouted, his hand going to his waist. Murugesan froze.

'Or else what, you will break my bones?' said the huge man, continuing to advance.

'Seeing that you outweigh me by at least sixty pounds, I would not normally attempt that. However,' said Panju, 'let me try.'

Panju spread his legs a little and crouched low. The big man stood, legs apart, crouching very little. Panju suddenly dived forward at the man's ankles. He wanted to use his body as a lever to take down the big man. But as he dived, the ankle was simply not there. The man moved out of Panju's way. Panju had to scramble up in a hurry. The big man was laughing.

'Listen,' he said, 'I am a champion wrestler. You are not going to take me down this way. Now watch,' he said as he reached for Panju's arm.

Panju took a couple of steps back.

'You are right, my teacher warned me never to go against a trained wrestler of a higher weight class. I may not be able to beat you in a wrestling bout, but,' Panju said, as he reached behind him and pulled out the revolver tucked in at his waist, 'I can drill a hole through you.'

The man stopped and remained still. Murugesan tried to hide behind him.

'Raise your hands above your head and keep them there.' Panju gestured with the gun. 'This is no drama pistol. This is a genuine Browning.'

Murugesan put his hands up quickly. 'Jean, do as he says. That's a real gun. He has been practising with it.'

Jean slowly raised his hands and shot a look of hatred at Murugesan. 'Nobody told me about guns. You knew he had one and didn't tell me. I don't like it,' he said, shaking his head. 'I definitely don't like it.'

'You just have to do exactly what I tell you, Jean. Then you won't get hurt. This is what you do first. Hold Murugesan's hand at the wrist tightly with your left hand. Don't let him squirm out.'

'Why would he want to?' muttered Jean as he held Murugesan's wrist as instructed.

'I suspect that he might want to at some time. But first, I must apologize to you for changing the script right in the middle of the scene. I understand how difficult it is for the actors, but I just can't help it. This is how the new script goes. Jean, you will take out from your trouser pocket, the bottle of chloroform that you have and, of course, the rag or whatever you planned to use—'

'—How do you know all this?' Murugesan spluttered, looking suspiciously at Jean.

'A pet imp of mine told me. Anyway, that's none of your business. Jean, take it out.'

Jean fished out a bottle and a cotton rag from his pocket. He managed to do it while retaining his hold on Murugesan.

'Now, no tricks. Don't try to fling it at me or something. The safety is off and my finger is on the trigger. You will be blown away before you start anything. Now soak the cotton in the liquid and hold it over Murugesan's nose and mouth until he is unconscious. However long it takes. You are the expert.'

Murugesan tried to pull himself loose. His squirming died down slowly as Jean pressed the rag over his nose and mouth and held it there. Jean released him after a while and Murugesan fell to the ground, bumping his head in the process.

'That's a job well done,' said Panju. 'But you could have stopped his fall, you know.'

'I know,' agreed Jean, his face showing no emotion.

'I am a little hazy about this part of the original script. What were you planning to do with me after I fell unconscious?'

'I was supposed to carry you back in the sack over there,' Jean said, pointing to the hessian bag that lay half-covered by the trunk of the tamarind tree. 'I was to take you back to the cart that is stationed just after the bend in this road and collect my balance payment.'

'Who is in the cart?'

'The two people who hired me. They sent Murugesan with me to point you out in case you were with someone else.'

'What was Murugesan supposed to do after you bagged me?'

'He was to be on his way as soon as you were unconscious.'

'This is what I want you to do. You will stuff Murugesan into the bag, tie its mouth and deliver him to the cart. I will be following along, taking cover in the trees alongside the road. So, no tricks. I can shoot fairly well up to twenty-five feet. I will be no farther than fifteen feet at any point of time and you present a fairly large target.'

'Can I collect my balance payment?'

'Of course, you will have earned it.'

Jean checked that Murugesan was breathing and stuffed him feet first into the sack, tied its mouth with a piece of jute string and hoisted it on to his shoulder with little effort. Panju followed him, keeping to the trees along the side of the road, as he walked up to the cart. The men in the cart took the sack. A brief altercation followed. One of the men ended up being pulled out of the cart. Then the man reached into his pocket and gave Jean some coins before getting back in. Jean waited till the cart was out of sight before he ambled back.

Panju joined him.

'I wish I could see their faces when they find Murugesan in the sack.'

'So do I,' said Jean. 'But it might take a while. According to the original plan, they are to open the bag only after they are in British-controlled lands. But the good thing is they have been instructed to kick the sack if there is any sign of life from within.'

'I think I like you,' said Panju. 'Aren't you upset I pulled a gun on you?'

'No. Anyway I got my money. In fact I was able to collect a little more by claiming you were far heavier than you were supposed to be. I had to use some persuasion.'

'I saw that,' said Panju.

'Can I go now?'

'Just one question. Won't the people who paid you be after you now? What are you going to do?'

'Them? They are British CID. They can't even wipe their arse properly. Anyway, I am from French Karaikal. I came here for a holiday for a week. I have been to all the night spots. I am done here. I am returning tonight. If they come to Karaikal, at least some of them won't return. In any case they do not know I am from Karaikal. And of course, my name isn't Jean.'

They walked in silence for a while.

'Can I go now?' the huge man asked.

'I suppose so.'

'Then, adieu,' the big man said as he walked away.

'Romba thanks monsieur,' Panju shouted after him.

Forty-three

'The sons of whores have botched it up again,' Hall fumed. 'We simply cannot depend upon them to get anything right.'

The story of a dazed Murugesan tumbling out of a sack at the small border town in Madras had already spread through the force and was threatening to become a huge embarrassment for the CID.

'Sir,' said Tulasi. 'I have some news. On the twenty-second one Mr Edmund Worthington is going to be travelling from Madras to Tanjore. The stationmaster has verified that he has booked an entire compartment.'

'Worthington? Wasn't he the Collector of Tirunelveli a couple of years ago? He scarpered and scurried back to England when things got too hot for him after that firing he had ordered.'

'Yes, Sir, I am told that he is taking charge as Collector of Tanjore,' said Tulasi.

'If he is the only British official travelling on that day, we can assume that he is the intended victim.'

'Should we warn him?' asked Chanduru.

'Warn that lily-livered poltroon? He will probably cancel his ticket and travel incognito. No, we will simply tighten our security net at all railway stations. Make sure that there are enough people at Villuppuram. That's the connecting station from Pondicherry, right?'

'Yes, Sir,' said Tulasi, consulting his diary. 'The train from Madras reaches Villuppuram at 23.16 and halts for fifteen minutes and arrives at Kumbakonam at 3.28 a.m.'

'So let us concentrate on people boarding the train at Villuppuram. They should be checked. Let two people travel on the train from Madras. We won't get any sleep on that day since we too, will be at Kumbakonam railway station as insurance. In the meanwhile, you two will be on continuous surveillance at that dancer's place.'

'It is not a problem at night,' said Chanduru. 'During the day, it is impossible to watch the place without being seen.'

'Maybe Tulasi can watch in disguise—perhaps as a blind beggar. If he takes his shirt off and shaves off his moustache, he will look like a regular beggar on the street.'

Hall watched with malicious glee as Tulasi's hand went to his moustache even as his eyes widened in horror.

'Sir, we can instead replace the beat constables,' said Chanduru quickly before Hall could dwell further on his plan.

'Yes, Sir,' Tulasi said, shooting a look of relief at Chanduru, 'the people of Attakkaran Street have bribed, I mean, persuaded the Circle Inspector to have two constables on duty, one during each shift, patrolling the road. I think we could replace either without raising any suspicion.'

'I will take the day duty and report to you at the end of the shift and Tulasi can do the night shift and report in the morning,'

'Fine, settle that among yourselves,' said Hall.

'Don't we need to have people at Tiruvaiyaru?' asked Tulasi.

'No, I don't think it's worthwhile to monitor that old Brahmin couple. Anyway, ask the local constable there to be on the lookout.'

20 June 2011

Hall went to bed early that night. He woke in the morning hearing a hubbub on the verandah and stepped out in his dressing gown. Tulasi stood there, bleary-eyed. He had another man handcuffed to him.

'What the devil is this?'

'This is Jatin. I was monitoring Ranjitham's place on Attakkaran Street, when I found him calling out and speaking to her. He asked her if she had any news from Panju. She said no. I heard her referring to him as Jatin. I waited till she had closed the door and nabbed and handcuffed him. It happened last night. I was waiting for a decent time to see you.'

'What does he say for himself?'

'Nothing. He has clamped his mouth shut.'

'Oh, we will fix that,' said Hall, perking up. 'Here's what you do. Take him to the empty room next to mine. Handcuff him, hands behind his back and tie him to a chair. I am sure you can find some good hemp rope somewhere. Then you are free to go home and get some sleep. I will see you later this evening along with Shandroo. Until then leave him to me. Oh, and stuff something in his mouth.'

Jatin stared at Hall. His eyes spat venom.

'You don't want him arrested, Sir?' asked Tulasi.

'All in good time. Just do what I asked you to.'

'Not a bad day's work,' thought Hall. He was particularly pleased that he had not even had to step out of the inspection bungalow to achieve all that he had. He lit a Trichinopoly cigar and leant back in his chair. He was still mellow when Chanduru and Tulasi entered.

'I have nothing to report, Sir,' Chanduru said.

'That is fine. We have made progress today.'

'Did Jatin talk, Sir?' asked Tulasi.

'He held out for nearly an hour. That was impressive and better than par for the course with me. He started singing only when I lit a fire under his toes. A little old-fashioned. But works every time. He admitted to sedition. By the way, Tulasi, this is the man who received the telegram about cooks and marriage. I managed to extract from him the date on which Panju is arriving. He was supposed to arrive on the twentieth. Now he will be arriving on the twenty-second. That alters our plans only very slightly. Unfortunately, he doesn't know much more. He is, of course, in cahoots with Iyer. But these extremists have learnt their lessons. They seem to operate in small cells entirely on a "need to know" basis.'

'So what do we do now, Sir? Search his present residence?'

'I have already sent out a constable to do that. We have recovered some seditious literature. I think we have the little bastard now. In any case, continue surveillance at Ranjitham's house.'

Hall paused to flick the ash from the cigar on to the ground and take a long pull.

'Oh yes, take the prisoner away to a police lock-up. Produce him before the magistrate in two days' time. Get the bugger some medical treatment. We don't want him limping too badly into the courtroom. He has burn marks on his toes. He has a cut under the eye that may require a stitch or two. He shouldn't have resisted arrest so violently. Right, Tulasi?'

'Yes, Sir,' said Tulasi.

JUNE 1911

PONDICHERRY, KUMBAKONAM

FORTY-FOUR

20 June 1911

All through the day, Panju found it hard to suppress his excitement. Iyer had said that he would take Panju to meet a spiritually advanced jnani.

'Are we meeting Sri Aravinda Ghose?' Panju asked, eagerness adding an octave to his voice.

'Yes,' said Iyer, smiling. 'It is Aurobindo Ghose.'

'The great revolutionary leader,' Panju said softly.

'No longer that,' said Iyer. 'He is now completely immersed in his spiritual sadhana.'

Panju saw him seated on a chair, in a white dhoti and a white shawl. He took in his long hair, parted slightly to the left, his small and slender frame, a scraggly beard that seemed to be growing preferentially on the lower part of his chin. Nothing exceptional, except that his eyes seemed to pierce right into Panju's soul.

'So, this is one of the promised younger generation.' Sri Aurobindo's voice was high-pitched, but seemed to follow its own mesmeric cadence.

'I don't understand, Sir,' said Panju. There was a question mark on Iyer's face too.

'This is what the voice in my mind told me while I was in prison. "This is the young generation," the voice told me, "the new and mighty nation that is arising at my command. They are greater than you. What have you to fear? If you stood aside or slept, the work would still be done. If you were cast aside tomorrow, here are the young men who will take up your work and do it more mightily than you have ever done." In fact, this is the reason I have taken up spiritual work, because it is His will.'

'Bless me, Sir, for I do not know if I am doing the right thing,' said Panju.

'If you are doing His will and consider yourself but an instrument, you will always do the right thing,' said the smiling Sri Aurobindo and closed his eyes, indicating that the interview was at an end.

FORTY-FIVE

21 June 1911

Panju noticed that Iyer was in a melancholic mood all morning.

'How did you know that Worthington's trip had been postponed?' asked Panju.

'I can't tell you that. We operate on the principle of the Russian patriots. You know only enough to carry out the task.'

Iyer kept quiet for a while before he continued.

'It is the lot of people like me to see young men go to their deaths. A burden that I cannot share with anyone else.'

'Are you talking about me?' asked Panju.

'I am talking about myself for a change. I am thinking of brave young men like Madan Lal Dhingra. And now you.'

'Sir,' said Panju. 'I respect you like my father. I deem myself privileged that you have given me this opportunity. Now that you have mentioned Madan Lal Dhingra, I must say that his last words before he was hanged for the assassination of Sir Curzon Wylie have been a source of inspiration for me. His words are engraved in my memory. I am repeating them, not for your sake but for my sake, to renew my inspiration.

"I believe that a nation held down by foreign bayonets is in a perpetual state of war. Since open battle is rendered impossible to a disarmed race, I attacked by surprise. Since guns were denied to me I drew forth my pistol and fired. Poor in wealth and intellect, a son like myself has nothing else to offer to the mother but his own blood. And so I have sacrificed the same on her altar. The only lesson required in India at present is to learn how to die, and the only way to teach it is by dying ourselves. My only prayer to God is that I may be re-born of the same mother and I may re-die in the same sacred cause till the cause is successful. Vande Mataram!"'

Iyer was crying openly now.

Panju looked on, a tightness forming in his throat, while Iyer sobbed like a child.

Forty-six

'I hope all the plans are clear. Gopal will accompany you to Villuppuram. Travel light. Don't even carry a bag. You will board the train there. You will meet Jatin at the entrance to Kumbakonam station and stay with him until the twenty-fourth. You will then go—'

'—I know. If it is on the twenty-fourth and not today as originally planned, won't the symbolism of it coinciding with the coronation be lost?'

'It doesn't matter that much. In fact, this is even better since the British will be more vigilant today, on the day of the coronation. They will be complacent afterwards till King George actually sets foot in India, much later. Anyway you have to leave, dressed as a sardar, complete with a red turban. I must say that your beard and moustache have grown a bit. We will have to make sure that the British CID don't see you leave. Please be very careful in the train. The entire police force has your description and will be on the lookout for you.'

'Which is why I have called for this last-minute visitor.'

A scrawny man with a small face and a pronounced Adam's apple entered, carrying a tin box with him.

Iyer saw him and exclaimed, 'Panju, why?' He thought for a moment and continued, 'I understand,' then added with a smile on his face, 'I don't know why I bother to make plans in the first place.'

Panju and Gopal travelled by road in a horse-drawn jatka. They got off well before the British Indian border and crossed over into the Indian side by making their way through fields. Panju was happy that he was not carrying any luggage. They were scratched badly by brambles and at one point of time Panju felt some liquid flowing down his leg and was horrified to find a leech on his leg. The liquid was his own blood. Gopal calmly lit a cigarette and got the leech off by touching it with the lit end. He held up the matchbox and declared, 'See the power of Swadeshi matches.' Finally, they reached Villuppuram station. It was not crowded. There were two men on the platform who were looking intently at every passenger boarding and getting off the train.

'This is where I say goodbye; farewell my friend,' said Gopal and left without turning back.

Panju was also subjected to the same scrutiny by the two men as he boarded. There were two padded benches, one opposite the other, in the compartment and on one of them sat three men, although the bench was meant for at least four. Panju asked the passengers to move a little and sat next to a young man with long hair tied in a topknot, an unruly beard decorating his chin. It was obvious that he was a swami of sorts. He wore orange robes and a necklace of rudraksha beads.

Panju attempted to speak to him. The swami conveyed to him through signs that he was observing a vow of silence. Panju noticed two of the people on the opposite seat, one of whom appeared to be staring at him. Panju sat in uncomfortable silence. The feeling of danger was palpable.

The train was leaving after its halt at the Mayavaram station when the two men opposite made their move.

'You are Panchapakesan, also known as Panju, aren't you?'

Panju was startled and was about to open his mouth when he realized that the question was addressed not to him, but to the swami seated next to him, and quickly closed his mouth tight.

The swami apparently did not understand the question and tried to indicate that he was observing a vow of silence. The two men were persistent and made the swami sit between them. One of them produced a pair of handcuffs and chained the swami's wrist to his. Panju was ready to bolt as he felt that any moment the swami would speak up and he would be caught.

As soon as the cuffs were produced, the swami's self-imposed silence evaporated and he started protesting. Panju recognized the language as Hindustani from the few Sanskrit words that he caught. The two men tried Tamil, Telugu and English in succession, but could neither understand him nor make themselves understood. Panju breathed in relief.

The train now approached Kumbakonam station and was slowing down for the stop. Panju realized that there would be more people at the station looking for him and came to an abrupt decision. He got out of the compartment, trying to make his exit seem as leisurely as possible, and reached the exit door. He leant out and saw from a distance that the platform would be on the other side of the train. He immediately went over to the door on the other side and as the train slowed down further, stepped out of the train, taking care to face the direction of the train's motion and kicking off backwards, running on the ground forwards for a short distance to restore his balance. He then turned around and started running, away from the platform.

As soon as his feet touched the ground, his thoughts turned to Ranjitham. His feet were leading him to her house.

FORTY-SEVEN

It was at least an hour before dawn when Panju reached Ranjitham's house. The western skies were tinted bright in a magic of refraction, but it was still too dark to see more than a couple of feet in front of him. Ranjitham's room had a window that opened out to the front of the house. It was constructed in such a way that it was easy to look out from inside but impossible to see into the room from the street level. Panju didn't want to wake the household; he certainly did not wish to see Ranjitham's mother. He decided to look through the window. He had to jump to catch hold of the narrow windowsill and pull himself up to be able to see into the room.

Ranjitham was asleep. An oil lamp cast a huge shadow of her body on the wall opposite.

'Ranjitham,' Panju called out in a whisper.

Ranjitham turned around, facing him, but did not open her eyes.

'Ranjitham.' This time he called out louder. His arms and fingers were tiring and he was not sure how long he would be able to hold his position, as the sill was narrow and he was practically hanging by his fingers.

Ranjitham awoke like a cat, all senses alert, and adjusting her sari on her shoulders in one fluid motion, grabbed the oil lamp and came to the window.

'It's me, Panju. I need to see you,' said Panju as he dropped back to street level.

'Wait, I'll open the door.'

'For a moment, I didn't recognize you,' she said, opening the door.

Panju was perplexed for a moment. Then he laughed.

'Oh, you mean this,' he said, rubbing his smooth chin with one hand and his scalp with the other. 'Before I left Pondicherry, I had a barber over who gave me a haircut and a shave. I am glad I did that because it saved my life on the train.'

'I think it suits you. But I thought as a Brahmin you are supposed to maintain a topknot.'

'I used to be proud of my kudumi and my Brahmin traditions until I met a man—a great poet—who convinced me that all living beings, even crows and sparrows, as he put it, are one species. Anyway, enough about me, let's talk about you. Didn't you miss me?'

Ranjitham, who was still holding the oil lamp, placed it next to a pillar on the thinnai. Now Panju could not see her expression.

'I think you should go,' said Ranjitham as Panju sat on the thinnai. 'It is not safe for you to be here. I think my house is being watched. I was called to the police station a week ago. They were asking about you, by name.'

'And they let you go?'

'Yes, probably to watch me and trap you or anyone connected with you who came to see me. Your friend Jatin came looking for you a couple of days back. As he left, I looked through the window and saw him being arrested.'

Panju felt cornered. Now he had nowhere to go.

'You have still not answered my question,' said Panju, an edge in his voice. 'Did you miss me?'

'Panju, I think you should stop meeting me. You should forget me.'

A flash of anger struck him. He got up abruptly and started pacing till the anger was replaced by an overwhelming sadness.

'What's wrong, Ranju, what has changed?' he asked softly.

'Nothing, I just changed my mind.'

'What do you mean?'

Ranjitham averted her eyes before she spoke. 'You don't know? You have no money. You have no job. The police hunt you. I am now committed to the Rajapuram zamindar. I need the money. My mother and I need the security.'

Panju did not catch the lack of emotion in Ranjitham's voice. The veins at his temples began to throb.

'You don't want me? I am not about to beg you. I promise you one thing. I will not see you again as long as I live.' He turned and walked away quickly. If he had continued looking at her, he would not have missed the tears that glistened in Ranjitham's eyes.

The anger evaporated to be replaced by grief and then determination, though the hurt remained. One more reason not to deviate from performing the task for which he had been brought into the world.

He felt eyes on him again. His peripheral vision had caught a movement in the bushes. He stopped and looked around. No movement. Must have been a freak gust of wind. He took stock of the situation. He must spend another day in hiding before the big day. With Jatin arrested, he had nowhere to go. And he had one more bit of unfinished business. *Meenakshi*. He walked on with a determined stride.

He couldn't get the image of Meenakshi with her dark kohl-smudged eyes out of his mind. There was one more thing that he had to do. He had to go to Tiruvaiyaru. It would be safe for him to take the train there since no one would be looking out for him in that direction.

JUNE 1911
TIRUVAIYARU

Forty-eight

22 June 1911, Tiruvaiyaru

He met Murugan in front of his house, cleaning the cart with straw and water.

'Is Chinnamma in?' he asked.

'Yes, Aiya. Chinnamma is in her room. Periya Aiya is not well. Periyamma has gone to the temple.'

Panju hurried to his room, not even bothering to wash his feet. Meenakshi saw him and her lips parted in a gesture of surprise and pleasure. She came running to him, pulling back at the last moment, overcome by shyness.

'How have you been?' Panju asked, holding her gently by the shoulders.

'You have lost weight,' said Meenakshi, head still bowed. 'You have not been looking after yourself. You are not eating properly.'

'Meenakshi, I came specifically to tell you something.'

The pleading tone in his voice must have emboldened Meenakshi.

'Don't tell me anything. I still haven't recovered from the last time you tried to tell me something.'

'I have treated you badly, haven't I? I want you to forgive me.'

'Did you say that to that…that…dancer too?'

'Meenu, I am completely out of her spell now. I have come to apologize before I do something worthwhile with my life.'

Meenakshi did not answer immediately. She went to the far wall of the room and spread out the jamakkalam that had been rolled up along with a pillow.

Meenakshi had a smile on her face as she said, 'Why don't we sit here and talk?' she went to the door, shut it and bolted it.

'Don't think I don't know anything,' Meenakshi looked at him archly. 'An Akka from my village told me everything, including how to behave with a husband.'

Fire started in his loins and spread as he kissed her. He carried her to the jamakkalam and their lovemaking was frenetic. Meenakshi cried out in pain once.

'This time I won't hurt you,' said Panju and they made love slowly. Meenakshi cried out again, but not in pain. They lay together, exhausted. Panju put his arm around Meenakshi and stroked her hair.

'Meenakshi,' said Panju.

'Mmm.'

'I have important work, I have to be on my way.'

'Enna, tell me something— '

'—Call me Panju.'

'I can't. A wife is not supposed to utter her husband's name. It will reduce her husband's lifespan.'

'Just once, why don't you say it?'

'All right,' said Meenakshi. 'Panju,' she said and giggled. 'Tell me something, when we were…busy, why did you whisper "Aravan"? Is that another girlfriend with a male name?'

'Did I say that? I don't know. The only Aravan I know is a character in the Mahabharata. He was the son of Arjuna, the great warrior. Aravan was a hero who offered himself as a sacrifice at the beginning of the Great War so that his side—the Pandavas— could win. However, he had a last wish. Since he was a virgin, he requested Krishna that he should have knowledge of sex and Krishna granted his wish. Now, I must be going.'

'It is inauspicious to say "I am going". Say you will go and come,' said Meenakshi.

Panju laughed as he slipped on his shirt, and unbolted the door. The laughter sounded hollow even to him.

As he went out the door, Meenakshi said, 'Please see your father before you go. He has not been well.'

'I know,' said Panju. 'I am doing just that.'

❖

Panju found Sambu lying down in his room, clearly asleep. He touched his forehead and withdrew his hand quickly in a reflex action. It was burning hot.

He was confused. There seemed to be two beings who sat in his head arguing.

It is your duty as a son to stay back and look after your father.

No, it is your duty, as the saint Tiruvalluvar said, to act in such a way that people will wonder what great austerities the father must have performed to be blessed with such a noble child.

Panju remembered the occasion years ago when he had fallen very sick and the doctor had prescribed a medicine that he said could have ill effects, but there was no other option. Sambu had taken the medicine himself and waited for a day to ensure that there were no ill effects before giving it to his son.

I have to do what I have to.

'I hope you are going to be here till your father gets better.' Bhavani held a tumbler of hot gruel as she entered the room.

'No, Amma. I have to leave now. Please send for Janaki to come and look after Appa.'

Bhavani was getting visibly angrier. 'Panju, you don't have to tell us what to do. Are you going to stay or not? Because, if you are not, I don't know in what shape your Appa will be, the next time you see him.'

'Amma, I have to go.'

Bhavani now switched tactics. 'Won't you stay at least for your mother's sake?'

'Amma, right now I have to go for the sake of a hundred million mothers.'

With that, Panju turned and left without looking back.

FORTY-NINE

23 June 1911

Janaki got up, as usual, before the sun was up and went to the front of the house to draw the kolam. She had decided on an elaborate one in a hexagonal shape starting with eight dots, increasing to fifteen dots in the centre and tapering to eight dots again. The pattern would be a repeating motif of birds and flowers. When she saw Murugan waiting with his cart, she felt a frisson of dread.

'What happened, Murugan?'

'Aiya is not feeling too well. Periyamma asked me to bring you home.'

She quickly drew a simple kolam in a square shape with a single loop at each of its corners and a dot in the centre. She wrote a note for Reverend Porter asking for a leave of absence and another for Arul. She washed and changed in a hurry. She informed Chittappa that she was going back to Tiruvaiyaru. Chittappa seemed very concerned that his brother was sick. 'Tell him I will see him next week,' he said.

Bhavani met her even before she got out of the cart.

'He keeps muttering in a delirium,' Bhavani said. 'There are only some moments when he is clear and lucid. He doesn't ask for food. I have been trying to feed him. He eats a little bit and refuses the rest, complaining of acute stomach ache.'

Bhavani rushed to her father's room. Sambu seemed weaker than before. His collarbones stuck out conspicuously and his breathing was heavy. He was muttering something. Janaki went closer, but could make out only a few words.

'Mangalam...I am sorry...the flowers are crushed...'

Janaki shook him a little. His eyes opened. 'Appa, this is me. Janaki.'

'Janaki,' he said, opening his eyes more fully. 'Hasn't Panju come?' He spoke with increasing clarity. 'I am sorry. I should have guided you better. I left you and Panju to yourselves. If I had spent some more time with Panju, he would not have gone away. And I should have got you married at the right time.'

'Appa,' said Janaki, 'you have given us the greatest gift a father can give. You have encouraged us to think independently. You have allowed us to make our own mistakes rather than you making them for us. In any case, Appa, I had vowed that I would not get married until I finished my education and that still stands.'

Sambu closed his eyes for a while, his forehead and eyebrows contorting with pain. He opened his eyes again.

'Please send word to Swamigal. Tell him he must come immediately. Tell the doctor to give me something to reduce the pain. I know he cannot cure me.'

'Appa, don't talk like that. In a few days you will be all right and you will be wondering if you were ever sick.'

Sambu's lips parted in what started as a smile and ended as a grimace.

'Janaki, I think you should go back. You will be missing your studies.'

'I am not moving from your side till you get better, Appa.'

'Thank you, Janu,' he whispered.

The physician came and examined Sambu.

'The only thing that you can do is try and keep him cool with a wet cloth on his forehead. I give him seventy-two hours,' he said.

'To get better?' Bhavani asked.

The physician shook his head.

FIFTY

24 June 1911

Sambu's fever had abated a little. He was no longer delirious, but the physician took one look at him and said, 'You should inform relatives.'

Janaki had already sent a message to Sambu's brother in Tanjore about his condition. Bhavani was upset at the physician. 'You shouldn't say something inauspicious like that,' she said.

Sambu indicated that he wanted to go to the riverside, but the vaidyan forbade that, saying he was in no condition to travel.

Janaki said, 'In any case, Appa, the main branch of the Cauvery has hardly any water. It is only a thin stream in a damp bed.'

'Don't worry, in a couple of months she will be in spate,' Sambu said. Or wanted to say.

At Sambu's request, Janaki moved him with the help of the vaidyan to the thinnai where they spread a mattress on a cot.

There were clouds in the sky, some of them dark, but there was no immediate rain.

He lay on his back thinking of another day just like this one. The thought of Mangalam brought the smell of kadambam to his nostrils. He thought of the times when he would teach, his resonant voice heard even at the end of the road. He thought of Panju, the son born of a hundred pilgrimages. But something had changed. The thoughts now seemed to belong to someone else. He felt neither happy nor sad.

My obeisances unto the ferocious and powerful Mahavisnu, the fiery one, who faces all directions, the fearful one, Narsimha, who is death to death itself.

He muttered to himself.

'Has Swamigal come?' he asked aloud. His voice was still such a low hoarse whisper that Janaki did not hear it.

He then heard the sound of Vedic hymns approaching the house. 'He has come,' he said.

The Swamigal was clad in his usual orange garb. A group of people from the ashram followed him. He gestured for his followers to stop and placed a hand on Sambu's head and said, 'At last I am going to do what you always wanted. I am going to give you sanyasa diksha.' He whispered the secret Karna mantra and the four Mahavakyas into his right ear.

Brahman is Awareness.

This soul is Brahman.

You are That.

I am Brahman.

Sambu's lips moved in repetition. He now had a smile on his face.

'Water,' he said, looking at Swamigal with effort.

Swamigal nodded.

'Shall I bring some water to drink?' asked Janaki.

'No, that is not what he wanted,' said Swamigal.

The smile on Sambu's face had now become fixed, his eyes open and staring.

Swamigal closed the open eyelids.

'There are two ways a sanyasi's body can be returned to the elements—by burying it in the earth or by immersion in water. He has just indicated that he wishes to be immersed in the Cauvery.'

Janaki and Bhavani watched as Sambu's body was placed on the banks of the Kollidam and washed by pouring pots of water over it. Meenakshi stood quietly to one side. Then one of the priests took a coconut that had been dehusked, leaving only a small cone of husk, raised it above his head and brought it down with an audible crash on the head. Janaki put her hands to her ears and Bhavani cried out despite Swamigal warning them. He had explained that this had to be done as the departing soul of a sanyasi needs to exit through the top of the skull.

A boat took Sambu's body to the middle of the Kollidam. A large stone was tied to his waist with a hemp rope and the body was lowered into the river.

Bhavani and Janaki had many callers the following day, including relatives whom Janaki had never seen. Vichu, too, had come. He said, 'I am truly sorry, little sister. I wish things had happened differently. I lost one sister and now I have the misfortune of seeing another widowed.' Janaki found the obvious overwhelming grief that he exhibited quite strange and not in character.

John Porter said, shaking his head, 'A great man, a truly great scholar. It's a huge loss for everyone.'

Janaki said, 'I am not sure when I can attend college. My mother will be alone here. Meenakshi is also a young girl. Her father died a month ago, orphaning her. We are not sure where Panju is at the moment. Until he comes back I cannot return.'

'Take your time,' said Reverend Porter, 'But, of course, you need to be back at least a month before the examination.'

Many others said good things about Sambu, most of them taking care to say—'in the previous phase of his life' as befits someone who had taken sanyasa.

'I have something to say to you in person,' Arul said, after condoling with her.

'Before you say anything, I have a question to ask of you. Will you first answer that?'

'Go ahead, I am willing to wait for my question,' said Arul.

'Look at this purely hypothetical situation. You want to do something that is very dear to your heart. You cannot because it will affect others around you. Will you still go ahead and do it?'

'Janaki, my God died on the cross for all of humanity, including me. Every day I witness this sacrifice being represented during Mass. As a Christian, I am supposed to imitate Him. Does that answer your question?'

'Well, yes and no,' said Janaki. 'I didn't expect you to answer from your particular viewpoint. Anyway, I'll take it.'

Arul hesitated a little before saying, 'I know this is absolutely the wrong time to talk of this. But I don't know when I will get an opportunity again. You know I travelled to Pondicherry and met the spiritual director at my seminary.'

Janaki kept silent.

'I told him about you. He advised me to pray and find the answer. I have been praying constantly ever since. I am now very clear in my mind that I want you even more than I want to be a priest. I travelled again to meet my bishop to tell him that I am clear about my vocation. He seemed disappointed, but understood. Janaki, will you marry me?'

Janaki replied after another prolonged silence. It wasn't clear whether the tears that brimmed over were for her father or for herself.

'Arul, you should know my situation. My mother and my sister-in-law live alone here. They cannot manage on their own. My mother has always had someone to look after her and Meenakshi is still a child. I don't even know where my brother is. Until he comes back, I cannot get married.' Janaki stopped, overcome. She dabbed at her eyes with the edge of her sari and continued, 'I would almost certainly be ostracized if I married you; but I don't care about what our society says. I cannot get a better, more considerate husband than you. It is just that I simply cannot abandon those who are dependent on me.'

'I will wait,' said Arul.

JUNE 1911

KUMBAKONAM

FIFTY-ONE

23 June 1911, Kumbakonam

'The bastards,' said Hall, 'I am going to demote each one of those sons of bitches. They have gone and arrested some weird bugger who can speak only Hindustani. Panju must have slipped right through their hands. Now we have to assume that Panju is already here. Since Worthington wasn't on that train, find out when he will be travelling.' Chanduru and Tulasi stood in front of him, heads bowed, as though atoning for their fatherless colleagues.

The awkward silence was broken by a man in uniform who came in and saluted smartly.

'Sir,' he said, addressing Hall. 'The station master asked me to deliver this to you.'

He handed over about a dozen sheets that were pinned together and left, saluting again.

'See what it is,' said Hall.

'It is the first class passenger manifest for trains passing through Kumbakonam,' said Chanduru, after looking at it for a while. 'It covers the next three days, Sir.'

'Look at trains originating from Madras and read out the list.'

For a couple of minutes Hall concentrated on Chanduru's reading.

Chanduru read: '... Edmund Worthington Mr and Mary Worthington Mrs—'

'—Wait. What date is this for?' asked Hall.

'That's today, Sir,' replied Chanduru.

'—That's it. We have got him now. I hope they don't postpone their travel plans again.' Hall took out his pocket watch. 'We still have some time to warn and detain them at the Madras station. But we won't do that. This is the ideal trap and Worthington is the perfect bait. According to the schedule, the train should be arriving tonight or rather early in the morning tomorrow by 3.28 a.m. We get to the Kumbakonam station by twenty-two hundred hours tonight.'

'We, Sir?' asked Tulasi.

'Chanduru, you and me. We will take two more constables along. We don't want too many people at the station scaring Panju off. As we discussed earlier, make sure that there are extra gaslights in the station.'

Hall could very nearly smell and even taste his quarry now.

FIFTY-TWO

Panju knew he had to get to the station early. He had made a mental note of the route he had taken through the fields when he last left the Kumbakonam station in a rather unconventional manner. He went back along the same route and reached the area where the platform sloped down to the ground level. The sun had just gone down, but the station itself was bright with gaslights. He walked a little further till he came to a point where he estimated the carriage would be when the train stopped. He lay down next to the wall of the platform after clearing the area of a few sharp pieces of granite jelly.

There wasn't much of a gap between him and the rails. He could get crushed between the train and the wall, but that was a chance he had to take. He satisfied himself that he was completely hidden from the view of anyone on the platform.

He checked his shirt pocket and made sure that the letter he had written was there. He could feel the cold steel of the pistol that he had tucked into the veshti at his back. He found it uncomfortable lying on his back. He turned around to face the wall. This would also reduce the chances of getting crushed by the train. At least he wouldn't be able to watch himself getting pulped.

He hadn't slept for over thirty-six hours. He very quickly fell into a trance-like state. He thought of his father. He wished he had a better relationship with him. He wished he could explain to him clearly why he did what he did. But how do you talk to someone who was upright in everything he did, even though he never applied his moral standards to others? He wished he had the same easy relationship that Janaki had with his father. He felt uneasy that he hadn't told Janaki with whom he shared everything, including his innermost thoughts. He suppressed all thoughts of Ranjitham. He hadn't done the right thing by Meenakshi...

He must have dozed off. He woke up with a start with the sound of the steam whistle. Soon the noise of the engine followed. He could feel the vibrations. He realized he could put a hand out and touch the rails. He huddled closer against the wall. As the engine approached, he heard its altered cadence as it slowed down and felt the vibration of the rails next to him. Now the steam from the engine singed him. The train stopped seconds after passing him, but those seconds seemed to last a lifetime.

He did not have a lifetime. He had four minutes. He started crawling in the direction of the engine, keeping as low as possible. Sharp stones tore into his ankles and knees. When he started to feel that he had been crawling all his life, he came to the point where one compartment was attached to the other. He got up, still keeping low, and ducked underneath the large couplings. *Now God is with me*, he thought, as he emerged next to the compartment that had I CLASS written on it. He rushed to the entrance door of the compartment without worrying about being seen, as the train now hid him from view. He put his hand on the handle and tried to twist it open. The door did not open.

It was bolted from inside.

FIFTY-THREE

24 June 1911

For a moment Panju is disoriented. He hears a window being opened in the compartment. He runs back the way he came, stumbling in the dark, slipping on the loose granite stones. He folds his veshti up to his knees. He reaches the gap between two carriages and vaults over the couplers. His right ankle lags just a bit, catching a sharp corner. Blood flowing down his ankle makes it slippery. He loses one of his slippers in the effort. He kicks off the other. Now on the platform side of the train, he jumps up on to the platform, into the glare of gaslights. He runs to the entrance of the compartment, scrabbling at his waist till he has the revolver in hand. A large man, about twenty feet away, utters a cry, 'There he is. Catch him!' Panju notices the English accent. The man starts running towards Panju. As he is opening the door, he sees with his peripheral vision two other men in uniform join the chase. He rushes into the compartment, slams the door behind him and runs along the aisle. He sees a curtained enclosure to his left. He rips the curtains open.

Edmund Worthington! The recognition is immediate. From the sounds that reach him, he knows his pursuers are already at the door. He raises his pistol and tries very hard to bring up hatred and loathing for the wild-eyed man in pyjamas before him. Nothing, no feeling at all. No hatred. No loathing. No exultation. Just weariness.

Edmund Worthington was unable to sleep. He sensed that the train was slowing down. He got up as the train stopped and opened the louvred window by pushing up hard on the handles. He craned his neck out. 'Can you see the name of the station?'

he asked Mary who had just woken up with the grinding noise of the locked wheels. Mary didn't reply. She hated to talk before brushing her teeth. She sat up.

'It's Kumbakonam,' said Worthington, reading the black letters on the yellow board 'The station is unusually bright. The train stops here for only a couple of minutes. We should be in Tanjore within the hour.'

They busied themselves rolling up their beds. Worthington finished first and sat near the window. He turned at the sound of someone tearing the curtains open and saw a short man clad in a veshti. There was a gun in the man's hand.

The man was young. 'Hey, put that down,' he shouted. 'Do you know who I am? You are in a lot of trouble, boy.' He threw his sola topi that was on a table at the intruder. It was a totally useless gesture. The hat did not even reach the man.

'Say your prayers,' said the man. The voice carried no inflexion.

Edmund was now certain he was going to die. No prayers came to his mind.

All of a sudden, he was three feet down the bowler's mark on the pitch at Lord's on a summer afternoon. He exulted in the smell of the fresh grass and heard the slow clapping of the spectators in the pavilion. He had just rapped the Australian left-hander on his back leg, the slope of the ground allowing the ball to speed up and turn sharply. He flung his hands out and appealed to the umpire, already sure of the decision.

In another world, another time, he heard and sensed a sharp crack simultaneously. The vision crumbled.

Panju lowers his pistol. Mary is all over Worthington, shaking his head back and forth as though to revive him, unmindful of the blood that splashes on her dress. Panju runs along the aisle. The pursuers are now inside the compartment. Panju jumps out of the compartment and starts running towards the station building, sprinting across the brightly lit station. He hears shouted orders. He is now in a small anteroom. He turns back to see the large white man behind him. He zigzags around a table laden with files to reach a larger room with curtains across the doorway. He needs to prepare in privacy for what he is about to do. He runs through the curtains. He hears footsteps. He needs to delay things a bit. He shoots at the curtain, a warning shot, aiming low so he won't hurt anyone by accident.

Chanduru and Tulasi, in that order, ran behind Hall, their thick boots clattering on the hard floor. Hall moved surprisingly fast for a large man. He was hurtling towards the entry door of the first class carriage. Two constables in uniform, young and agile, were able to keep pace with him. Chanduru was at least ten feet behind them. Hall hesitated a little before the door, but was hastened by the sound of a shot from within the carriage. He pulled out his Webley revolver from its holder and continued into the compartment, followed by the constables. Chanduru slowed down and let Tulasi take a lead over him. Tulasi, too, entered the compartment. Chanduru waited for some time, looking at the exit door and saw Panju emerge. He nodded to himself and entered the compartment behind Tulasi and Hall. He heard Hall shouting orders to the young constables. 'One of you stay here. You,' he said, pointing to the other, 'go get the railway doctor.'

They made their way down the aisle, allowing the constable who was looking for a doctor to go through. They noticed in passing that Worthington's face was full of blood. Mary sat, her face a frozen mask, rocking on her haunches. She kept saying, 'So much blood'.

As Chanduru stepped down from the other exit of the compartment behind Hall and Tulasi, he saw Panju disappear into an office complex that was part of the railway station. Hall was some ten yards behind Panju while Chanduru and Tulasi were a couple of yards behind Hall. They entered a room with tables heaped with files and bunches of documents tied with red cotton tape. A curtain on the opposite wall was drawn. This obviously led to another room. As Hall prepared to rush through the screen, Chanduru heard the crack of a bullet. The next second, Hall's body hit the floor. Chanduru ran to Hall who was on his back, writhing in agony. Chanduru saw immediately that his right kneecap was shattered. Blood pooled on the floor, drenching his khaki trousers. The pistol that Hall was carrying lay some distance away. Chanduru bent down and picked it up. Tulasi was squatting near Hall trying to see how badly he was hurt.

Chanduru now held the pistol. He pointed it at Hall and said, 'I have no choice but to kill you.' Tulasi got up, astonishment showing clearly in his rounded eyes. Chanduru waved the pistol at him and said, 'You keep out of it and you won't be hurt.'

Hall spoke with difficulty, but the words were enunciated clearly, 'So, you were the traitor. You were a part of them. You kept the opposition informed of all developments. That is why the kidnapping failed. I should have suspected you when all our plans started going awry. And you tipped off Jatin the first time.'

'You are absolutely right. But you missed another thing, Hall. The other night, when I was watching Ranjitham's house, I saw Panju meeting her and I could have taken him into custody if I wanted. Anyway, I now have to kill you. I have no problem in ridding the world of a monster. If you believe in God, you can pray.'

'I don't believe in anyone but myself,' said Hall. 'In any case, if you are going to shoot, shoot and be done with it. My knee is hurting like hell and this will be a relief.'

For a moment, Chanduru admired the man who faced death without flinching.

'Listen—' Tulasi started to say something.

'Don't worry. You won't be involved. I am going to shoot myself after I kill this demon,' said Chanduru and pointed the gun at Hall's chest. Hall closed his eyes.

Chanduru would have squeezed the trigger if he hadn't heard another crack from the other room. Chanduru ducked involuntarily, lowering the gun.

'Oh God!' shouted Tulasi and ran into the other room, through the curtain. Chanduru stood over Hall, uncertain what to do next.

For a moment, Panju is desolate that he has committed the sin of taking another's life. He finds solace in recollecting what Sambu quoted often—

Sins committed in other places are destroyed at holy places;
Sins committed in holy places are destroyed at Varanasi;
Sins committed at Varanasi are destroyed at Kumbakonam;
Sins committed at Kumbakonam are destroyed at Kumbakonam.

Panju also remembers the fifth verse from the eighth chapter of the Bhagavad Gita—'He who remembers me at the time of his death will attain Me.' He sits down, crossing his legs in the lotus pose. He centres himself by steadying his breath and starts chanting the five-syllabled mantra of Siva. He raises his pistol, places it against his right temple and squeezes the trigger.

The pistol falls from his hand and he topples sideways, the lotus pose intact.

By the time Chanduru recovered from the shock of hearing the shot, Tulasi was back. He now held a pistol in his hand.

'Drop your gun,' Tulasi said.

Shoulders slumped, Chanduru let the Webley fall from his hand.

Tulasi took a few steps towards the fallen Hall and shot him twice in his chest as Chanduru watched, amazed. Hall's body bucked twice and lay still.

'I've decided to join you,' said Tulasi. 'I have had enough of watching this monster's atrocities. In any case, this is a better solution as fewer people wind up dead. For the record, I will tell you what happened. First let me put this revolver where it belongs.'

Tulasi went back through the now open door, the curtain ripped aside. He wiped the revolver fastidiously with a handkerchief that he pulled out of his trousers. He then pressed it against Panju's hands and placed it carefully next to the body. He then came back, picked up the Webley revolver from where it lay, wiped it methodically and placed it in the holster strapped to Hall's body after pressing it once against the dead man's fingers.

'Now, it should be clear,' he said, addressing Chanduru, 'what precisely happened here. For the record, let me tell you.'

'In a heroic move,' said Tulasi in the sing-song voice that he normally reserved for reading out English text, 'Deputy Inspector General Hall chased after the assassin, not even drawing his weapon, lest he should hurt an innocent bystander. Being British and extremely athletic, he was very much ahead of us even though we were running hard after the criminal. The assailant ran into the room and fired a shot through the screen at the doorway to prevent being followed. The bullet hit the DIG on his right knee and he fell down. Hearing the commotion, Panju came out and shot him twice in the chest, thereby bagging two white men for the price of one. Then the coward went into the room and shot himself.'

'Is that clear?' asked Tulasi.

'He shot five times with the pistol,' Tulasi continued. 'Once at the Collector. Once through the door, twice to kill the DIG and once at himself. That should leave two bullets in the magazine.'

'Yes,' said the dazed Chanduru, his brain trying to catch up with the fast-moving events and failing.

'This is what I found in Panju's pockets,' said Tulasi as he handed over a slightly crumpled piece of paper to Chanduru.

Chanduru smoothed out the piece of paper and read it:

'The English have clapped Bharata Mata in irons and have made slaves of all of us, trampling over our traditional Sanatana Dharma, sabotaging our educational systems so that Indians will only be fit for poring over files for their masters. They have impoverished a glorious nation. They are a big leech, sucking our economy dry, a dangerous predator in our midst. They have, however, badly miscalculated. They have thought of Indians as effete and powerless. I am but the least among the three thousand south Indians who have signed a pledge in blood to kill at least one Englishman. If the only thing that my death serves is to inspire one more Indian to do his duty to drive out these foreigners, my dying, unlike my living, will not have been in vain. The mlecha George V not only declares himself Emperor of India, but also has the gumption to come to India to gloat before our eyes. My compatriots and I can promise one thing; he won't go back alive.

Vande Mataram!'

AUGUST 1911
TIRUVAIYARU

FIFTY-FOUR

22 August 1911

Meenakshi and Janaki sat on the sands of the Cauvery, watching her flow past, swirling and eddying.

'Akka,' Meenakshi said, 'I have something to tell you.'

Janaki turned away from the river and looked at Meenakshi. Meenakshi's eyes brimmed with tears. Her hands were tracing arabesques in the sand.

'I have missed two periods now.'

Janaki looked up. No thoughts that she would never be able to complete her education or marry Arul arose in her. Just wonder.

'We will name the baby Bharati, whether it is a boy or a girl. We will raise the baby together,' Janaki put her arms around Meenakshi.

The Cauvery knows now that she has done this before and must do it again. She remembers how in the past she has impacted the culture of the people. She remembers the magnificence of the Chola architecture, the brilliance of the Carnatic music trinity, the dance rhythms of the Tanjore quartet, the rich splendour of the region's paintings that she gave birth to in her previous lives.

She knows that she will be reborn again when thunderclouds fill the sky and the land and the sky are connected by torrents of water. In the meantime, she lives in the minds and spirits of the people of the lands she has so completely drenched. She has suffused the minds with the spirit of sacrifice, which too, will be reborn again and again in the land that she has blessed.

ENDNOTES

The following books helped me in fashioning the background to the story.

Bipin Chandra et al., *India's Struggle for Independence,* Penguin Books, 1989.

David Gilmour , *The Ruling Caste: Imperial Lives in the Victorian Raj*, Pimlico, 2007.

Padma Seshadri and Padma Malini Sundararaghavan, *It Happened Along the Cauvery*, Niyogi Books, 2012.

Lakshmi Viswanathan, *Women Of Pride: The Devadasi Heritage,* The Lotus collection, 2008.

The oath of the Bharat Samman is largely the oath of the Abhinav Bharat from http://www.savarkar.org/en/armed-struggle/oath-abhinav-bharat.

The climactic event in the story is inspired by Vanchinathan's shooting of the Tirunelveli Collector, Robert Ashe, at Maniyachi on 17 June 1911, when Ashe and his wife were on their way to Kodaikanal.

V.V.S. Iyer probably trained Vanchinathan in shooting.

The meetings with Subramania Bharati and Sri Aurobindo are completely fictional.

The translations of Sanskrit and Tamil poems in the book are mostly mine.

Acknowledgements

To Dr Karthik Kalyanaraman for looking at the initial chapters and giving me very strong motivation to go on.

To Anita Nair for invaluable suggestions regarding the structure and flow of the book.

To my brother Santhanam and sister-in-law Kanchan, Dr Rajini Srikanth, Dr John Mathew, Varun Agarwal and Netra Srikanth for valuable feedback and suggestions on the first draft.

To Leela, Raghava, Kaesava, Karthik, Chris and Sneha for being a part of the focus group and giving useful suggestions on many aspects of the book.

To my editor Dharini Bhaskar, for the edits with a light yet sure touch.